"IF YOU TOUCH THAT BOWSTRING, I'LL TAKE IT AWAY FROM YOU AND WRAP IT AROUND YOUR THROAT."

At Karl's words, the two bowmen turned their horses and galloped away in opposite directions.

At close quarters he could have taken both of them on. But with just a few yards between them, one of the bowmen could drill him through while Karl was killing the other. Yet there was no choice, he would have to take one of them out, and worry about the other later.

The bowman to the left was already wheeling his horse about. Two tugs at his saddle straps and he had unlimbered his crossbow. Forty yards separated Karl from him. If he could get to the bowman quickly enough . . .

Thirty yards . . . twenty yards . . . ten . . . the bowman took aim, four fingers curled around the crossbow's long trigger . . . .

With an upward slash, Karl knocked the crossbow aside, and speared the bowman through the chest. But even as Karl tried to jerk his sword loose, agony blossomed like a fiery flower in the middle of his back. As he fell to the ground, his body twisted. The last thing he saw was a glimpse of the fletching of the crossbow bolt that projected from his back . . . .

Great Science Fiction from SIGNET

BOOK TWO OF GUARDIANS OF THE FLAME

THE SWORD AND THE CHAIN

JOEL ROSENBERG

for **Harry Leonard**
who, thankfully, still doesn't know when
to stop haranguing me

Acknowledgments

I'd like to thank the people who helped me through this one: Kevin O'Donnell, Jr., who insists that I think it through before I write it; Mary Kittredge, who demands that I get the words written, and then worry about whether or not they're the right ones; Mark J. McGarry, who swears that both of them are leading me astray; Jim Drury, who makes me feel that I know what I'm doing; Robert Lee Thurston and Judy Heald, whose support is always invaluable; Bob Adams, whose timely advice on blacksmithing was not nearly so important to me as his friendship; Darrell Sweet, cover artist extraordinaire; Susan Bissett, who, for the second time, has turned my barely legible scribblings into a fine map; my editor, Sheila Gilbert, who has the good grace to trust me; and Cherry Weiner, my agent for this work, who asked for more of Ellegon.

And, most particularly, I'd like to thank my wife, Felicia Herman, who not only gets more beautiful every year, but knows how to separate what's important from what isn't.

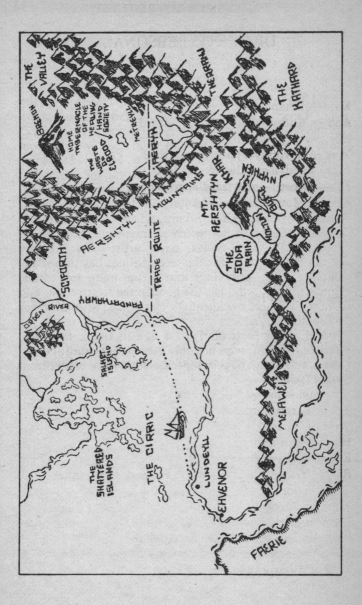

DRAMATIS PERSONAE

Karl Cullinane—warrior
Andrea Andropolous—novice wizard
Ellegon—a young dragon
Walter Slovotsky—journeyman thief
Ahira Bandylegs—dwarf warrior
Louis Riccetti—ex-wizard/engineer
Rhêden Monsterhunter—hunter
Teerhnus—blacksmith
Ch'akresarkandyn ip Katharhdn—warrior, soldier of
    fortune
Orhmyst—master slaver
Kirah—freed slave
Aeia Eriksen—freed slave
Tennetty—freed slave, apprentice warrior
Chton—freed slave, farmer
Ihryk—freed slave, farmer
Fialt—freed slave, farmer, sailor, apprentice warrior
Ahrmin—slaver
Wenthall—master wizard
Zherr, Baron Furnael
Sammis—master wizard
Hivar—man-at-arms
Enna—fealty-servant
Rahff Furnael—heir to barony Furnael, apprentice
    warrior
Thomen Furnael
Beralyn, Lady Furnael
Bren Adahan—heir to barony Adahan
Avair Ganness—captain and owner of the *Warthog*
Thyren—journeyman wizard

Jheral, Hynryd, Raykh, Lensius, Fihka—journeyman
    slavers
Seigar Wohtansen—Clan Wohtan wizard and warleader
Estalli, Olyla—Seigar Wohtansen's wives
Peill—elf warrior
Jason Cullinane

I find that the great thing in this world is not so much where we stand as in what direction we are moving; To reach the port of heaven, we must sail sometimes with the wind and sometimes against it—but we must sail, and not drift, nor lie at anchor.

—Oliver Wendell Holmes

Introduction

It started as a game. Just a quiet, pleasant evening for seven college students.

Karl Cullinane, Jason Parker, James Michael Finnegan, Doria Perlstein, Walter Slovotsky, Andrea Andropolous, and Lou Riccetti sat down for an evening of fantasy gaming. It was going to be fun. That's all it was supposed to be.

But then gamemaster Professor Arthur Deighton somehow transferred them to the Other Side. Without warning, they found themselves in the world they thought existed only in their imaginations, in the bodies of the characters they had been pretending to be. Short, skinny Karl Cullinane became a tall, well-muscled warrior; crippled James Michael Finnegan became the powerful dwarf, Ahira Bandylegs. All seven of them changed into different people with unusual talents.

Suddenly it wasn't a game anymore.

Jason Parker was the first to die. He spent the last few moments of his life kicking on the end of a spear.

The others survived, but now they weren't playing, they were fighting to stay alive, to escape the wrath and weapons of warriors and wizards, slavers and lords.

They had to find the Gate Between Worlds and return home.

They had to, and they did—but in the doing, they lost far too much. Ahira died at the Gate. Doria went catatonic. Nothing could be done about that at home. But, back on the Other Side, the Matriarch of the Healing Hand Society could bring Ahira back to life, could cure Doria's shattered mind.

So they returned to the Other Side. And, yes, the Matriarch was willing to help them, just this once.

But nothing is ever free. There were prices to pay, and promises to make. Promises that would be kept.

No matter what the cost.

PART ONE:
Metreyll

CHAPTER ONE: *Profession*

"Where we do go from here?" Karl Cullinane asked, sitting next to Andrea Andropolous on the largest of the flat stones surrounding the ashes of supper's campfire. He squinted at the setting sun as he sipped his coffee.

Andy-Andy smiled. Karl always liked that smile; it brightened up what had been an already bright day. "Do you mean that metaphorically?" she asked, tossing her head to clear the wisps of hair from her face. Extending a slim, tanned forefinger, she stroked his thigh. "Or are you asking where the two of us can slip off to, to get some privacy?" She looked up at him, her head cocked to one side. "I would have *thought* that last night would have been enough for a while. Let's wait until dark, shall we?"

He laughed. "That wasn't what I meant—I was talking about how long we're going to stay here on the preserve. The Hand Society isn't going to let us live here forever." *And I was also wondering how the hell we're going to keep our promise to the Matriarch.* "But . . ." He took her hand. "As long as you've brought the subject up, I wouldn't mind—"

A firm, reedy voice sounded in Karl's head: *This is ridiculous.*

Lying on the grass twenty yards away, Ellegon opened his eyes. Then, raising his head from his crossed forelegs, the dragon glared at the two of them. *Can't you think about anything but sexual intercourse? I know you're only humans, but must you *always* be in heat?*

Curling and uncurling his leathery wings, he rose to all fours, sending a flock of birds fleeing from their perches in a nearby elm and into chittering flight. Ellegon was small, as dragons go: He measured barely the length of a Greyhound bus from the grayish-green tip of his pointed tail to the saucer-sized nostrils of his saurian snout.

His cavernous mouth closed, then opened, releasing wisps of smoke and steam. *I would think that people who were recently college students could have other subjects on their minds. Now and then, at least.*

Ellegon, Karl thought. *You're not being reasonable. I—*

No, never mind. Pay no attention. Don't bother with me. I'm only a dragon, after all. The dragon turned and lumbered away.

"Ellegon," Karl called out. "Come back here."

The dragon didn't seem to hear.

Karl shrugged. "I wish he'd be a bit less—"

"—of a pain in the butt," Walter Slovotsky finished, as he walked up. "But it's your own fault, you know." He was a big man, although not quite as tall, broad-shouldered, or well muscled as Karl. Here, at least. Back home, Walter had been a half a foot taller than Karl, and much stronger. But Karl had been changed in the transfer between worlds, receiving added height and muscle, as well as skills that he hadn't possessed at home.

There had been changes, but not everything had changed; Walter still could figure things out faster than Karl could, most of the time. And that still rankled.

"What do you mean?" Karl asked, irritated.

"Tell you in a moment; I need some coffee." Picking up a rag to protect his hand from the heat of the battered coffeepot's handle, Slovotsky poured himself a cupful. He seemed oblivious to the chilly wind that blew across the meadow, despite the fact that he was shirtless, as usual, dressed only in blousy white pantaloons and sandals, a tangle of knives and straps at his hip.

With his free hand, Slovotsky rubbed at the corners of his eyes. Their slight epicanthic folds gave him a vaguely oriental appearance, although his features were clearly

Slavic, and his black hair was slightly curly. "You're just asking for a hard time, Karl. There's no reason for it. He's jealous, that's all."

"Jealous?" Andy-Andy arched an eyebrow. "Of me? Why? I wouldn't think—"

True.

"—that dragons would get jealous," she finished, as if she hadn't been interrupted. Perhaps she hadn't been; Ellegon could easily have turned her out.

Karl turned to see the tip of Ellegon's tail vanish as the dragon disappeared into a stand of trees on the far side of the meadow.

Don't eavesdrop. You want to join the conversation? Fine. Come on back and chat. Otherwise, keep out of it.

No answer.

Walter shrugged, the corners of his mouth turning upward in an amused grin. "It's just a matter of attention from Karl. Which you're getting, and he's not."

He jerked a thumb toward Lou Riccetti, who sat propped against the base of a tall elm, his arms crossed over his blue workshirt, lost in thought. "Slovotsky's Law Number Thirty-seven: Some people need less attention than others." He shrugged. "Some want more. It all depends on—"

"Ohgod." Perched in a high branch of a dying oak, Ahira the dwarf shook his head. "*Everyone*, get your weapons; Lou, you take my crossbow. Karl, on your horse. *Move.* There's a bunch of riders galloping toward the preserve—I think we're about to be attacked."

As he spoke, Ahira was already climbing clumsily but quickly down the tree, supporting himself by the pressure of his blunt fingers against the rough bark, not bothering to look for branches to hold on to.

Karl dropped his cup as he jumped to his feet. With a quick, reflexive pat at his swordhilt, he ran across the meadow to where his chestnut mare stood, idly grazing in the ankle-high grasses.

Unless Ahira was jumping at shadows, there probably

wasn't time to saddle her. He took the bridle down from the branch where it hung and quickly slid the bit between her teeth as he slipped the crownpiece over her poll and tightened it behind her ears. Reins in his left hand, he grasped her rough mane in his right and eased himself to her back, swinging his right leg over and seating himself firmly.

He flicked the reins and dug in his heels. *What the hell is going on?* he thought.

I can see it a bit better, and—

Make it quick. We're about to be attacked.

No, we are not. This is what is going on. Ellegon opened his mind.

Craning his long neck to see over a rocky outcropping, Ellegon stared out over the Waste of Elrood. Off in the distance, five shapes moved quickly across its cracked, dusty surface.

He concentrated on them; they zoomed into view. All five were filthy humans, mounted on horses. Quite possibly tasty horses.

Three of the humans rode together as they pursued a fourth, a half-naked, skinny one, wearing a metal collar with a dangling length of chain. The fifth rider, dressed like the other pursuers in matching green tunic and leggings, galloped in toward the quarry from a different direction.

Thanks, Ellegon, Karl thought. *The fifth one probably took a different route than his friends; he's trying to cut the slave off before he reaches the tabernacle grounds.*

He will. His horse is much fresher than the other four.

"Andrea!" Ahira shouted. "Get up to the bluff. Hide in the bushes, and when they get close enough, hit as many as you can with your sleep spell. We'll sort it out later. Right now, I just want to—"

"No," Karl said, reining in his horse next to the dwarf. "They're not after us. It's four soldiers, chasing an escaped slave. They're not going to come close to the clearing. Andy, how far can you reach with your sleep spell?"

She waved her hands helplessly. "Two, three hundred feet. At best."

Ellegon, do any of them have bows? You didn't notice before, and I couldn't tell.

Two of them do. Karl, we've got to talk about—

Save it for later. He turned to Andrea. "No good. They'd cut you down before you got in range. Ellegon and I'll take care of it." *Get airborne, and give me a hand.* Karl had the only horse among the five of them; depending on how far away the hunters and their quarry were, he might have to hold the fort all by himself for several minutes before the others could arrive.

Karl had a great respect for his own fighting skills, but a single man successfully taking on four or more was a longshot, no matter how handy that one man was with a sword. But with Ellegon overhead, there probably wouldn't be a fight at all; few people would risk being roasted in dragonfire.

No.

What?

I thought I made that clear. No, I will not get airborne. They have bows. I'm scared.

That was bizarre. Ellegon's scales were as hard as fine steel; he was almost immune to any nonmagical threat.

But there was no time to discuss that. "Ellegon's out—I'll slow them up. Catch up with me as soon as you can."

Andrea reached out and grabbed at his leggings. "*Wait.* I've got a—"

"No time, didn't you hear me? *escaped slave.* Stay out of it; I don't want to have to worry about your getting hurt." He jerked his leggings out of her grasp.

Ignoring Ahira's shouts from behind, he kicked his

horse into a canter. Galloping her down the incline to the edge of the Waste was tempting, but Karl wasn't used to riding bareback; best to ensure arriving rather than take the chance of being bounced off his horse's back.

He cantered down the slope toward a break in the trees. Beyond it, touched with the red light of the setting sun, the Waste of Elrood lay in harsh, bright flatness. Long ago, what now was the Waste had been covered with lush greenery like the wooded sanctuary surrounding the tabernacle of the Healing Hand. A thousand years ago, a death duel between two wizards had ended that; now a vast ocean of sun-cracked earth spread across the horizon.

A quarter of a mile ahead, a dustcloud roiled. At its head the lone rider, keeping a bare hundred-yard lead on three others, dodged his horse to avoid the fourth rider coming from the side.

Four on one. I hate four on one. But that was the way it had to be, at least for a while; it would take Walter, Ahira, and Riccetti a good five minutes to catch up. Karl would be hard pressed to hold off four warriors for that length of time. A five-minute swordfight would be an eternity.

Then again, the dragon's voice sounded dimly in Karl's head, *you might just be able to* talk *to them.*

Bets? He dug in his heels.

As he neared the quarry, the man swerved his horse away. A half-naked, skinny wretch with a badly scarred face, rivulets of sweat running down his dust-caked chest, he jerked on the reins with his cuffed hands, the dangling links of chain tinkling in bizarre merriment.

"N'vârl!" Karl called out in Erendra. *Don't run.* "T'rar ammalli." *I'm a friend.*

No good. The man obviously figured that Karl was with the others; his clothing was similar to theirs. To him, it must have looked like a trap, as though yet another horseman had appeared to cut him off just a few hundred yards away from the sanctuary of the tabernacle

grounds. A low moan escaped his lips as he cut perpen-
dicularly across Karl's path.

As though he had waited for just this chance, the
fourth pursuer let fly a whirling leather strap, weighted
at both ends. Twisting through the air, it spun across the
intervening yards and tangled itself in the rear legs of the
quarry's horse. Whinnying in pain and fear, the horse
tumbled to the ground, sending the rider flying. He
tumbled head over heels on the rough ground, and then
fell silent.

There wasn't time to see to the fallen man. If he was
dead, there wasn't anything to do. Injured, he probably
could keep for a while; Slovotsky, Ahira, and Riccetti
would be along with the bottle of healing draughts.

Reaching across his waist, Karl drew his saber. "Easy,
now," he whispered to his horse, while he settled the
reins in his left fist. "Just stand easy." He waited for the
four soldiers.

As their horses pranced to a panting halt, he took a
quick inventory of their weapons. All four were swordsmen, wearing the wide-bladed shortsword popular in the
Eren regions. Karl could probably handle that, on horse-
back. His ruddy mare was a large and powerful animal;
likely he could dance her around that tired assortment of
lathering geldings while his saber's greater reach took its
toll.

But the two at the rear of the group had crossbows
strapped to their saddles. That could be bad.

Very bad.

But . . . crossbows? If they had them, why hadn't they
used them?

Stupid. Dead . . . isn't worth . . . much. Ellegon's
voice was dim now that Karl was on the very edge of the
dragon's range; worse, the flow of words had developed
gaps when Ellegon wasn't concentrating.

Right, he thought, wondering if the dragon could hear
him. He faced the four men. "Ryvâth`ed," he said, letting
the guttural Erendra r roll off his tongue. *It stops here.*

The leader, a burly, bearded swordsman, answered him in the same language. "This is none of your concern," he said, moving his horse closer to Karl's. "The slave is the property of Lord Mehlên of Metreyll, whose armsmen we are—laws regarding abandoned property do not apply."

Karl could just barely hear Ellegon. *Stall. Just stall.*

He couldn't stall for long. The younger of the two bowmen had unstrapped his crossbow and was fumbling for one of the bolts in the wooden quiver strapped to the cantle of his saddle.

But it was at least worth a try. "You," he said in Erendra, "if you touch that bowstring, I'll take it away from you and wrap it around your throat." The largest of the four was almost a head shorter than Karl; perhaps he could intimidate them for a few minutes, until the odds evened up.

The bowman, a blond youth who looked to be in his late teens, sneered. "I doubt that," he said. But his fingers stopped their search for a bolt.

Good. Just a few more minutes. "Now, we can talk," he said, lowering the point of his sword.

He listened for sounds from behind him. Damn, nothing but the clattering of hooves as the quarry's horse got to its feet. The escaped slave was, at best, feigning unconsciousness.

At best . . .

To hell with it. "He is *not* a slave. Not anymore. He is under my protection." It was only fair to give them a chance; Karl had made a promise to the Matriarch, but he could hardly fulfill it by killing everyone in this world who tolerated—or even supported—the ownership of people. It wouldn't work, even if Karl was willing to wade through a sea of blood.

Dammit. There had been a time when the most violent thing Karl could remember doing was blocking too hard during a karate lesson.

But there have been some changes made. "You're not going to take him."

The leader snorted. "Who are you?" He raised an eyebrow. "You don't look like a daughter of the Hand. You're ugly as most of them, granted, but—" He cut himself off with a shrug. "What do you suggest we do? We have chased him a long way—"

"Turn around and ride away," Karl said. "We will just leave it at that."

The leader smiled, his right hand snaking across his body toward the hilt of his sword. "I doubt—"

His words turned into a bubbling gasp as the point of Karl's saber sliced through his throat.

One down. Karl kicked his horse over to the next swordsman, a pock-faced beardless one, who had already drawn his sword.

There was no time to waste; he had to take this one out and get to the bowmen quickly. As the other slashed down at him, Karl parried, then thrust at the man's swordarm.

No-Beard was ready for that; with a twitch of his arm, he beat Karl's sword aside, then tried for a backhanded slash to Karl's neck.

Karl ducked under the swing and used the opening to thrust through to his opponent's chest, the flat of his blade parallel to the ground. The point slid through the leather tunic as if through cheesecloth.

Karl jerked his saber out. Wine-dark blood fountained, covering his sword from its tip to its basket hilt and beyond, staining Karl's hand and wrist. He had gotten through to either the aorta or the heart. It didn't much matter which; No-Beard would be dead in seconds.

Karl spun his horse around to face the others. Like mirror images, the two bowmen turned their horses and galloped in opposite directions.

He hesitated for a moment. At close quarters, he could take both. But with just a few yards between them, one of the bowmen could drill him through while he killed the other.

There was no choice. He would have to take out one, and worry about the other later.

The bowman to the left wheeled his horse about. Two tugs at his saddlestraps unlimbered his crossbow; he reached down to his waist for a three-pronged beltclaw.

Forty yards of broken ground separated Karl from him. Karl dug in his heels and kicked his horse into a gallop. If he could get to the bowman quickly enough . . .

Thirty yards. Bracing the butt of the crossbow in a notch in his saddle, the bowman slipped the claw over the bowstring and pulled it back, locking the string into place. The beltclaw fell from his fingers.

Twenty yards. With trembling hands, the bowman drew a foot-long feathered bolt from his quiver, slipped it into the crossbow's groove, and nocked it with a practiced movement of his thumb.

Ten. He raised the bow to his shoulder and took aim, four fingers curled around the crossbow's long trigger.

With an upward slash, Karl knocked the crossbow aside, the bolt discharging harmlessly overhead. As the bowman reached for the dagger at his belt, Karl speared him through the chest.

The sword stuck.

Damn. Karl had been in too much of a hurry; he hadn't made sure that the flat of his blade was parallel to the ground—the damn sword had wedged itself in between two ribs. As Karl tried to jerk it loose, the blood-slickened hilt twisted out of his fingers.

The limp body of the bowman slipped from the saddle, carrying Karl's sword with it. He swore, and—

Agony blossomed like a fiery flower in the middle of Karl's back. His legs went numb and lifeless. As he started to slip from his mare's back, he tried to hold on to her mane, but a spasm jerked the rough hairs from his fingers.

He landed on his side on the hard ground, his body

twisted. From the corner of his eye, he glimpsed the fletching of the crossbow bolt that projected from his back.

He felt nothing, nothing at all from the waist down. *My spine. Ellegon, help me. Please.*

No answer.

Nothing.

Through a red cloud of pain, he saw the other bowman still his horse's jittery prancing and reload his crossbow, taking the time to aim carefully. It was the blond boy he had threatened before. Beyond him, Ahira, Walter, and Riccetti ran across the sun-baked plain, weapons carried high. But there was no way that they could reach the bowman in time.

The point of the bolt drew his eyes. Shiny though rust-specked steel, glistening in the ruddy light of the setting sun. It bore down on him; the bowstring—

—*snapped*, sending the bolt looping end over end in the still air. A long red weal drew itself across the boy's leg; as he lowered his hands to protect himself from his invisible attacker, he was jerked out of the saddle.

He collapsed in a heap as Walter Slovotsky ran up and took up a position standing over the boy, one knife in each hand.

"Go take care of Karl," Slovotsky addressed the air. "I'll see to this . . . trash."

A staggered line of dust puffs drew itself across the ground toward where Karl lay. "Easy," Andy-Andy's voice murmured. "Lou has the bottle of healing draughts. It won't hurt much longer." Gentle, invisible fingers cradled his head.

Quietly, she spoke harsh, awkward syllables that could only be heard and forgotten while Karl watched Lou Riccetti puff and pant his way across the plain, an ornately inlaid brass bottle cradled in his arms.

And then, as her dismissal of the invisibility spell began to take effect, the outline of her head appeared, superimposing itself over his view of Riccetti.

The image solidified: first the brown eyes, faintly misted with tears. Then, the slightly too-long, slightly bent nose, the high-boned cheeks, and the full mouth, all framed with the long brown hair that was now touched with red highlights in the light of the setting sun. Karl had always found Andy-Andy beautiful, but never more so than now.

"Andy, my legs—"

"You stupid *shit.*" She slipped an arm under his shoulder and clumsily flipped him over onto his belly. "Quick, give it here." A cork popped.

A wrenching pain forced a scream from his mouth as the bolt was drawn from his back. But, horridly, the pain still vanished in mid-back. He was paralyzed.

No. Please God, no. He tried to talk, but his mouth was as dry as the Waste.

And then a liquid coolness washed the pain away. It vanished, as though it had never been.

"Twitch your toes, Karl," she commanded.

He tried to.

And they moved.

He was all there; he felt *everything,* everything from the top of his aching head all the way down to where his right great toe throbbed. *Probably sprained it when I fell.* "Thanks." He tried to get his arms underneath him, to push himself to his feet.

"That will be enough of *that,*" Andy-Andy said. "We're running short of the healing potion. I had to give you most of it to take care of the hole in your back. We can't afford to have you swallow any more just to take care of the shock to your system. So you just lie there. I've got to go see to the man that got knocked off his horse."

"Don't bother," Ahira said, his voice a low rasp. "Must've snapped his neck in the fall. He's dead. *Damn.*"

But, Ellegon's voice sounded in Karl's head, *he died free. You gave him that gift.*

Wonderful. Tears welled up. He hadn't done anything right. He should have listened to Andy-Andy: If he had only waited a few moments, she could have cast her spell of invisibility on him; the escaped slave would never have been scared into turning aside; the bola would have missed. And Karl would never have been shot, not while he was invisible. It could have all been done so easily, if only he had waited.

And, now, it's all a waste.

No. It was not.

That's easy for you to say. Coward.

Listen to me, Karl. He was too far away; I couldn't hear much of his mind as he tried to escape; I don't even know his name. But I did hear one thing, when he saw you, and mistook you for one of the pursuers. I heard him thinking, "No—I'd rather die than go back."

And if I'd waited—

He still would have died, sometime soon. Perhaps ten years from now, perhaps fifty. No time at all; you humans are so . . . ephemeral. But he might not have died free. Always remember that he died a free man.

And was that so much?

He thought so. What right have you to dispute it? The dragon's mental voice became gentle. *You've had a difficult time. Go to sleep now. Lou will rig a travois, and we'll bring you back up to camp.*

But—

Sleep.

Weariness welled up and washed him in a cool, dark wave.

Ahira looked down at the bound form of the blond bowman and swore softly under his breath. "What the hell are we going to do with this?"

The youth didn't answer; he just stared listlessly at the ground.

The dwarf rested his hands on the hilt of his double-bladed battleaxe. The axe was the simple answer, and probably the best one. But possibly not. In any case, there was enough time for a leisurely decision whether or not to kill the bowman; with his hands tied to the roots of an old oak, he wasn't going anywhere.

Walter stooped to check the knots. "It'll hold him. Do you want me to have Ellegon keep an eye open?"

Ellegon. That was another matter. If that damned dragon of Karl's hadn't turned coward suddenly—

Two points. I belong to myself, not to Karl Cullinane, or anyone else. Secondly, I did not suddenly "turn coward," dwarf. I am a coward, James Michael Finnegan. I have been, for more than three hundred years.

Don't call me that. My name is Ahira.

Now it is. And what scares you the most?

"What does that have to do with anything?"

I will show you, if you insist. But I suggest you save it for later, Ahira. For the time being, let it rest that there is one thing that frightens me just as much as the thought of being crippled James Michael Finnegan frightens you.

Slovotsky chuckled. "I'd take him at his word, were I you, little friend. You weren't around when he gave Karl a taste of what being chained in Pandathaway's cesspit felt like. Check with Karl before you let him show you." He raised his head and addressed the air. "Ellegon? Do me a favor and tune us out; I want a private conversation with the dwarf."

Very well. The dragon's mental voice went silent.

Slovotsky shook his head. "Not that I trust him to keep out of our heads. It's just that since he's agreed to, he probably won't let the cat out of the bag to Karl. Cullinane's going to be a problem."

Ahira looked over to the far side of the meadow. Under a pile of blankets, Karl Cullinane lay sleeping in the twilight. A few yards away, Andrea and Lou Riccetti sat talking quietly.

"Cullinane's going to be a problem," Ahira echoed, as he and Slovotsky walked to the far edge of the clearing, away from the bound bowman. "Big deal."

Slovotsky cocked his head. "You don't think so?"

"Cullinane's the least of my worries, Walter. We've

got bigger ones." Ahira jerked his head at the bound form of the blond bowman. "Like what we're going to do with William Tell here. Or how long we can stay on the preserve before the Healing Hand Society kicks us out." He shrugged. "Right now, I'm more worried about Riccetti. I told him to take my crossbow. All he ended up doing was bringing along the healing draughts for after. Not exactly a big help. If we'd really needed him in the fight, we would all have been in deep trouble." Ahira pounded his fist against a tree, sending chips of bark flying off into the night.

"Don't get so bent out of shape about Riccetti; you're missing the big problem." Slovotsky laid a hand on his shoulder. "But take it easy. Try and deal with one thing at a time, as you used to when you were writing computer programs—just one step, one problem at a time.

"Take Riccetti. So what if he wasn't any good in a fight? Can't blame him. The rest of us have the abilities we gained in the transfer. I've got *this*." With a smooth, flowing motion, he pulled one of his four throwing knives from the tangle of straps at his hip, caught the tip of the blade between thumb and forefinger, and threw it at a nearby tree. It quivered as it sank into the trunk five and a half feet above the ground.

Slovotsky patted at his hip. "And while I'm not in Karl's league, if we can get a sword for me, I could use it reasonably well. Not to mention my thieving skills." He walked over and pulled the knife from the tree, taking a moment to clean it on a fold of his blousy pantaloons before replacing it in its sheath. "You've got your strength, your darksight, and your skills with crossbow and battleaxe. Karl's damn good with his sword; Andy-Andy has her spells."

"But Riccetti's got nothing." Lou Riccetti had been a wizard; he had given up his magic as his part of the payment to the Matriarch of the Healing Hand Society for bringing Ahira back to life.

Which means that I'd be an ungrateful ass if I gave him hell for not getting involved in the fight. If it wasn't for me—

No. That wouldn't do; recriminations wouldn't be any help. The question, as usual, was what to do next. "Any ideas on what we do with Riccetti?"

A shrug. "We hand that problem to Karl. Let him work it out; he knows more about weapons and martial arts than both of us put together. For all I know, he might be able to turn Lou into a decent swordsman, if the two of them work at it." Slovotsky seated himself on a waist-high boulder. "Leave that one alone for the time being. As you pointed out, we've got bigger problems staring us in the face. Like what we're going to do with the bowman there. If we let him go, we're just asking for trouble. On the other hand, slicing his throat in cold blood doesn't exactly thrill me."

"I don't think it matters whether or not it thrills you. Not if—and I say *if*—we have to do it. He'll keep for a while. . . . You were saying I missed the big problem?"

"Yup." Slovotsky nodded. "Have you taken an inventory of our supplies lately? It's not just that we're down to our last pound of coffee and last fifth of Johnny Walker—if we don't get some food, and soon, we're going to be eating bark in a little while."

"Good point. Make a list tonight, and we'll talk it over in the morning, all five—"

Six.

"—all six of us." He spun around, startled at the interruption. "I thought you agreed to let us talk privately."

Sorry. The dragon's mental voice held no trace whatsoever of sincerity.

Tell me, do you give Karl as much trouble as you do me?

More. I like him better.

Slovotsky threw back his head and laughed. "I told you he'd eavesdrop." His face grew somber. "But I'm still worried about Karl. What the hell are we going to do about him? He could easily have gotten himself killed today, dashing off like that. And in case you weren't paying attention, the Matriarch said that she won't help us anymore. Any further deaths are as final as . . ." He furrowed his brow as he searched for an analogy.

"A temporary rate hike from the phone company?" Ahira suggested.

"Right."

"As for Karl," Ahira said, shrugging, "I've got to try to get him to show a bit of restraint. He has this thing about freeing slaves—and it's already put a price on our heads. We can't have him just rushing off and slashing away every time he sees someone in a collar."

Not that Ahira had any complaint about Karl's feelings; as James Michael Finnegan, Ahira had been raised in a world where slavery was generally considered a wrong. Or, at least, the prerogative of governments, not individuals.

But slavery had been the way of things in this world for millennia; they couldn't change things overnight, no matter what Karl had promised the Matriarch, as his part of the payment for Ahira's revivification.

You can be sure that Karl won't be restrained, Ahira.

Oh? And why is that?

Mmmm, just call it professional pride.

Walter Slovotsky nodded. "The dragon's got a point." He rubbed the back of his hand over his eyes and yawned.

Ahira clapped Slovotsky on the arm. "It's been a long day. Ellegon, you keep an eye peeled on the Waste; Walter, I'll take first watch. Go get some sleep; I'll wake you in a couple of hours. We'll worry about all this tomorrow."

"At Tara?" Slovotsky didn't wait for an answer; he walked off, whistling the theme from *Gone with the Wind*.

CHAPTER TWO: *"That Isn't Much, Is It?"*

We should be careful to get out of an experience only the wisdom that is in it—and stop there; lest we be like the cat that sits down on a hot stove lid. She will never sit on a hot stove lid again—and that is well; but also she will never sit down on a cold one anymore.

—Mark Twain

Back when he was in school, pursuing one of his many majors, Karl Cullinane had avoided the sunrise religiously; he saw the dawn only accidentally, unintentionally, through cigarette-smoke-tearing, caffeine-aching eyes after a night spent among a pile of books and papers, throwing together a last-minute term paper, or cramming for a final exam.

Whenever he could, he arranged his classes—the ones he didn't intend to skip regularly; the others didn't matter—to let him sleep as late as he could. Often he rose at the crack of noon.

Back then, he could sleep through anything.

Seems there've been some changes, he thought, sitting tailor-fashion beside Andy-Andy's sleeping form, blankets piled around him as protection against the dawn chill.

The sun rose across the Waste, touching the sky with pink and orange fingers. When he looked at the Waste through half-closed eyes, it was almost beautiful.

I see you're awake, the reedy voice sounded in his head. *Finally.*

"I'm awake," he whispered, rubbing at the middle of his back. No pain; none at all. It wasn't pain that kept him awake. When a distant breeze had wakened him, Karl had been afraid to let himself fall asleep again; his sleep had been filled with visions of himself as half a person, chopped off at the middle of his stomach. And nightmares of wading through unending pools of blood and gore.

"Just leave me alone, Ellegon." He lay back, pillowing his head on his hands. The dragon had deserted him yesterday; Karl felt no inclination to talk to him now.

You're being very immature about this, the dragon said petulantly.

"Leave me *alone*."

"What is it, Karl?" Andy-Andy whispered, her breath warm in his ear.

"Nothing. Go back to sleep." He closed his eyes. "That's what I'm going to do."

But I have to talk to you.

No.

Andy-Andy cuddled closer, her long brown hair covering his face with airy, silken threads. Karl put his arms around her and held her to him.

He drew in his breath to sigh, then spent several long seconds trying to spit out her hair without waking her.

God, how I hate mornings. He opened his eyes. *Then again . . .*

Andy-Andy lay sleeping, the blanket's ragged hem gathered around her neck, her features even more lovely in repose. Her long lashes, the olive tone of her skin, the slight bend in her slightly too-long nose—an inventory of parts didn't do her justice.

Then again, maybe I'm prejudiced. He reached out a hand to pull the blankets down—

*And, then again, maybe you should give both your hormones and your mammary fixation a rest, and talk to me. You don't understand. Maybe I should *make* you understand.*

Don't. Ellegon's mindlink could carry more than the dragon's phantom voice or images; it could also transmit feelings, experiences. And not just pleasant feelings, either.

Will you listen to me, then?

Carefully brushing her hair away, Karl sighed. *Just give me a minute.* He untangled himself from Andy-Andy's sprawling limbs and slipped out of the blankets, taking a moment to slip his breechclout on, step into his sandals, and strap their laces around his calves. He eyed his leggings and tunic, debating with early-morning laziness whether or not to put them on now.

Later. After coffee.

Absently, he picked up his scabbarded saber and slipped the belt over his left shoulder, resting his right hand for just a moment on its sharkskin hilt. Karl had a tendency to lose things, one way or another, but here, in this world, losing his sword could quickly mean losing his life.

Near the downhill edge of the clearing, Riccetti and Slovotsky slept under their blankets, their snores barely reaching Karl's ears.

Beyond them, on a flat stone next to the smoldering remains of last night's fire, Ahira sat, drinking a cup of coffee, keeping watch over the sleeping form of the captive bowman. His head turned, and he lifted an aluminum Sierra cup in a silent invitation.

Nodding gratefully, Karl walked down the gently sloping clearing, the morning dew clutching at his feet with damp, chilly fingers. That felt good, in a strange way; the clammy cold was a physical confirmation that his legs weren't numb.

He glanced at the ashes of the fire as he seated himself on a flat rock, silently accepting a hot cup of coffee from Ahira.

He shook his head. Ahira shouldn't have been so care-

less with the fire. Maybe, by adding enough tinder and
kindling, they could tease the embers back into a roaring
fire, but maybe not. And they had only a couple of books
of matches left. Once those were gone, the only way they
would have to light fires would be with flint and steel.
Which was a pain, no matter how easy his old Boy Scout
manual had made it look.

*I imagine it is. But if I were you, I wouldn't worry
about it. Consider for a moment the fact that the fire is
dead, but the coffee is hot.* Beyond a stand of trees, a
gout of orange flame roared skyward. *Think it
through.* Another blast of fire cut through the lightening
sky.

Karl sipped his coffee. It was just the way he liked it:
too sweet for most people to stomach, with just a touch of
creamer. "Ellegon? Just take it easy on me, please? I
don't think all that well in the morning."

Ahira chuckled. "Who does?" He sobered. "Sleep
well?"

"No." He looked down at his right hand. Somebody
had washed the blood from it while he slept, but there
were dry, reddish-brown flecks under his nails and in
the hairs on the back of his hand. "Had a few bad
dreams."

"I can't feel too sorry for you; I was up all night."

"Slovotsky didn't relieve you?"

The dwarf shrugged his improbably broad shoulders.
"I didn't wake him. He's going to need his sleep. You, too
—you've got a long trip ahead of you. We're short of
almost every kind of supply, and somebody's going to
have to go into Metreyll and do some shopping." He furrowed his heavy brows, peering up at Karl. "And scout-
ing—we've got to figure out what to do when the
armsmen are missed. To do that, we've got to know what
the situation is, in Metreyll. Yes?"

"Not really. We really have a way to fix things so we
don't get blamed: We leave the dead men where they are,
and put a sword in the hand of the dead slave." *I wish I*

*knew your name. I'm sorry, whoever you are, but you
don't have any further use for that body. As a decoy, it
might help to save our lives.* "If anyone comes around to
investigate, he'll have to decide that the slave had turned
to fight, driving one off, killing the other three; their
horses just wandered away."

Ahira snorted. "You *do* wake up slow—the locals are
going to think that an unarmed, half-starved slave killed
three swordsmen?"

"As long as there aren't any other suspects around, they
will. Either that, or they'll have to decide that somebody,
for no apparent reason, came from God knows where to
the slave's defense."

"Hmm. That doesn't sound likely."

"No, it doesn't. Happens to be true, that's all. Occam's
Razor, Ahira. Most people use it all the time, even if they
can't tell you what it is." Karl drank some more coffee.
"Got another idea?"

"No."

"Then let's give mine a try."

"Agreed." The dward nodded. "Andrea, Riccetti, and
I will take care of it. We'll keep their horses, yes?"

"Yes." Not that the poor assortment of fleabags would
be of much use. "But there's something you're missing,"
Karl said. "We're low on healing draughts. Someone has
to go over to the tabernacle and see if we can pry some
loose. Besides, I want to see how Doria's doing."

Ahira nodded. "I'll give it a try. Tomorrow. Although
. . . the Matriarch did say we're on our own. No more
help. And that could mean—"

"That they won't *give* us any. Not that they won't *sell*
us some. We do have the coin Walter and I took off
Ohlmin—"

*Only because I brought it here. You abandoned it
near the Gate Between Worlds.*

Karl ignored the dragon and spoke to Ahira. "We
should be able to meet their price."

"You hope. I'll check it out. *And* see how Doria is. If I can. You get the Metreyll shopping trip."

"Agreed." Karl stood. "I'd better go saddle up my horse and get going."

"No." Ahira shook her head. "Not until dark. You're taking Walter with you."

"I know," Karl said, irritated, "that you don't know much about horses, but putting two men our size on one isn't good for a horse, even when there's no hot sun beating down. And we can't take one of the new horses; they might be recognized. So I'd better ride in alone, just me and my horse. I *like* her. She did good, yesterday."

Meaning that I didn't.

Exactly.

Ahira scowled. "First of all, you're not taking your horse; Ellegon's going to fly both of you over tonight, and drop you off outside Metreyll. I want Walter to go along, to keep an eye on you. You've got a tendency to get into trouble." He swigged the last of his coffee, then set the aluminum cup down gently on a flat stone. "As far as Ellegon goes, Karl, I wish you'd learn to be a bit more patient with the people you care about.

"I had a long talk with Ellegon last night. He had his reasons. Dammit, Karl, that dragon may be more than three centuries old, but by dragon standards, he's still a baby. You don't expect a child to do the right thing, not when he's scared out of his wits."

"And what the hell did he have to be scared about? All those soldiers had were bows and swords. Nothing for him to be afraid of."

*There was *so*. I'll *show* you.*

"Don't." Karl stood. "Stay out of my mind." Ellegon had opened his mind to Karl before, letting Karl feel what it had been like to be chained in a Pandathaway sewer for three centuries. A dragon's mind couldn't edit out familiar smells the way a human's could. Three centuries of stench. . . . "Maybe you had a good reason. Just *tell* me, for God's sake."

Very well, then—

"*No.*" Ahira shook his head slowly. He lowered his voice. "Karl has to learn not to make snap judgments, Ellegon. It could get any number of us killed. Show him. Now."

Don't—

Ellegon opened his mind . . .

. . . and flew. *That* was the secret, after all: Alone, his wings weren't strong enough to lift him; he had to reach inside and let his inner strength add itself to the lifting power of his fast-beating wings.

Slowly, he gained altitude, as he circled around the craggy vastness of Heiphon's reaches until the ledge where he had been born was far beneath him, the hardened shards of his shell only vague white flecks, barely discernible.

Ellegon worked his wings more rapidly, until the wind whistled by him. He began to tire, and let the frantic beating of his wings subside until they barely kept him flying. Then it occurred to him that if his wings weren't sufficient, possibly they were superfluous; perhaps his inner strength alone could support him in the air. So Ellegon curled his wings inward, and lifted even more with his inner strength.

And dropped through the sky like a stone.

In a panic, he spread his wings against the onrush of air and worked them, scooping air from in front and above, whisking it behind and below.

For a moment, it seemed as though his frenzied effort had no effect, but then the craggy peak slowed its menacing approach, stopped, and began to fall away.

Another lesson learned, he thought. It seemed that his inner strength couldn't support him all by itself, either. It would have been nice if there were someone to tell him that, instead of letting him learn by trial and error.

But that is the way it is for dragons. We have to learn for ourselves. It didn't occur to him to wonder how he knew that, or how he knew that he was a dragon.

A mile below him, a gap in the clouds loomed invitingly. He eased the frantic beating of his wings until he started to lose altitude and dropped slowly through the gap, letting the cottony floor of clouds become a gray ceiling.

Below him, lush greenery spread from horizon to horizon, broken only by the brown-and-gray mass of the mountain called Heiphon, a blue expanse of water to the south, and a dirty brown tracing that wormed its way across the grassland, through the forest.

What was that brown line? It cut across the forest and dirtied the tops of the rolling hills, sullying the greenery. It had to be unnatural, as though someone or something had deliberately chosen to make the land ugly.

He couldn't understand that. Why would anyone spend time on the ground soiling the greenery, when one could fly above it and enjoy it?

Ridiculous. He eased back with his inner strength, spreading his wings as he glided in for a closer look. There was something moving on the dirt line. . . .

There. A strange sort of creature, indeed. Six legs and two heads; one head long and brown and sleek, the other pasty flesh only partly hidden by greasy fur.

No, he was wrong. It was *two* creatures, not one. Both four-legged, although the smaller one's forelegs were stunted. If it got down on all fours, its backside would stick up in the air. No wonder it chose to ride on the back of the other; even a creature as ugly as that would not want to look more foolish than necessary.

But why did the larger one carry it? Perhaps the smaller was the larval form, and the larger its parent.

He flew closer, and as he did, their minds opened before him. Ellegon began to understand. The smaller creature was a *Rhêden Monsterhunter;* at least, that was what its small mind said. And the larger had no choice about carrying it; it was compelled to, under threat of leather and steel.

Another absurdity. No matter; Ellegon would end the silliness, by eating them both.

As he stooped, the Rhêden Monsterhunter's head snapped up. It reached for a strange contraption: two sticks, one bent, the other straight. That was a *bow and arrow*, but what was *dragonbane?*

The Rhêden Monsterhunter pulled back the arrow, and then released it. The stick flew toward Ellegon.

He didn't bother flaming it, and there was no point in dodging it. He was a dragon, after all; surely this puny stick couldn't hurt him.

Its oily head sank into his chest, just below the juncture of his long neck. A point of white-hot pain expanded across his torso.

Ellegon fell.

He crashed through the treetops, branches snapping under his weight, not slowing his fall. The ground rushed up and struck him; his whole body burned with a cold, cruel fire that faded only slowly to black.

When he awoke, a golden cage surrounded his face, a golden collar clamped tightly around his neck. He lay on his side on the hard ground, his legs all chained together. Tentatively, he tried to flame the chains, using just a wisp of the fire of his inner strength. He screamed as his neck burned.

Safely beyond his reach, the Rhêden Monsterhunter stood smiling. "It'll take me some days to rig a cart for you, dragon. But it will be worth it; they'll pay a fine price for you in Pandathaway."

Karl shook his head, trying to clear it. So, that was why Ellegon hadn't helped him. It wasn't really coward-ice. It was sheer, unreasoning terror. Definitely un-reasoning; if Ellegon had looked into the bowmen's minds, he would have seen that none of their arrows were tipped with extract of dragonbane. Dragons were nearly extinct in the Eren regions; the cultivation of dragonbane was a dying skill.

But he couldn't. As a young dragon—no, as a *child*—he had been so badly hurt by that crossbow bolt that the thought of facing another dragonbane-tipped arrow chased all rationality from his mind. The pain of the bolt cleaving through his chest . . .

*Yes. It *hurt*.*

Karl looked down at his own chest. A wicked round weal over his heart stared back at him like a red eye.

Karl, I'm . . . sorry. I was just so scared.

It hadn't been fair to expect the dragon to leap to his aid. Ellegon wasn't an adult, not really. Applying adult standards to him was wrong. The dragon was a curious mix of infant and ancient: By dragon standards, three and a half centuries of age put Ellegon barely out of babyhood, but Ellegon had spent almost all of that time chained in a cesspool in Pandathaway.

How do you handle a child who's frightened? *Not* by shutting him out of your life; that was clear. Maybe there wasn't a hard-and-fast rule, but the answer had to start with listening.

Karl nodded. *So I'll start listening now.* "It's okay, Ellegon. My fault; I should have known you had your reasons. Are you sure that you're willing to fly us into— *near* Metreyll, once it gets dark?'"

I'll try, Karl. I'll try to do better, next time. I will.

He sighed. "See that you do," he said out loud, while his mind murmured, *I know you will.*

Ahira stared up at him, his heavy brow furrowed. The dwarf sat silently for a moment. "I've written down a shopping list, some of the things we're going to need. All of us had better go over it."

"No problem. Something else on your mind?"

Ahira nodded. "What are we going to do about Riccetti? He's practically helpless in a fight, and I'm willing to bet that we're going to go through more than a couple before this is all over."

"Sorry, but there's no easy solution to that one. As soon as I get back, I'll start him on swordsmanship. But I can't make a swordsman out of him overnight. At best, it'll be months before he develops any kind of proficiency. Mmm . . . he's not left-handed, is he?"

"No. Why?"

He sighed. "It doesn't matter, then. Lefties have an edge in swordplay, just as they do in tennis, back home. The rest of us aren't used to having the blade come from the other side. It's—" He stopped himself. Of course. An opponent's unfamiliarity was a huge advantage; it had helped a Japanese police society disarm numerous samurai at the end of Japan's feudal era. But the name of the weapon they carried—what the *hell* was it called?

It hovered just at the edge of his mind. A length of chain, weighted down at both ends—

Manriki-gusari.

Thanks. But how did you know?

I read minds, fool.

Ahira laughed. "Get some breakfast. And take it easy for the rest of the day; you'd better be on your toes in Metreyll. Karl?"

"Yes?"

"I want your word on something. No fighting unless it's in self-defense."

"Fine." Self-defense was a loose term, one that could be applied to almost any situation by a sufficiently flexible mind. "That sounds reasonable."

Hypocrite.

Huh?

You have nightmares about wading through blood, and then the next day you try to wiggle out of Ahira's suggestion that you not shed more unless you really have to.

Ellegon—

"Excuse me," the dwarf said. "I wasn't finished. You've been known to have a liberal imagination; *Walter* decides what constitutes self-defense, not you."

"Understood."

"Do I have your word?"

"You're not leaving me a lot of leeway." Karl sighed. "Yes."

"Good." Ahira spread his hands. "Just stay out of trouble. That's all I'm asking. That isn't much, is it?"

That, friend Ahira, depends.

CHAPTER THREE: *Metreyll*

> *I was never attached to that great sect,*
> *Whose doctrine is, that each one should select*
> *Out of the crowd a mistress or a friend,*
> *And all the rest, though fair and wise, commend*
> *To cold oblivion, though 'tis in the code*
> *Of modern morals, and the beaten road*
> *Which those poor slaves with weary footsteps tread*
> *Who travel to their home among the dead*
> *By the broad highway of the world, and so*
> *With one chained friend, perhaps a jealous foe,*
> *The dreariest and the longest journey go.*

> —Percy Bysshe Shelley

The preserve was miles behind. Half a mile below, the Waste of Elrood lay in the starlight, a solid expanse of baked, cracked earth, the blankness relieved only by an occasional stone outcropping.

Shivering only partly from the cold, Karl clung to Ellegon's back. The cool night air whistled by, whipping through his hair.

He looked down and shuddered. Even if the Waste had not held bad memories, it would still have been unpleasant; a landscape like something out of the pictures the Apollo astronauts had brought back, with none of the charm of accomplishment those pictures carried with them.

Behind him, Walter Slovotsky chuckled. "I wouldn't

worry about it, Karl," he called out, his voice barely carrying over the rush of wind. "It's an advantage—as long as we're at the preserve, anyone who wants to give us trouble would have to cross forty miles of the Waste to do it."

He has a point, Karl. And, powerful as they are, I'm willing to bet that the Hand clerics are grateful for that protection.

That was probably true. And it pointed up one of the troubles in this world: Anytime you had anything, be it a piece of land, a horse, a sword—even your own life— you always had to consider the possibility that someone would try to take it away from you.

Just because he wanted it.

And is that so different from your world? For a moment, Karl's head felt as though it were being stroked by gentle fingers—from inside. Then: *Or don't you consciously recall the Sudetenland, Lithuania, Wounded Knee, or—*

Enough. You made your point. Just leave it at that, eh?

But, dammit, there *was* a difference. Back home, there was at least an acknowledgment that the strong preying on the weak was wrong. It was reflected in laws, customs, and folktales, from fables about Robin Hood to the legends of Wyatt Earp.

He chuckled. Well, it was the *legend* that counted, anyway. Back when he was majoring in American history, Karl had found several accounts that suggested that the Earp brothers were just another gang of hoods, as bad as the Clantons they had gunned down—from ambush—at the O.K. Corral. The Earps had managed to wangle themselves badges, that was all.

And when you think about it, quite probably Robin Hood robbed the rich to give to himself.

Which made sense; in the holdup business, robbing the poor had to be easier than robbing the rich—but it was bound to be financially unrewarding.

That's why they call them "the poor," Karl. If it was rewarding to rob them, they probably would be known as "the rich."

Funny.

Only to those with a sense of humor.

The boundary of the Waste loomed ahead, a knife-sharp break between the scarred ground and the forested land beyond. In the starlight, the huge oaks would normally have seemed to be threatening hulks, but by comparison with the Waste, their dark masses were somehow conforting.

You don't have to go any farther. Set us down anywhere near here.

Just a short way. Ellegon's flight slowed. *Let me put you a bit closer; this way, you won't have so far to walk.*

Why the sudden concern for my sore feet?

I have my reasons, the dragon responded, with a bit of a mental sniff. *But since you're so eager to be on foot . . .*

The dragon circled a clearing among the tall trees, then braked to a safe, if bumpy, landing.

Karl vaulted from Ellegon's back, landing lightly on the rocky ground. Reflexively, he slipped his right hand to his swordhilt as he peered into the night.

Nothing. Just trees in the dark, and a mostly overgrown path leading, he hoped, toward Metreyll.

Walter climbed down to stand beside him. "My guess is that we're about five miles out," he said, helping Karl to slip his arms into the straps of a rucksack. "We *could* camp here and walk into town in the morning, I guess," Walter said, frowning. He brightened. "Or maybe we should just walk in now."

Karl slipped his thumbs under the rucksack's straps. "Do I get two guesses which you'd rather do?"

Be safe. Take three.

"Well?" Slovotsky jerked a thumb toward a path.

"Why not?" *Ellegon, you'd better get going. But do me*

a favor: Circle overhead, and see if the path leads to the Metreyll road.

I didn't set you down here by accident, fool. Of course it does.

As Karl and Walter moved away, the dragon's wings began moving, beating until they were only a blur in the darkness, sending dust and leaves swirling into the air. Ellegon sprang skyward and slipped away into the night, his outline momentarily visible against the glimmer of the overhead stars.

Be careful, he said, his mental voice barely audible. And then he was gone.

"Let's walk," Karl said.

They walked in silence for a few minutes, carefully picking their way along the dirt path through the trees. Finally, Walter spoke.

"I've got a suggestion, if you don't mind."

"Yes?"

"Look, this is just a supply trip." Slovotsky patted at the leather pouch dangling from his belt. "Right?"

"You have a keen eye for the obvious." Karl shrugged. "What's your point?"

"Hmm, let me put it this way: I'm not going to take the chance of lifting anything. Granted, as long as we're based in the sanctuary, we've got a nice buffer zone between Metreyll and the Waste, but there's no need to push it. We don't want to get the locals angry at us. Too risky."

"Fine. So you're not going to use your skills." That made sense. There was enough to do in Metreyll, and with all the coin they had, money wouldn't be a problem for a long while. They had to buy provisions and supplies, as well as some hardware. And weapons; the party was short of spares.

"That wasn't what I meant." Walter ducked under an overhanging branch, then made a show of holding it out of the way so that Karl could pass.

Sometimes, it seemed as though Walter made too

much of Karl's being larger than he was. Then again, maybe that was understandable; Slovotsky had long been accustomed to being the biggest man in almost any group.

"What I meant," Slovotsky went on, "is that *you* have to watch it. There's liable to be some sort of slave market in Metreyll. Not as big as the one in Pandathaway, granted, but something—the whole economy of this region is based on slavery."

"So?"

"So we give Metreyll a bye. No interfering with local . . . customs, no matter how repugnant. At least for the time being. My guess is there's still a reward out for you in Pandathaway. We don't want reports getting back there about your still being alive."

"Thanks for your tender concern about my health."

Slovotsky snorted. "And thank you for the sarcasm. I don't particularly care if you believe it, but I *am* worried about you. As well as me. If you start swinging that sword in Metreyll, we're both in deep trouble."

"Walter, where did you get the idea that I'm some sort of bloodthirsty monster?"

"Mmm . . . yesterday was kind of a clue." He held up a hand to forestall Karl's objection. "Okay, that was a cheap shot. Look—I'm not saying that you really enjoy slicing open someone's gut. With the exception of the time we killed Ohlmin and his men, I don't think you've ever liked violence.

"But it doesn't bother you the way it used to. What it comes down to, Karl, is something you said in Pandathaway, after you freed Ellegon. Something about if what you're doing is important enough, you worry about the consequences later."

"Wait—"

"No, you wait. Slovotsky's Law Number Seventeen: Thou shalt *always* consider the consequences of thy actions. You could make a lot of trouble for all of us, if you don't keep your head on."

He understood Walter's point. And it did make a kind of sense; the time he had freed Ellegon had cost them all much. But to commit himself *not* to do anything about people in chains . . .

Karl shrugged. "I gave Ahira my word. Just leave it at that."

Walter sighed deeply. "Unless I can convince you that I'm right, I wouldn't trust your reflexes, Karl. I've seen the way you clap your hand to your sword whenever you're irritated about anything. When you know there's no reason to cut someone up, you're safe to be around, granted; I'm not worried about your stabbing me if I don't put enough sugar in your coffee. . . . The trouble is, you're thinking as if you were the only one who can suffer from your actions, dammit."

"You sound scared."

"I am." Walter snorted. "Not just for my own tender hide. I didn't want to tell you this, but . . . Ellegon told me something, on our way over; he tuned you out. Wasn't sure whether you should know or not. He left it up to me whether and when to clue you in."

"And what's this great secret?"

"Well, you know his nose is more sensitive than ours." Walter shook his head slowly. "It must have made it hell for him in the sewers. But the point is, he can pick up on things that you and I can't. Even things that a medical lab back home would have trouble with. Slight biochemical changes, for instance. Hormones, like that."

A cold chill washed across Karl's back. "*Whose* biochemical changes?"

"Andrea's. Nobody knows it but you, me, and Ellegon, Karl. She's pregnant, although only a couple of day's worth. I guess congratulations are in order, no?"

Ohgod. "You're lying." He turned to face Slovotsky. "Aren't you?"

"Nope. Now, did that drive the point home? If you screw up, you're not just endangering you and me—and Andy, for that matter. You get yourself killed or put the rest of us on another wanted list, and you're putting an unborn child's life in danger. Yours." Slovotsky snorted. "So are you still interested in playing Lone Ranger right away? If you call me Tonto, I swear I'll stick a knife in you."

His head spun. *A baby?*

"Karl, you—"

"Okay. You made your point." *I'm going to be a father.* He rubbed his knuckles against the side of his head. *There's going to be a baby depending on me.*

"Hope so." Slovotsky said solemnly. Brightening, he clapped a hand to Karl's shoulder. "Hey, can I be the godfather?"

"Shut up."

Slovotsky chuckled.

"You want what?" The blacksmith turned from his forge, bringing the redly glowing piece of metal over to his anvil, holding it easily with the long wrought-iron pincers. He picked up his hammer and gave the hot metal a few tentative blows before settling down to pounding it in earnest.

Wary of flying sparks, Karl moved a few feet back. "I want a length of chain," he said in Erendra, "about this long." He held his hands about three feet apart. "With an iron weight on either end—those should be cylindrical, about half the size of my fist. If you can do that sort of thing."

"It wouldn't be difficult," the smith said, returning his worked iron to the forge. "I can have that for you by noon, if you're in a hurry."

Sweat running in rivulets down his face and into his sparse red beard, he pumped the bellows for a few moments before pausing to take a dipperful of water from an oaken barrel. The smith drank deeply, clearly relishing every swallow. He took a second dipperful, tilted his head back, and slowly poured the water onto his upturned face, then shook his head to clear the water from his eyes.

"What do you want it for?" he asked, offering Karl a dipperful of water with a gesture of his hand and a raised eyebrow.

"Religious artifact." Karl accepted the dipper and drank. "I'm an apostle of the metal god."

The smith cocked his head. "There isn't a metal god."

"Then I'm probably not one of his apostles."

The smith threw back his head and laughed. "And Teerhnus is liable to get his proud nose cut off if he puts it where it doesn't belong, eh? Very well, have it your way. Now, as to the price—"

"We're not done yet. I'll want two of them. And I'll also want to buy some of your other equipment. I'll need . . . a general-purpose anvil, some basic tools—hammer, tongs—and a hundred-weight of rod, sheet, and bar stock, a bit of—"

The smith snorted. "Granted, there is enough work for another smith in Metreyll, but you don't look the type." He set his hammer down and reached out, taking Karl's right hand in both of his. "From this ridge of callus I'd say you've spent much time with that sword in your hand, but none with a hammer. And you're too old to apprentice."

Karl drew his hand back. "It's for a friend. Now, what sort of coin are we talking about for all this?" It was hard to concentrate on the transaction with the back of his mind shouting, *A father—I'm going to be a father!*

Teerhnus shook his head. "You don't know what you're talking about." He gestured at the seven different anvils scattered around the shop, each mounted on its own tree-trunk stand. They ranged dramatically in size and shape, from a tiny one that couldn't have weighed more than thirty pounds to an immense, almost cubical monster of an anvil that Karl probably couldn't have lifted. "Even a brainless farrier needs at least two anvils to do any kind of work at all. If your friend wants to be able to do more than shoe horses, he'll need at least three. And I'll need quite a bit of coin for each. *Damn*, but it's a pain to cast a new anvil. You are planning to travel with them?" He peered at Karl from under heavy brows. "I'd be a fool to help you set up a friend of yours in competition with me, no matter what the price."

Karl shook his head. "That's not what I'm planning to do. I swear it."

The smith nodded. "On your sword, if you please."

Karl slowly drew his sword, then balanced the flat of the blade on his outstretched palms. "What I have sworn is true."

The smith shrugged. "I guess that settles it. Nice piece of workmanship, that sword. Are those Sciforth markings?"

"I don't know. Would you like to see it?"

"Of course." Teerhnus accepted the hilt in his huge hands. He held the sword carefully, stroking a rough thumbnail along the edge. "Very sharp. Holds the edge well, I'll wager." He flicked the blade with his finger, smiling at the clear *ting!* "No," he answered his own question, "that's not a Sciforth blade. They make good steel in Sciforth, but not this fine. Could be Endell, I suppose; those dwarves know their alloys." He rummaged around in a wooden bin until he found a soft wool cloth, then handed sword and cloth to Karl. "Where did you get it?"

Karl shrugged as he used the cloth to wipe the blade; he replaced his sword in its scabbard. He couldn't answer honestly; the smith wouldn't believe him. Or possibly worse, he might. Back home, on the Other Side, the sword had been a skinning knife; it had translated well. "I just found it somewhere." Better an evasion than to be caught in a lie. "Now, when can you have the anvils and such ready?"

"Hmmm . . . you're planning to be in Metreyll long?"

"Not past sunset. I'm en route to . . ." Visualizing

Ahira's map of the Eren regions, he picked a city at
random. " . . . Aeryk. I plan to be out of Metreyll by
nightfall."

"Can't be done." The smith shook his head. "I do have
work to do. I could spare some rod stock, I suppose, but I
don't have any spare hammers, and casting anvils is just
too much trouble to bother with."

Karl produced a pair of platinum coins, holding one
between thumb and forefinger. The obverse showed the
bust of a bearded man, the reverse a stylistic rippling of
waves. "Are you sure?"

"Pandathaway coin, eh?" The smith spread his palms.
"Well . . . those two are fine as a down payment, but I'll
need six more on delivery."

"This *is* platinum, after all—and Pandathaway coin,
at that. I thought you'd be happy to take these two, and
give me some gold back, as well as the iron."

"I doubt that." The smith grinned. "I wouldn't call
that thinking at all. Let's agree on seven platinum, and
we'll both be happy."

The money wasn't really a problem, but there was no
need for Karl to draw attention to himself by seeming to
have too free a purse. "Three. And you will give me five
gold back. Pandathaway coin, not this debased Metreyll
coinage."

"Six platinum and six gold. And *you* will stay in
Metreyll, along with your strong back, long enough to
help me cast three new anvils."

Karl sighed, and resigned himself to a long bargaining
session. "Four . . ."

Five pieces of platinum, six of gold, four of silver, and
a bent copper poorer, Karl waited for Walter Slovotsky
in the town square, near the lord's palace.

Metreyll was laid out differently than the other cities
they had seen. Unlike Lundeyll, the city itself had no
protecting walls. Unlike Pandathaway, it was both land-
locked and apparently unplanned; Metreyll's streets

radiated out from the central palace like a misshapen
web, woven by a demented spider.

Although calling it a palace might have been too
generous an assessment: It was a cluster of nine two-
storied sandstone buildings, surrounded by narrow,
crumbling ramparts. The raised portcullis showed its
age: The timbers were splintering, the pulley chains and
spikes so rusty that it was clear that the portcullis was
lowered rarely if ever.

Two mail-clad guardsmen at the gate eyed him
casually as they sat on three-legged stools, their spears
propped up against the wall nearby, but well out of
reach.

Karl nodded to himself. Ill-kept, unattended defenses
were a clear sign that Metreyll hadn't known warfare for
a while, and the lack of challenge from the bored guardsmen meant that the locals were used to the presence of
strangers.

"Are you going to sleep just standing there?"

Squinting in the bright sunlight, Walter smiled down
at him from the bench of the half-filled flatbed wagon.
"You'll be glad to hear that beef is cheap—seems the
ranchers had too good a year. I picked up about four
hundred pounds of jerky for a song." He snorted. "Not
exactly 'This Way to Cheap Street,' but a song."

He set the brake and dismounted, patting the two
hitched mules in passing. "Although horseflesh—even
muleflesh—is at a premium. I bought a stallion and
another gelding—the hostler will hang on to them until
dark—but they set me back a nice piece of change.
Apparently it's going to be another bumper crop of cattle
this year, and the tributary ranchers are paying nice
prices for labor—all kinds of labor."

Karl smiled as he took off his rucksack and tossed it
into the wagon. "I almost wish we needed a bit of money.
When I was a kid, I fully intended to be a cowboy." He
shrugged. "Maybe we could look into all of us hiring out
as hands, anyway. Just for a while." Of course, they

would have to figure out how to keep Ellegon out of sight.

No, that probably wouldn't do. He had responsibilities now. Fulfilling childhood fantasies was something he would have to set aside.

Walter shook his head. "I don't think that's such a good idea. All the hiring is for a cattle drive—and guess where that's headed."

"Pandathaway?"

Slovotsky nodded. " 'Everything comes to Pandathaway'—except us, I hope. I doubt they go easy on felons' accomplices."

"Good point. So you keep your eyes open, too."

"They never close, Karl. Now, how'd you do at the smith's?"

"Fine, I guess. Although he struck a hard deal. Come to think of it, I probably was taken. But he did throw in a couple of used swords." He shrugged. "In any case, we can pick up that gear at sunset, too. West end of town." He eyed the noon sun. "Any ideas on what we should do until then?"

Slovotsky raised an eyebrow. "Joy Street? Or whatever they call it. It's down this way—" He held up a palm. "You don't absolutely *have* to cheat on Andy, you know. Just a few beers, while I see what's available. Prisoner of my hormones, I am."

Karl laughed. "Why not? I could use a beer." He boosted himself to the bed of the wagon and sprawled on a sack of grain. "You drive."

The unpaved street twisted gently through the markets, past a drab tarpaulin where a sweaty grain seller hawked his muslin sacks of oats and barley, a ramshackle corral where a well-fleshed hostler groomed his tattered assortment of swaybacked mares and half-lame geldings, an open-air workbench where a squinting leatherworker and a bewhiskered swordsman haggled angrily over the price of a fore-and-aft peaked saddle.

Wagons creaked through the street, as farmers and

their slaves brought sacked grain and caged chickens to market. Some wagons were drawn by dusty mules, or slowly plodding oxen; others were handcarts, pulled by slaves.

Karl gripped his sword. He fondled the sharkskin hilt for a moment, then sighed and let his hand drop. *Damn Walter for being right. This wasn't the time or place to get involved in a swordfight. And besides, I can't solve the problem by chopping up everyone who owns a slave. That just wouldn't do it.*

That thought didn't make him feel any better. "God-dammit."

"Just keep cool," Slovotsky whispered, urging the mules on.

The street widened as the slave market came into view. Surrounded by a hundred bidders and spectators, a noisy auction proceeded in front of a boxlike wagon bearing the wave-and-chain insignia of the Pandathaway Slavers' Guild.

The auctioneer accepted a handful of coins from a farmer, then, smilingly, snapped the farmer's chains around the wrists of a skinny, bearded slave before removing his own chains. "You should have no difficulty with this one; he has been well tamed," the auctioneer said, as the farmer looped a hemp rope around the slave's neck. As the slave was led away, Karl shuddered at the old scars that crisscrossed his back. *Well tamed . . .*

"Easy, Karl," Walter whispered. "There's nothing you can do about it."

One of the slavers brought the next slave out of the wagon. This slave was a short, dark man in a filthy cotton loincloth. His whip scars were fresh; livid red weals were spattered randomly over his hairy torso and legs. Lines around the edge of his mouth and eyes suggested that he used to smile often. But he wasn't smiling now; chained at his neck, wrists, and ankles, he stared sullenly out at the crowd.

A cold chill ran up Karl's spine. "Walter, I know him."

"No kidding?" Slovotsky's expression belied his calm tone; he looked as if he had been slapped.

"The Games in Pandathaway—he was my first opponent. Took him out in a few seconds."

This was horrible. An expectant father had no business risking his own life, forgetting the danger to the others, but this man was somebody Karl *knew*. Not a close friend, granted; he didn't even know the other's name. But someone he knew, nonetheless.

He turned to Slovotsky.

The thief shook his head. "Karl, do us both a favor and get that expression the hell off your face. You're starting to draw stares." He lowered his voice. "That's better. We're just a couple of travelers, chatting idly about the weather and the price of flesh, got it? I don't know exactly what harebrained scheme you're working on, but we're not going to do it. No way. Remember, you gave Ahira your word."

"Walter—"

Slovotsky raised his palm. "But this isn't the time to put your honor to the test. We've got plenty of coin. We'll *bid* on him. Sit tight for a moment." Tossing the reins to Karl, he vaulted from the wagon and moved into the crowd.

The bidding was stiff; several of the local farmers and ranchers forced the price from the initial twelve gold up to more than two platinum. The most persistent, a stocky man in a sweatstained cotton tunic, followed each of his bids with a glare at Slovotsky, as though challenging him to go on. When the bidding topped two platinum, the stocky man threw up his hands and stalked off, muttering vague curses under his breath.

Finally, the auctioneer raised the twig above his head, holding it delicately between his thumbs and forefingers.

"Will anyone challenge the price of two platinum, three gold for this man?" he asked the crowd in a practiced singsong. "A worthy, well-mannered slave, no doubt useful both in the field and as breeding stock. Both he and his sons will work hard, and require little food. No? I ask again, and again, and—" He snapped the twig. "The slave is sold; the bargain is made."

He nodded down at Slovotsky. "Do you want to claim him now? Very well. No chains? Two silvers for the ones he wears, if you want them. I'd advise it; this one hasn't quite been broken to his collar. Yet. And watch the teeth—he's nasty."

Walter reached into his pouch and handed over the money, accepting the slave's leash and an iron key in return. A few cuffs and curses moved the man down the platform's steps and over to the wagon.

The slave's eyes widened as he saw Karl. "You're Kharl—"

Slovotsky backhanded him across the face, then drew one of his knives. "Keep your tongue still if you want it to stay in your mouth." The point of his knife touching the smaller man's neck, he urged him onto the back of the wagon. The auctioneer smiled in encouragement before calling for the next slave to be sold.

"Just keep quiet," Karl whispered. "And relax. Everything's going to be fine."

"But—"

"Shh." With a clatter, the wagon began to move. "I know a smith on the edge of town. We have to make a stop first, but we'll have the collar off you in just a little while. Just be patient."

"You mean—"

"He means you're free," Walter said, giving a flick to the reins. "It just won't show quite yet."

The little man's mouth pursed, as though he were bracing himself for a slap. Then he shook his head, puzzled. "You mean that, Kharlkuhlinayn." It was half an unbelieved statement, half a terrified question.

At Karl's nod, his face grew somber. And then his gap-toothed mouth broke into a smile. A special sort of smile.

Karl didn't say anything. Nobody else would have understood how beautiful that smile was.

Unless they had seen it on the face of someone they loved.

Or in a mirror.

"Ch'akresarkandyn ip Katharhdn," the little man said, as he sat on a sack of wheat in the bed of the wagon, rubbing at the lesions left by his chains. The sores were infected, oozing a hideous green pus in several places. Undoubtedly, his wrists and ankles ached dreadfully, but the light rubbing was all he allowed himself. "It's not so hard to pronounce, not as difficult as Kharlkuhlinayn."

"Call me Karl."

"You can call me Chak, if you'd like. You can call me whatever you want." Chak nodded slowly. "I owe you, Kharl. I don't understand why you freed me, but I owe you."

Walter chuckled. "So your only objection to slavery is when you're the slave."

Chak's brow furrowed. "Of course. It's the way of things. Although . . ." he shook his head. "There's times when it turns my stomach. Then again, it doesn't take much to turn my stomach. I'm a Katharhd; we've got delicate digestion."

"What happened to you?" Karl asked. "When we met, you were living off your winnings in the Games, but—"

"You put an end to that, Karl Cullinane, and I've spent many an hour cursing your name. When you knocked me out of the first round, I was down to my last couple of coppers. Fool that I was, I signed with this shifty-eyed Therranji; said he was taking on guardsmen for Lord Khoral. Damn elves can't help lying.

"In any case, fourteen of us rode out of Pandathaway. Took a while until we were past Aeryk and clear of the trade routes. One night, we camped and had dinner— with an extra ration of wine. Spiked wine; we all woke up in chains, got sold off in small lots. Seems the Therranji was a clandestine member of the Slavers' Guild, not a recruiter for Khoral." Chak shrugged. "He was just trying to get us clear of Pandathaway. That way, chaining us wouldn't bring the Guilds Council down on him for ruining the damn city's reputation as a safe place to be." His eyes grew vague. "Not that it'll stay safe for him."

A clattering came from around the bend, accompanied by a distant snorting and whinnying of horses.

Chak's nostrils flared. "I know that bloody mare's whining. It's the wagon of my former owners." His right hand hovered around the left side of his waist. "Wish I had a sword." He eyed the two scabbarded weapons lying on bed of the wagon. "Would you be willing to lend me one?"

Karl nodded. "Sure."

"*No.*" Walter shook his head. "We don't want any trouble. Karl, give him your tunic. I don't want them to see Chak out of his chains; we don't need loose talk about two strangers who bought and freed a slave."

Karl shook his head. "I never gave my word about not—"

"Karl. It comes down to the same thing. Now, is your word good, or not? Give him your tunic, please."

Nodding slowly, Karl complied. "Just sit tight for a moment." He tossed the tunic to Chak, who slipped it on without comment, although the hem fell well below his knees. Chak sat down, tucking a loose blanket around his legs to hide that, and began a careful study of the contents of a muslin sack.

Karl snatched the rapier from the bed of the wagon and tossed it to Walter.

Slovotsky raised an eyebrow; Karl shook his head. "I'm not looking for trouble," Karl said. "But slip this on anyway. We don't need to look helpless, do we?"

"Well . . ." Walter conceded the point, belting the rapier around his waist. "Let's look busy."

Karl jumped down from the wagon and busied himself with offering bowls of water to the mules, while Walter checked the leads of the trailing horses.

The slavers' wagon passed without incident, although the two slavers riding beside it gave practiced glances at Karl's and Walter's swords. Karl nodded grimly; when the smith had agreed to throw in a pair of swords, Karl had deliberately picked a slim rapier for Walter, one with a well-worn, sweat-browned bone hilt. Since Slovotsky wasn't good with a blade, it had seemed a sound precaution to pick a weapon that advertised a non-existent expertise.

Several grimy faces peered out through the barred windows of the boxy slave wagon. Chak kept his face turned away, although he couldn't resist sneaking a peek.

As the wagon pulled away, he sighed. "Damn." The word was the same in Erendra as in English, something Karl occasionally wondered about.

Karl took his hand off the pommel of his sword. Walter and Ahira were right; they couldn't afford to draw attention to themselves here and now. But . . .

But that doesn't excuse it.

Walter peered into his face. "I'm sorry, Karl." He spread his palms. "Slovotsky's Law Number Nine: Sometimes, you can't do anything about something that sucks." He sighed. "No matter how *much* it sucks," he murmured.

Chak was already pulling off Karl's tunic. "That child is what bothers me. Just too young."

Karl raised an eyebrow as he slipped on the tunic.

"She's only eleven or so. But Orhmyst—he's the master; the rest are just barely journeymen—likes his women young. Says they're more fun. He's had this one for better than a year, ever since he raided Melawei; kept chattering about keeping her, even after they get to Pandathaway. Said she wouldn't bring much coin, compared with the pleasure."

Karl's heart thudded. *"What?"*

Walter's face whitened. "He's raping an eleven-year-old girl?"

Chak rubbed at the back of his neck. "Every night.

And she spends her days whimpering, and begging for some healing draughts to stanch her bleeding; Orhmyst isn't gentle." Chak pounded his fist against the bed of the wagon. "In the Katharhd Domains, we'd cut off his balls for that, and not worry about whether the girl was slave or free."

"Walter," Karl said, "we can't—"

"Shut up, dammit. Give me a minute." Slovotsky brought his fist to his mouth and chewed on his fingers for a long moment.

Then he threw up his hands. "Cullinane, if it were possible that you set this up . . . never mind." He glared at Karl. "You remember what I was saying, about how you sometimes can't do anything about some things that suck?"

Karl nodded slowly.

"Well, you can just forget it. Sometimes I don't have the slightest idea of what I'm talking about—"

"We agree on something, at least."

"—but for now, how do you want to handle this? You're the tactician, not me."

"I promised Ahira I wouldn't get in any fights, unless it was a matter of self-defense." He chuckled, knowing what Walter was going to say.

"And you also agreed that I'd decide what constitutes self-defense. This does." Walter flashed a weak grin. "We'll work out an appropriate rationalization later. Tactics are your department: How are we going to do it?"

Karl smiled. "We'll follow them, but lag behind. Until it gets dark. Then you get the pleasure of skulking around, doing a nice, quiet recon." He turned to the little man. "Do you want in on this? You can have a share of their coin."

Chak shrugged. "I wouldn't mind. Always could use a bit of extra coin. Particularly," he said, patting at a phantom pouch, "now." He took the other sword from the wagon and drew it partway out of the scabbard. It was a wide, single-edged blade, more of a falchion than anything else. Chak nodded. "As long as my share includes this, it might be worth it."

Karl raised an eyebrow. "And maybe you've a score to settle with these folks?"

"That too." Chak smiled grimly. "There's always that."

Karl sat back against the base of a towering pine, his sword balanced across his lap. Deliberately, he twisted the chain of the manriki-gusari between his fingers. It helped to keep his hands from shaking.

Overhead, the branches and pine needles rustled in the wind, momentarily revealing, then hiding the flickering stars. A cool breeze blew from the west, sending a shiver across his chest. Half a mile down the road, almost hidden by a stand of trees, a campfire burned, sending gouts of sparkling ashes soaring into the night sky.

Chak grunted. "That friend of yours is taking too long," he whispered. "Probably tripped over his feet. Got himself killed." He tested the edge of his falchion's blade, then sucked at the cut on his thumb for the twentieth time. At least. "Good blade."

Karl shook his head. "No, we would have heard something."

"We would have heard that it's a good blade? Truly?"

"No, if he'd gotten into trouble—" Karl stopped himself, then gave Chak a sideways look. The little man's face was a caricature of puzzlement. "Seems you're getting your sense of humor back."

Chak smiled. "I always joke before a fight. Helps to steady the nerves. Now, my father, he always used to drink. Claimed it sharpened his eye, tightened his wrist. And it did, at that."

"Oh." Karl was skeptical; he let it show in his voice.

A snort. "Until the last time, of course. His wrist was so tight it was still straight as an arrow after a dwarf chopped his arm off." He bit his lip for a moment.

"Which is why I don't drink before a fight—joking keeps the arm looser." He looked over at Karl. "Now that you know all about me, tell me where you're from. The name is unfamiliar, although you look a bit like a Salke. A tall Salke, but they do grow them high."

Karl shook his head. "It's kind of complicated. Perhaps I'll go into it sometime."

"As you wish." Chak took one end of the manriki-gusari. "But you *will* tell me about this metal bola you're holding. Please? Never seen one like that before; doubt even you can throw it far."

"You don't throw it, usually. And as to what it can do, I suspect I'll have a chance to show you, in a while."

"Damn sure of yourself, Kharl."

"Of course." He smiled genially at Chak as he knitted his fingers together to keep them from shaking. *In fact, it's all I can do to keep my sphincters under control.* But he couldn't say that. "We were talking about that valley of yours."

"Not mine. Not really; I just passed through it once. But it is pretty. And not occupied, as far as I was able to tell. At least, not as of a few years ago. It's just too far away from any civilization; if anyone wanted to settle there, he'd have to travel for ten, twenty days to get to the nearest cleric. And since it's in Therranj, it'd be a bitch for humans to do business. Damn elves'll take you, every time."

"But people could live there."

"Sure." The little man shrugged. "Like I said, if they were willing to do without civilized necessities. I'm—"

"Making far too much noise," a voice hissed, from somewhere in the darkness.

Karl leaped to his feet, his sword in one hand, the manriki-gusari in the other.

Walter Slovotsky chuckled as he stepped from the shadows. "Relax. It's just your friendly neighborhood thief."

Karl quelled an urge to hit him. Dammit, he had asked

Walter, more than once, not to sneak up on him. And Walter was usually good about it.

Just nerves, I guess. "How are they set up?"

Slovotsky squatted and picked up a twig. "This is the wagon," he said, making an X on the ground.

"The road runs here." He drew a gentle arc to the left of the X.

"Campfire here, on our side of the wagon; throws light on our side of the road. Chak, there are four of them, no?"

"Yes."

"Well, I could only see three. One's on watch on top of the wagon, a bottle of wine and a cocked crossbow to keep him company. There's a huge one sleeping on our side of the fire—he's got a bow, which isn't cocked." Slovotsky shrugged. "But he's sleeping with his sword in his hand. The third one's in a hammock strung up *here*, between two trees."

He spat on the ground. "Couldn't find the fourth. He could be out in the brush relieving himself, but if he is, he's either got the runs or is constipated as hell. I gave him plenty of time to show up; no sign."

"Maybe he's in the wagon?"

Walter shrugged. "Could be."

Chak shook his head. "They don't sleep in the wagons. Too dangerous. And if one of them was with the women, you would have heard. They don't use gags. But I wouldn't worry about it; they've only got the two bows, and we've accounted for those. As soon as the fight starts, the fourth one will pop up, and we'll cut him down."

"So?" Walter asked. "How do we do it?"

Karl stood. "We'll play it as we did with Ohlmin and his friends, with a bit of the way we handled Deighton thrown in. Conceal yourself close to the wagon—close enough to be sure you can get the watchman with your knife—and wait. Chak and I will work ourselves in, as close as we can. Give us plenty of time to get into position, then start things off by throwing a knife, taking the watchman out. That'll be the signal for Chak and me."

"Fine," Walter said. "But we don't know what their watch schedule is. What if they switch off before we get there?"

"Good point. If all they do is change places, don't worry about it; just take out whichever one is on the wagon. On the other hand, if the crossbow moves from the wagon, or if the slaver by the fire cocks his bow, we'll need to know that before we take them. If that happens, just slip away; when enough time has passed and Chak and I haven't heard anything, we'll head back here, re-think the attack, and try again."

He turned to Chak. "You kill the one in the hammock. I'll take the one by the fire."

The little man nodded. "Should be easy. What do I do after?"

"Just grab one of their bows, see if you can find the fourth one. Or help me, if I'm in trouble."

"Walter, when you take the watchman out, try for the chest—but any good disable is fine. Don't expose yourself to go in for the kill; as soon as you get the watchman, look for the fourth man."

He clapped a hand to Walter's shoulder. "Remember, football hero, you're free safety. We've got to be damn sure we get them all; if one of the bastards escapes, we're in deep trouble. We don't need for word to get back to Pandathaway that I'm still alive."

Walter's mouth quirked into a smile. "Bloodthirsty, aren't we?"

"You got any goddam objection?"

"That wasn't an accusation. I did say *we*, after all."

CHAPTER FOUR: *On the Aeryk Road*

Those who know how to win are far more numerous than those who know how to make proper use of their victories.

—Polybius

Walter Slovotsky crouched in the tall grasses surrounding a huge oak, his belly hugging the ground, one of his four teak-handled throwing knives in his right hand. His palm concealed the blade; a reflection from the steel could alert his target, twenty yards away.

Beyond the boxy slave wagon with the sleepy-eyed guard sitting cross-legged on its flat roof, the campfire burned an orange rift into the night. From where he lay, Walter couldn't see beyond the wagon to where Karl and Chak were—

—*should be*, he reminded himself. *Should be.* They were supposed to have moved silently into place by now, but Walter had long ago learned that things didn't go the way they should around Karl. Not that things always went badly, just differently.

Too bloody much of the time.

He slipped his thumb along the cool slickness of the blade and decided to wait just a few more minutes, to make sure they had gotten to the right places.

This had to work just right.

If it didn't, the fact that Karl was still alive would soon be common knowledge, even if a surviving slaver caught

only a glimpse of him. No other men six and a half feet
tall made a habit of taking on slavers on the trade routes
of the Eren regions. Come to think of it, no shorter men
got into that habit; the Pandathaway guilds had long
made that an ill-advised profession to get into.

*So why the hell am I in this? Not because of some
eleven-year-old girl I've never even laid eyes on.*

It was because of goddam Karl Cullinane. As usual.
Walter could have tolerated knowing that somewhere,
some little girl was being mistreated, even raped. People
were being mistreated everywhere; cutting the number
by one or two wasn't going to change that.

You had to take the long view. Maybe there was a way
to change things, but it couldn't happen overnight. Risking everything for a moment's gratification just didn't
make any sense at all.

So why did I agree to this?

He sighed. *Goddam Karl Cullinane. If I had just
shrugged and dismissed it, he'd have looked at me as if I
were a piece of shit.*

And was that such a big deal? Was Karl Cullinane's
opinion so important?

Yes. Ahira was Walter's best friend, and Karl had
worked out a way to bring Ahira out of the grave. That
counted for something.

That counted for a lot.

And Karl's growth over the past months counted for
more. When they had arrived on This Side, Karl had
been a directionless flake; Walter had watched him
grow, seen him strip away his shield of not caring, of
choosing not to understand others, not to commit
himself.

It all added up to respect. The simple fact was that
Walter respected Karl, and wanted to receive the same in
turn from him. Walter Slovotsky had always been
respected by everyone whose opinion he cared about, and
he wasn't about to learn how to live without that.

He shook himself. *If I don't pay attention to what's*

*going on, I may have to learn how to live with a bunch of
crossbow bolts in me.* He rubbed at a slim scar that
curved around the left side of his collarbone. A knife had
left that as a remembrance of Lundeyll; it hadn't been
any fun at all. One of his own knives, and it had cost
quite a bit to get it replaced in Pandathaway. In fact—

Enough. It was time to stop stalling, and get it done.
One way or the other.

He set the knife down with the bulk of the oak's trunk
between it and the view of the watchman, and raised
himself on his toes and fingertips, inching slowly, silently,
into the cover of the tree. *Aim for the chest,* Karl had
said. Very well; the chest it would be.

Picking up the knife between the thumb and first two
fingers of his right hand, he stood and moved quickly to
his right. Raising the knife to shoulder level, he threw,
then dove for the cover of the grasses.

With a flicker of steel, the knife tumbled end over end
through the night air.

The guard must have seen the sudden movement; with
a grunt, he jerked back and to the side. The knife's hilt
caught him a glancing blow in the left arm, then fell
away in the dark.

"Datharrrrti!" the guard called out as he reached for
his crossbow and jumped to his feet. *Raiders!*

Oh, shit. Karl had said to hide in the shadows, but he
hadn't been counting on this. With a functioning crossbowman on the roof of the wagon, the fight would be
over before it began.

The bowman, a blocky little man, leveled his crossbow
at Walter.

Ignoring the rustle of branches overhead, Walter broke
into a staggered sprint, snatching another of his knives
from his belt and throwing it, still on the run. At least it
might distract the bowman for a second or two.

With a meaty thunk, the knife sank into the watchman's thigh. His leg crumpled; he fell to the roof, a sound
halfway between a scream and a groan issuing from his

lips. Clapping his hands to his leg, he dropped the cross-bow.

Walter reached the side of the wagon. Without a pause, he grasped the edge of its roof and pulled himself up.

Below, steel clashed against steel. Karl fought with the gigantic swordsman who had been sleeping next to the campfire. Swords flashed in the firelight; screams and shouts filled the air.

Groaning, the watchman pulled the knife from his thigh, rose to his knees, and lunged at Walter, stabbing downward.

Walter caught the descending arm with both hands, stopping the razor-sharp point just inches from his left eye. A clout to the side of his head set the world spinning, but he held on as they rolled around the rough wood.

The watchman's free hand clawed at Walter's throat; the rough fingers fastened on his windpipe. Walter tried to drag air into his lungs as they struggled face to face, gasping as he drew in the foul reek of wine on the other's breath.

Inexorably, the knife moved toward his face, the point seeking his left eye, as if on its own volition.

Walter pushed against the knife arm. The blade's progress slowed; the point stopped four inches from his eye.

His hands started to tremble. The point moved closer. Three inches away, then two, then—

With a heave, Walter lurched on top of the slaver, driving his knee into the open wound on the other's thigh.

The watchman screamed; his fingers loosened from Walter's throat. Just for a moment, the watchman's right arm lost its strength.

Walter didn't wait for him to recover; he twisted the knife arm behind the watchman's back and up, past the hammerlock position, until he felt a sickening, wet pop as the arm separated from the shoulder socket, the knife falling from the slaver's limp fingers.

The slaver whimpered; feebly, he kicked at Walter, trying to slide away on his belly.

With one smooth motion, Walter snatched up the knife and stabbed downward into the other's kidney. He pulled the knife out and stabbed again, and again, and again, as the blood poured from the slaver's wounds.

With a muffled scream, the slaver twitched, then fell still.

Walter's stomach rebelled; he fell to his hands and knees, sour vomit spewing from his mouth. Wiping his mouth with a bloody hand, he willed his body back under control.

Below, Cullinane sliced down at his huge opponent's swordarm; as the other parried, Karl whipped the manriki-gusari around the slaver's blade and jerked, sending both the manriki-gusari and his enemy's sword flipping end over end into the night. He lunged in full extension; his blade slid into the slaver's throat, almost to the hilt. Blood fountained as Karl kicked the slaver off his blade; the giant gave a bubbling groan and fell face down onto the campfire.

As he lay there motionless, the fire hissed, sending up clouds of smoke and steam. A reek of scorched flesh reached Walter's nostrils. He gagged, but quelled the urge to vomit again.

"Walter," Karl shouted, "are you okay?"

Walter nodded.

Chak walked slowly into the dwindling firelight, his falchion dripping with blood. "Mine's taken care of. But where's Ohrmyst?"

Walter vaulted to the ground, letting his knees give to absorb the shock. "We've got to find him. *Quickly!* If he gets away—"

"I know, dammit. I know." Karl looked from side to side, his face a snarling rictus. "Chak, you go that way, I'll—"

He stopped, lowering the point of his sword.

Cullinane smiled. He scanned the ground for a

moment, then walked over to the fire and picked up a
water bucket and a soft cloth. Ignoring the body that lay
smoldering in the ashes, he dipped the cloth in the water
and started washing his hands. "There's another cloth
here—clean yourself up. You can use it."

What was this nonsense? This wasn't any time to relax.
"Karl—"

"I wouldn't worry about the fourth man," Karl said,
cleaning, then resheathing his sword. "Wouldn't worry
about him at all."

A distant flapping of leathery wings sounded from the
direction of the road. "Although," Cullinane went on,
"next time, I wish you'd look a bit more closely; Orhmyst
was sleeping in a hammock slung way up high in that oak
tree." He pointed at the tree Walter had hidden under.
"When the alarm sounded, he lit out."

A dark, massive bulk came into view overhead; the
wind whipped up dust and burning embers from the
campfire.

Chak shouted and dove for the concealment of the
woods.

Relax, Walter. Ellegon hovered overhead. *I don't
think Ohrmyst will be talking to anyone. And would you
tell your friend that I'm harmless? Please?* He landed on
the ground with a thump, then lowered his massive head
so that Karl could reach up and pat it.

Karl's laugh sounded forced as he scratched vigorously
against the dragon's jaw. "Only relatively."

True. Ellegon burped.

"What are you doing around here, anyway?"

*I told you I'd do better this time. And Ahira figured
you might get into trouble; he sent me out to check the
road from the sanctuary to Metreyll. When I didn't spot
you, I started checking this road.*

Walter nodded, then knelt over the water bucket,
looking away from the body sprawled over the coals. He
splashed water on his face; the sudden cold helped quell
the last traces of his nausea.

"That was nice timing, Ellegon," he said.

A clattering from inside the wagon jerked his head around. "Karl, what say we free some people?"

Karl shot a glance toward the woods. "Chak, it's safe. You can come out now."

No answer.

Don't worry; he'll come out when he calms down. Then, accusingly: *You didn't tell him about me, did you?*

"Well, no. It didn't exactly come up. I wasn't thinking ahead."

Not thinking ahead. That was Karl, all over. In fact—

Ohmygod. "Karl—we're going to free these people, no?"

Cullinane cocked his head, puzzled. "Of course. That's the purpose of the exercise, after all. What—"

"Bear with me a minute." A cold wind sent a shiver up his spine. "There's fifteen, sixteen slaves in the wagon, right?"

"Not slaves anymore." Cullinane stooped to pick up his manriki-gusari, then twirled it easily. "Not anymore."

"And, I assume, some of them will want to join up with us. At least for a while."

Cullinane nodded as he pulled the smoldering body of the dead slaver from the campfire. He dragged him a few feet onto the bare dirt before riffling through his pouch. "Gin," he said, dangling a brass keyring. "And you're right, but so what? We've got enough food."

"And some might *not* want to come with us. They might want to go home."

"So what?"

"So," Walter said, impatient, "we give them some coin, maybe a horse if we can spare one, and wave as they go on their merry way. Right?"

"Right." He lifted his head and raised his voice. "Stand easy in there," he said in Erendra. "You will be free in a moment."

"*Dammit*, Karl, listen to me. What happens when they

start talking about the nice, big man who—teamed with a dragon, of all things—took on a bunch of Pandathaway slavers, and then *freed* them? Word gets back to Pandathaway, somebody puts two and two together, and—"

Cullinane's face went ashen. "And the hunters are on our tails again."

Including Andy-Andy's rather pretty one, which isn't going to be all that mobile in a few months. I care about her, too, Karl. "Exactly what we've been trying to avoid. So what do we do?"

Karl Cullinane drew himself up straight. "We free them. Period."

Walter shrugged. "Fine. And what do we do about the aftermath?" *Karl, if you aren't scared shitless, you don't understand the situation.*

"We work it out. Somehow. Just like we work out what to do with that Metreyll armsman." He started toward the wagon, then caught himself. "Of *course.*" As he turned back to face Walter, his face was creased in a huge smile. "Did you ever study economics?"

"No." What the hell did that have to do with anything?

"I did. For a while." A mischievous grin replaced the friendly smile. "And economics is, my dear friend, the answer."

"Well?"

"I'll tell you later. C'mon, we've got some locks to unlock, some chains to break. I think I'm going to enjoy this. You coming?"

"Sure." Why not? Besides freeing them, the only choice was to leave them as slaves, and Cullinane wouldn't accept that.

Probably have to cut their tongues out, as well. And I wouldn't stand for that.

So I might as well get what pleasure I can out of this; sure as anything I'm going to be in front of the blades when the shit hits the fan.

As they walked toward the wagon, Karl threw an arm

around Walter's shoulder. "You know, there are times when I enjoy this profession. A lot." A half-shudder went through Cullinane's body, but his smile remained intact.

Understandable. It was one thing for Karl to feign shrugging off his revulsion for violence, but another matter to truly take bloodletting for granted. *The day you can kill without any twinge of conscience, Karl, is the day I want to get as far away from you as I can.* "You've really got a solution?"

"*The* solution, Walter." Cullinane smiled. "By the way, in case I didn't mention it, you did just fine. If the watchman had been able to use his bow, all three of us would have been in deep trouble. The rest of it doesn't matter." With a sniff, he dismissed Walter's vomiting as irrelevant.

"Thanks." Respect; that felt good. *Next question: is Cullinane's respect worth going through* this *again? Next answer: I'll duck that issue for as long as I can.* "But this idea of yours—you're not going to tell me yet, are you?"

"Nope. A little frustration is good for the soul."

"I'm not going to like the answer, am I?"

Nope. Ellegon snorted. *Not one little bit.*

CHAPTER FIVE: *The War Begins*

If ever there could be a proper time for mere catch arguments, that time surely is not now. In times like the present, men should utter nothing for which they would not willingly be responsible through time and in eternity.

—Abraham Lincoln

Ahira sighed, shaking his head. *I should have known better,* he thought. *I really should have.*

Correct.

Thank you, Ellegon. The dwarf spat. *Thank you very much. Any sign of trouble on the Waste?*

I would have mentioned it if there were.

"Is. There. Any. Sign. Of. Trouble. On. The. Waste?"

No. There is nothing visible on the Waste.

Good. Stay on watch. The dragon didn't answer; Ahira decided to take that as an assent. "Karl?"

"Yes?" The big man turned from his conversation with Andrea and the grimy little girl.

"We need to talk. Take a walk with me."

"Sure. Give me a minute." Karl patted Andrea on the arm and smiled down at the silent little girl, who clung to Andrea's arm as though it were a lifeline. "See if she'll let you give her a spongebath—and dig up something else for her to wear." He switched to English. "Push for the bath," he said in a low voice, "and give her as thorough a going-over as you can. She's been through a rough time, and we'd better know if there's anything physically wrong with her."

Andrea pulled the girl closer. "Why not just give her more healing draughts? We've still got some left from what you found in the slavers' wagon, no?"

"Only three bottles. I don't know how long they'll have to last. We can't afford to dispense the stuff when it isn't necessary, just as a precaution."

"And if she does need some?"

Ahira grunted. "Then we give to her. Karl, I do want a word with you. Now."

"One more thing." Karl switched back to Erendra and raised his head. "Chak, keep an eye on the bowman. It won't be for much longer."

Sitting across from the bound youth, Chak nodded, then jerked his thumb at a large wooden trunk next to the boxy slave wagon.

"Yes, Kharl, but do you mind if I go through this trunk while I do? I might find something. Maybe another bottle or two of the healing draughts; maybe some more coin."

"How do you plan on opening it?"

Chak smiled. "I think I can find a key."

"Go to it, then."

Across the clearing, five other former slaves sat talking with Walter and Riccetti. Three men, two women, all of them filthy, although none were apparently injured; despite his protestations, Karl had been generous with the bottles of healing draughts he had found in the slavers' wagon.

There wouldn't be more of that coming their way, at least not from the Healing Hand Society; the Hand acolyte had been more than clear on that point.

"Well?" Karl raised an eyebrow. "What is it?"

"I sent you into Metreyll to pick up provisions and supplies, not six—no, seven more mouths to feed."

He shrugged, his shoulders threatening to split the seams of his worn leather jerkin. "I would have brought back all of them, if most hadn't wanted to—

Crunch!

Ahira snatched his battleaxe from his chest, tearing the handle right through the straps that bound it to him. A thumb-flick sent its leather sheath spinning away.

Cullinane drew his sword and spun around into a crouch. "What the—?"

"Sorry," Chak called out, as he stood over the shattered trunk. He hefted the sledge. "But I told you I'd find a key."

Ahira looked down at the torn leather thongs that had secured his battleaxe to his chest. "Nice friend you've got there, Karl."

He chuckled. "Take it easy, Ahira, you're all tensed up."

Ahira stared pointedly at Karl's naked blade. "And, of course, you're not."

"Well . . ." He slipped the saber back into its scabbard.

"Never mind." Ahira raised a palm. "Never mind. What *is* this insane plan of yours?"

Karl shook his head. "In a while. First, how's Doria doing?"

Ahira spat. "They wouldn't let me see her. The acolyte I spoke to said that she's being 'fully integrated into the body of the Society,' and that any contact with outsiders —*outsiders*—was forbidden." *Be well, Doria. May you find with the Hand all that eluded you with us.*

"You think she's okay?"

"Hope so. If she isn't, there's not a damn thing we can do about it." Frustrating, but true. The Matriarch of the Healing Hand Society had protected the Hand preserve against the powers that had devastated the Forest of Elrood, turning it into the Waste. Handling a few warriors and a novice wizard wouldn't cause her to work up a sweat. "Unless you feel like storming the tabernacle."

Karl snorted. "Fat chance. As to how I think we ought to proceed, how about you gathering everyone around, while I have a talk with Andy, so that—"

"Kharl! Kharlkhulinayn!" Chak ran toward them, a long, thin piece of metal held high in his hands. "Look!" He jerked to a halt and handed it to Karl, holding it carefully as though it were a fragile piece of glass. Chak smiled broadly, as though he had just presented Karl with the Hope diamond.

Ahira looked at it. It looked like an oversized butterknife, actually; the flat blade was almost three feet long. He reached over and tested the edge against his thumb. Dull as a butterknife, too. "What is this?"

Chak stood back. "You don't know? *That*, Ahira, is a woodknife."

Karl cocked his head to one side. "I'm no wiser; what is a woodknife?"

"Look." Chak lifted it from Karl's outstretched palms and walked to a nearby sapling. Holding the handle with just thumb and two fingers, he slashed at the trunk, as though in slow motion.

The blade passed through the trunk as though it weren't there.

With a rustling of leaves, the sapling crashed to the ground.

"See?" Chak said, bouncing the blade off his own neck. "It cuts only through wood. Nothing else. Quite a find, eh? I expect we're going to find quite a bit of use for this, where we're going."

What the hell did that mean? "Karl? Would you please tell me what you're—"

Cullinane raised a palm. "Tell you what: Why don't you gather everyone around, so I only have to go through this once. No rush; I've got to talk to Andy first, soon as she's finished bathing the girl. Private matter."

What's going on with the two of them now? I thought they'd worked things out. Ahira opened his mouth, then closed it. *None of my business.* He nodded. "Fair enough, but this had better be good."

"It will be. I hope."

* * *

Karl led Andy-Andy well away from the camp before sitting both of them down on a fallen log. "How's she doing?"

"Not too bad, at least physically. A few bruises, some abrasions were all I could find. But I'm not up on anatomy . . . it's too bad you can't check her over." She left the obvious unspoken; a little girl who'd gone through that particular kind of hell didn't need any man poking and prodding at her.

He chuckled thinly. "Two weeks of premed doesn't make me an internist. If you can't find anything wrong with her, I probably couldn't. Well . . . just keep an eye on her; we can always dose her again later if she needs more.

"But that's not why I needed to talk to you." *I wish I could put this off a bit longer, but—* "I've got a question for you."

She smiled up at him. "I can guess what it is. I've heard that fighting hikes up the ol' hormones, eh? Well . . ."

"Shh." He shook his head. "This is serious. I've got something to ask you, then something to tell you." *And I hope I'm doing this in the right order.*

Her face matched his somber tone. "Okay, Karl. You are serious. About something."

He took a deep breath. "The question is this: Will you marry me?"

Her eyes opened wide. "Will I *what?*"

"You heard me." All of a sudden, he didn't quite know what to do with his hands. They clutched aimlessly at the air in front of him. "I know we don't have a priest around, but we could improvise some sort of ceremony. Marry me—you know: live together, have kids, the whole bit."

She threw up her hands and laughed. "Karl, just 'cause we've slept together a couple of times . . ."

"It's not that." *Not just that,* he amended silently.

"If it's not that, then it has to be something else, something that's pretty impor—*no.*" Andy-Andy paled. "I'm pregnant? I must be, but how do you know?"

"Ellegon. He can detect the pheromonal changes. But how did you guess?"

"It's the only thing that makes sense. We haven't discussed this before. . . ." She shook her head. "Dammit, Karl, I'm not *ready* to be a mother, and—"

He raised a palm. "And we can take care of that. If necessary."

"How?"

"Do I have to go into details? Just take my word, please. It can be done."

"How?"

He shrugged. "This isn't exactly the way this was supposed to go, you know . . . Okay, think about it: We've got a lot of healing draughts, and I think I can improvise the tools for a D&C. I know I'm not a doctor, but we've got room for error. It'd hurt, but the draughts can protect you from any risk of infection, any permanent damage. If you want an abortion, you can have it. Up to you," he said, trying to sound casual, failing miserably. The thought of himself performing the abortion bothered Karl, not the notion of an early abortion itself. He'd never bought the idiotic notion that a microscopic blastula was a human being.

Doing a primitive abortion here isn't the only choice. We could try to sneak you back home, through the Gate. But I really don't want to try getting past The Dragon again, and I'm sure as hell not going to suggest that.

She tented her hands in front of her mouth and chewed on a forefinger. "Let me think, okay?"

"Fine. Take your time. Is . . . is there anything I can do?"

"Just leave me alone for a while."

"Andy—"

"Please?"

He stood. "Okay—but I've got to go talk to everybody

else;. Ahira's on my back. Join us in a few minutes?"

"Maybe. Just . . . just give me some time."

He nodded. "I love you, you know."

"I know." She smiled weakly. "Now get lost for a while."

"Please listen," Karl said in Erendra, as he stood in the center of the circle of faces. "I've got something to say." He paused to look at them. With one exception, all of the former slaves still looked scared. The exception was Chak. His smile almost radiated trust as he sat tailor-fashion, his right hand never straying far from the hilt of his falchion.

Lou Riccetti's round face beamed up at him. Trust to Lou to work things out, if they involved numbers. And those economics courses he'd taken didn't hurt either. Riccetti nodded reassuringly.

Ahira scowled. As usual. He didn't like being kept in the dark. Probably he wouldn't like what came next any better.

And then there was Slovotsky. *Walter, if I can ever figure you out, I'll admit to being a genius.*

Actually, Walter's easy. He's—

Shh. Karl went on: "For those of you who don't know, there are people after my head. When I met Ellegon, he was chained in a cesspit in Pandathaway. I didn't like that; I freed him.

"The Pandathaway guilds didn't like *that*. They sent slavers out after me. After all of us. They caught up with us in the Waste.

"We managed to get away, and then kill all of the bastards. By now, Pandathaway probably thinks that I'm dead." The Matriarch had said that he couldn't be located while on the Hand preserve, and certainly a location spell couldn't have spotted him during the period that he had been home, on the other side of the Gate. "They will soon be hearing that I'm alive.

"There's probably nothing that we can do to prevent that." Twenty yards behind Ahira, the bowman glared over at him. "Even if we killed him; the other freed slaves will talk.

"I propose that we don't even try. Instead, I suggest that we do two things. First, Chak knows of an uninhabited valley in Therranj. I propose that we move there, and settle down; raise food and cattle, everything. We'll have to send another party into Metreyll to pick up some more supplies and animals, cattle, sheep, goats, chickens, whatever we need. The trip will take a while; and building houses, clearing fields, planting crops, all of it will be hard work. But once we're settled in—"

Walter shook his head. "That won't do it. Pandathaway is ticked at you, Karl; they won't let a bit of distance stand between them and revenge." He shrugged. "It might buy us some time, but that's all."

Notice the "us"?

Yes. Now, shh. Karl held up a hand. "No. I'm not going to spend much time there for the first couple of years; certainly not enough to be located and found. Instead . . . Lou: Explain a bit about supply and demand, and how that effects economic utility."

Riccetti picked up his cue as though they had rehearsed it. Which they had, of course.

He stood. "The price of anything depends on two things: how much of it is available, and how badly people want it; supply and demand. If anything—*anything*—gets too expensive, then people start to find substitutes. That applies to swords, to grain, to cattle—and to slaves. Karl's talking about making slaves too expensive."

"Exactly." Karl folded his arms across his chest. "And we'll do that by making slave-taking too expensive, too risky a business. I'm talking about doing the same thing that we did yesterday, but on a larger scale. We'll hit every caravan we can, force the Slavers' Guild to beef up their caravans, adding more and more guards, cutting down on the profits from slaving. And we'll *keep* doing that until the system starts to collapse."

Shaking his head, Ahira spat. "That's just plain silly. There are a lot of slaves, Karl; you won't affect the price of slaves one whit. Figure that Pandathaway alone imports, say, three, four thousand slaves per year. Right now, they get them via raids on Therranj, Melawei, and so forth. Let's say that each caravan has twenty slaves, and that you hit—and free—one caravan each tenday. And let's assume that every one of the freed slaves either joins us in this valley of yours or finds his or her way home.

"That's only a thousand or so freed slaves each year." He shrugged. "It'll drive up the price a bit. But that's all."

Smiling broadly, Walter Slovotsky nodded. "Beautiful, Karl. Dammit, James, you're wrong; it'll do more. Once we've demonstrated that *we* can take on slavers and get away with it, others will start doing it, too. Everyone has shied away from crossing the Slavers' Guild because of the fear of retribution. Once we show that we can get away with it, most of that fear will be gone.

"It's a sure bet that some of these unemployed mercenaries will try to get into the business. And since they'll have stolen the slaves, they'll be afraid to sell them. They'll have to free them, making their profit off money that the slavers carry. Just as we did." He hefted his now-full purse. "A nice bit of thinking it through, Karl. That is what you're talking about, isn't it?"

"Yes."

From across the clearing, Andy-Andy's voice called, "It's crazy, you know." She walked quickly toward the group.

How did she hear?

I echoed your words. A mental smirk. *And if you're really nice to me, I won't relay your thoughts without permission.*

I didn't know you could do that. Although it really wasn't all that surprising, come to think of it.

You didn't ask.

He scowled. *Well, then, relay this.* He stopped himself. *Never mind.* "Andy—"

"Later." She smiled. "We'll have plenty of time, on this trip to that valley of yours. But we'd better move quickly." She placed the flat of her hand on her stomach. "Before I start to swell."

Karl couldn't help smiling.

Ahira shook his head. "This is insane, you know, but . . ."

"But what?" Riccetti frowned. "It makes perfect sense."

"But let's try it." The dwarf bounced to his feet and stuck out his hand at Karl. "You can count me in." As they shook hands, Ahira shrugged. "It's worth a try." He turned to the freed slaves. "You may either come with us, or leave. Anyone who wishes to leave us should see me later."

Slovotsky smiled. "All we have to do is take on a few thousand slavers."

Andy-Andy shook her head. "There's one other thing."

"Oh?" Ahira cocked his head. "What am I missing?"

"We've also got to stay alive."

Karl nodded. "That *is* the keystone of the whole plan, after all."

A gout of fire roared into the sky. *Nice keystone.*

Ellegon at his side, Karl smiled down at the bowman. "I'm going to turn you loose. We'll give you a waterbag and a knife; start across the Waste tonight. I want the extra time to get clear of here." As the youth glanced over at the string of horses, Karl shook his head. "If you try to leave before then, or raise a hand to any of us, or steal a horse, I'll have Ellegon eat you."

The dragon leered. *Please try to leave early. I could use a snack.*

The bowman glared up at Karl. "The Pandathaway Guilds Council will hunt you down like an animal. They will find you, Karl Cullinane. And, my Lord Mêhlen willing, I will travel to Pandathaway to watch you die."

Karl smiled. "Have Lord Mêhlen give them a message from me. Tell them: Karl Cullinane is alive, and . . ." He let his voice trail off.

Did this make any sense? *Here I am, an expectant father, and I'm asking for trouble. Ahira was right; this is absolutely insane.*

"You made a promise to the Matriarch. And though she will not help you further, will you keep that promise, or not?"

Karl looked across the clearing to where the little girl was smiling at Andy-Andy over a bowl of stew. Not much of a smile, but a smile nonetheless. And a very special sort of smile. . . .

Yes. Hell, yes. He cut the bowman loose. "Tell them this: I'm hunting *them.*"

PART TWO:
The Valley

CHAPTER SIX: *Settling In*

All things are artificial, for Nature is the art of God.

—Sir Thomas Browne

The valley took Karl by surprise, although that morning Ellegon had told him they would reach it shortly after noon.

He led his mare up a gentle incline, through the charred remains of what once had been a stand of trees. There was no way of knowing what had caused the fire that had burned a black slash across the surrounding miles; possibly someone's carelessness, possibly a lightning strike.

The fire had been years before; rain had since reduced the burned trees to a flat ash surface that allowed easy passage for both the flatbed and the former slave wagon.

Life was starting to return; impudently, thumb-thick saplings rose chest-high, as though in a promise that this area would be wooded once again. In the light breeze, leafy ferns nodded their agreement.

In further confirmation, the grasses had started to reclaim the ground at the top of the hill.

His horse snorted, nudging him from behind.

"Dammit, Carrot, we're moving fast enough." He turned to stroke her neck before resuming their slow pace through the rubble. "You take it easy, hear? I don't want you breaking a leg."

She whinnied as if she understood, and agreed that breaking a leg was, indeed, not the ultimate goal of her horsy life.

Hmmm, *would* the healing draughts work on a horse?
Possibly. Quite possibly.

But would Ahira object to his experimenting, even if it
meant the difference between preserving and having to
kill the horse?

Certainly; the dwarf and the horses had something less
than a deep and abiding affection for each other.

Behind him, Ahira grunted as he pulled on the reins of
his gray gelding. "Move, you filthy little monster. *Move*,
I said." The small horse towered above the dwarf, drawing back its head to the limits of the reins and snorting at
Ahira as it gave ground, inch by inch.

Quite a horseman, eh? The mental voice was faint.
Quite.

Following Ahira, Slovotsky sat in his usual place on the
bench of the flatbed, with blond Kirah close beside him.
A few weeks of freedom had done Kirah's appearance
good; she actually was quite pretty, although a bit too
skinny for Karl's tastes.

Deep in quiet conversation, Walter smiled, and patted
her knee. Karl found that vaguely reassuring, and was
ashamed of himself for feeling that way.

*Walter's my friend, dammit. I should be happy he's
found someone, not relieved that I don't have to worry
about him and Andy-Andy anymore.*

*To the best of my knowledge, Walter has never been
accused of practicing exclusivity.*

Ellegon!

*If you're going to trust either or both of them, then do
so. If not, don't. But whipping yourself with worry suggests that you don't think you have enough real problems
to worry about. Would you like to hear my list?*

*No thanks, Ellegon. . . . I can always turn to you for a
spot of reassurance, eh?*

Think nothing of it.

I won't.

Behind Slovotsky and Kirah, Lou Riccetti napped

under a light blanket, with a sack of grain for his pillow. The wind carried his snores to Karl's ears.

Hmph. Riccetti was *supposed* to be keeping an eye on the bull, who was secured to the flatbed by a length of rope tied to his brass nose ring. Karl thought about waking Riccetti, then dismissed the idea. No need, the lumbering beast followed without complaint.

From its high seat, Andy-Andy drove the former slave wagon, little Aeia huddled next to her, the five chicken cages tied down on the flat roof. The bars were gone from the wagon's windows, having joined the other rod stock in the back of the flatbed.

Trotting along beside the wagon, the two goats voiced their unflattering opinion of the whole party. Aeia turned to give them a few reassuring words. She liked the goats, although the smelly creatures didn't return her affection.

Aeia was still a problem; she had yet to make it through a night without waking up crying, not going back to sleep until Andy-Andy held her for at least an hour.

What it came down to was simple: Aeia was homesick. There was a solution to that, but Andy-Andy wasn't going to like it; she had practically adopted the girl.

Spread out behind the wagon, Tennetty, Chton, Ihryk, and Fialt led their horses, occasionally switching the five cows to make them keep the pace. The cattle were brakes on the whole procession; they could barely walk fifteen miles on a good day. Goddam splay-footed beasts—

Stop worrying; the trip is almost over.

Last was Chak, who insisted on riding his horse through the charred rubble, swearing at her when she balked.

Karl stroked Carrot's neck as they walked up the hill. "Easy, now."

A carrot works better than a stick, most of the time. This time Ellegon's voice was louder, clearer.

Karl looked up. High overhead, the dragon circled, a dark speck against the blue sky. *True. Which is why I finally got around to naming my horse Carrot.*

A suitable name. She is probably very tasty.

"Ellegon, you are *not* eating my horse. Case closed."

Hmph. I would have thought I deserved some sort of reward for finding a route you can take your wagons over. The mindlink grew tighter for a moment, then loosened. *Lewis and Clark didn't have aerial reconnaissance. Neither did Cortez, or Pizarro. You may have noticed that you haven't had to turn around and try a different route once over the past three months.*

"I noticed. Honest. And I noticed it the first day, even before you mentioned it. So would you please—" He cut himself off. Snide comments were not the way to handle a child asking for praise. *You've done one hell of a job, in case I haven't mentioned that recently.*

You haven't.

The crest of the hill lay just a few yards ahead; the slope steepened. On an impulse, Karl dropped Carrot's reins and ran up, onto the summit, and over the hill.

And into wonder.

The valley opened up below him, trees and grasses spread out in a welcoming green embrace. In the distance, silvery threads of streams wove their way down from the far, snow-peaked mountains, tumbling through stands of pine and maple, finally emptying into the mirror-bright lake that cupped the valley floor.

Half a mile below, seven deer drank at the lake's edge. The water was still, mirroring the fluffy clouds and blue sky. A five-point buck looked up at him; then the group sprinted gracefully into the forest, leaping high over the grasses as they ran.

The wind blew across the valley, bathing him in the warm tang of sunbaked grasses, and the cool scent of pines.

He didn't notice Chak walking up. One moment, Karl

was all alone; the next, the little man stood beside him, Carrot's reins in one hand, the reins of his own gray mare in the other.

"Like it?" Chak smiled, handing him the reins.

Karl didn't answer him.

It wasn't necessary.

"Ready, Lou?"

Riccetti nodded, smiling inside. *Ready? I've been waiting my whole life for a moment like this.*

Ahira beckoned him to his feet. "You go first."

Riccetti rose and walked to the campfire. He turned to face the others, his back to the crackling flame.

"The two main considerations in this sort of construction," he said, "are water supply and defense."

All the others looked at him, listening intently.

Which was nice; Lou liked being the center of attention. For once.

Slovotsky nodded. "Good point, but what does that do for us?"

The fire was hot; sweating, Riccetti moved away from it, the heat still pressing against his back. "Form follows function, Walter," he said. "What we've got to do is figure out what sort of complex to make, given our present limitations of materials and the lack of power tools. I wish we had a few dozen tons of concrete mix, steel girders, PVC pipe, and such. But we don't." '

Both Chton and Fialt frowned, while the other new people stared back blankly; Riccetti realized that he had lapsed back into English.

Item, he thought, *English, teaching of. Discussion: Many useful concepts are not available in Erendra, absent a great deal of neologism or circumlocution. Examples: concrete, suspension bridge, gunpowder, steam engine, railroad. Question: Should we actually teach English, or settle for supplementing Erendra vocabulary?*

Sprawled on the ground behind the others, Ellegon raised his head. *Noted, Louis. I will remind you of this later, when you have time to consider it.*

Don't forget.

Dragons don't forget, stupid. We leave that sort of thing to humans.

"My apologies," he said in Erendra, both to Ellegon and to the natives. "I was saying that we don't have many different materials to work with, nor do we have . . . magical tools, other than the woodknife."

Chak spat. "And you should be grateful for that, instead of complaining that we don't have any other magical tools. Woodknives are rare, Richetih; takes a master wizard to make one, and it takes him *years*. I don't know where Ohrmyst bought—or, more likely, stole—his. I've traveled far; only heard of a few in existence. Only seen one other, in Sciforth, and that one heavily guarded. You couldn't have bought that knife for a wagonload of gold."

Cullinane raised a palm. "Stand easy, Chak. Lou was just commenting, not criticizing."

That seemed to settle the matter for the little man; Chak listened to Karl the way Riccetti would have listened to Washington Roebling himself.

Riccetti went on: "How and what we build has to be planned with that limitation in mind. We also have to consider the problem of the water supply."

Tennetty shrugged, sending her straight black hair flipping about her face.

She was a slim woman, with an almost impossibly thin nose, and a permanent expression of distance on her drawn face. The daughter of a poor farmer on one of the Shattered Islands, on her fifteenth birthday she had been sold to a slaver's ship. The ten intervening years hadn't treated her kindly, as she passed from owner to owner; it showed in her lined face.

Riccetti found her profoundly unattractive, even when her mouth was closed. Which was usually, but nevertheless all too seldom.

"What problem?" She gestured at the lake, which lay shimmering in the starlight. "If we build our houses close to the lake, then we have a short walk for water. If we are stupid enough to build them far away, then we have a long walk for water. What is so complicated about how far you have to carry a bucket?"

Sitting on the other side of Andrea from little Aeia, Cullinane shook his head, grinning. "I'd really like to have running water, myself. Taste of home, and all that. You've got a way?"

"Yup." Riccetti smiled. "I took a quick look this afternoon, while the rest of you were lolling around camp. So far, I've counted seven streams that feed into the lake. I've found one with a waterfall." He pointed. "About a quarter-mile that way. The waterfall's small— it's not much taller than Karl is. But if we set up the compound over part of that stream, surrounding the waterfall, we can divert it, and still have a bit of flow to play around with. We'll want a mill, for one thing . . . and in the future, I might be able to rig up some sort of water heater."

"Hot showers," Andrea said, sighing. She bent her head toward Aeia's. "Have you ever had a hot shower?"

She shook her head. "What's a shower, Andy?"

"But in the short run, we can have flowing water inside, for washing, cooking, and for privies."

Ahira's forehead furrowed. "How are you going to build a flush toilet?"

Riccetti shrugged. "That's years away. For now,

you're going to have to settle for a constant-flow one, sort of like an outhouse with some water from the stream running underneath. Open pipes like the Romans', but we'll use wood instead of lead."

Slovotsky nodded his approval. "That's not bad. Constant-flow toilet, eh? It's so simple, it'd be hard to think up, if you didn't already know about it. I guess you weren't wasting your time in your engineering courses."

Cullinane threw back his head and laughed.

The dwarf glared at him. "What's so funny?"

The big man shook his head. "Never mind." His expression went vague.

*Louis, Karl has asked me to tell you that he remembers lending you his copy of *Farnham's Freehold*, and that he's glad he did.*

That's nice.

And he also said to mention that he won't tell anyone that you swiped the notion of constant-flow toilets from Heinlein. If you build the first one for him and Andrea.

Tell him to go to hell. I'm running the construction here, and I'll do as I see fit. He waited for Ellegon to replay the message. Cullinane glared at him for a moment, then relaxed, his hand miming tipping a hat.

Good. It was best to start things off by letting everyone —Cullinane particularly—know who was in charge of the building.

"In any case," he went on, "that's the first part of it. The other thing is that the waterfall is in a stand of pines. We can save a lot of effort by building there; even green, pine is good to build with. It's a bit tricky, but I've read about how to use it."

I'd give any digit you care to name for one-tenth of the library Farnham had. Or even for Robertson's Green Wood Construction. Or the Britannica, or the Rubber Handbook, or anything.

All that stood between him and all of those books was about five hundred miles of forest, plains, mountains and

Waste, plus the warrens surrounding the Gate Between Worlds.

And The Dragon, guarding the Gate.

Ellegon snorted. *You had best learn to live without those books, Louis. He is still awake. And will be, for much longer than you will live.*

Riccetti shuddered. No *way* was he ever going near The Dragon again. "So we build there," he said. "Agreed?"

"Sounds right to me," Cullinane nodded. "You were talking about defense. Some sort of castle?"

"No. We don't have the tools or the manpower for stonework, even if we could find stone worth quarrying. My suggestion is that we go for something like a western fort. It'll look a bit crude, but—"

Fialt spat. "I am *from* the west. I was born and raised on Salket. We build with stone there; we are civilized." He was the oldest of the group, a grizzled graybeard of fifty or so.

Slovotsky chuckled. "Not your west—ours. But it sounds like a lot of work, Lou."

"It will be. But it should give us some defense. If the colony grows a lot, we won't be able to put all the houses inside, of course, but it still makes sense to have some sort of fortification to retreat to, if necessary. We may not need it, but . . ."

Chak nodded. "Kharl's plan should keep us relatively safe, as long as he doesn't spend too much time here. But you're right, Richetih: no sense in taking a chance for no payoff."

Ahira cocked his head to one side. "That's easy for you to say—you're going on this first expedition with Karl; little of the sweat will be from your brow. Not more than a tenday's worth, at best."

"Damn, but I like your positive attitude, Ahira." The little man smiled. "Pointing out another nice part of Richetih's plan."

Riccetti spread his hands. "That's the broad outline. If

we do it this way, I'll mark out the boundaries in the morning, and we can get right to work. Should be able to have three walls of the palisade up within a—"

"Palisade?"

"The outer wall. We'll put a walkway around the inside, around the top. As I was saying, it should be done within two, maybe three tendays. Ahira, you're still the leader. It's up to you." *And if you don't want to do it my way, I'd like to hear what idiocy you have in mind.*

Andrea raised an eyebrow. "Why just three-quarters of the wall? It seems to me it'd be more efficient to do the whole thing at one time."

"No. The gate will be the hard part; by leaving that wall for last, we can have a way of bringing wood in to build the houses and such. We could do the houses first, but I think we'll save some effort by using the palisade as the fourth wall for some of them, and for the grainmill, when we build it. Besides, we'll want to set up a smithy and make some nails before we do the houses; we can build the palisade walls with just wood and leather.

"And sweat, of course." He turned to Ahira. "That's my proposal. There'll be lots of details to work out, but it seems to me this is the best way."

"Any objections?" The dwarf waited silently for a moment. "We'll do it. Lou, you're in charge of construction. Complete charge; you don't ask anyone, you tell them, unless you think you need another opinion. Refer any discipline problems to me." He tapped his thumb against the blade of his battleaxe.

Cullinane snorted. "That include you?"

"Lou, if I give you any trouble, you can refer it to Karl."

Or me.

"Or Ellegon." The dwarf turned to Slovotsky. "Now, Walter, what are your thoughts about crops and animals?"

Riccetti sat down, barely listening as Slovotsky stood

and began to talk about slash-and-burn agriculture, and where he wanted to put the first field.

For more than four years, Lou Riccetti had been an engineering student in a world that really didn't want things built. The days of great construction had passed from his world; the future of engineering was with piddling little electronic circuits, not big structures, not great things. There would be no more Brooklyn Bridges built, no more Hoover Dams.

But here, it was different. A world to conquer.

He smiled.

I'm going to be building things, he thought, his heart beating audibly in his chest. *It's a small start, but it's a start.*

He shook his head. This was ridiculous. Getting all excited about putting together a bunch of log cabins and some stockade fencing? And some sort of smithy, come to think of it. That would have to be done early; the flatbed contained fifty or so pounds of thin nail stock, but no nails. Then again, nailmaking shouldn't require a full-fledged smithy; a hot fire, a bellows, a hammer, and the smallest of the anvils would do. And—

Ridiculous. It had to be done, granted, but getting excited about it?

I disagree. Ellegon lifted his head from his crossed forelegs, curling and uncurling his wings. *It is not ridiculous, friend Louis. Not if it makes you feel this good.*

Build and enjoy.

The first wall went up much more quickly than Karl would have believed possible.

It wasn't just because of the woodknife's ability to turn the felling, stripping, and shaping of a tall pine from a tedious affair into something that took only minutes, helpful as that was.

And it wasn't just Ellegon's great strength, although that certainly helped, too.

Ellegon would seize the blunt end of a stripped log in his massive jaws and drag it from where it fell to where the empty post hole was. That made harnessing the horses unnecessary, although Riccetti could and did rig a block, tackle, and twenty-foot-tall tripod. With that, and with the aid of the mules and the cannibalized harnesses from the flatbed, Karl, Walter, and Ahira could raise the upper end of a log into its proper position and lower the flat end into its hole, before packing dirt around the now-upright log to keep it steady.

And it wasn't just that all of them worked hard, although they certainly did.

Ellegon hauled logs, beginning work when the sky grew light, not quitting until well after dark. Fialt, Kirah, and Chak took turns with the woodknife, felling and stripping pines, keeping a constant supply of twenty-foot posts coming, as well as stacking the scraps for the cooking fires. Karl, Walter, and Ahira dug the holes and raised the posts. Andy-Andy and Aeia kept bowls of hot stew and pitchers of cold water coming from dawn to dusk. Ihryk and Tennetty hunted deer, duck, and rabbit, gathered wild garlic, onions, chotte, burdock, maikhe, and tacktob for the stewpot, stretching the supply of dried beef and putting off the time when it would become necessary to start converting to chickens from egglayers into roasters.

What really made it all work was Riccetti.

Lou always seemed to be at Karl's elbow, any time he needed a bit of advice or instruction. At times, he wondered if there weren't really three or four Lou Riccetti's; others reported the same.

Riccetti was the one who knew how to lash together a tripod of logs and throw together a wooden block and tackle to raise and support a pole, or turn a dozen saplings and a few hundred yards of rope into a double-lock bridge across the deep-bedded stream.

He was the one who withheld a portion of the scrap wood, for Ellegon to roast slowly into wood tar, to be later distilled down to creosote, which would protect the palisade against insects and rot.

Riccetti showed them how to lash the poles together at the top of the wall with wet leather strips, so that as the leather dried, it shrank and linked the individual poles together solidly.

More important, he knew how to apportion the work so that no bottlenecks developed; Karl, Walter, and Ahira always had just enough poles to work with, without worrying about falling behind while unused ones accumulated, or letting valuable time go by while they waited for the next.

Riccetti was, finally, in his own proper environment; Karl smiled at the little swagger his walk had developed.

The sounds and smells of the dying were far away; the days passed quickly, filled with the sweet smell and unwashable stickiness of freshly cut pine, the stink of his own sweat, and the deep sleep brought on by hard labor.

CHAPTER SEVEN:
Moving On

Now hollow fires burn out to black,
And lights are guttering low:
Square your shoulders, lift your pack,
And leave your friends and go.

— Alfred Edward Housman

It was a clear night. Andy-Andy lying still beside him, Karl stared up at the dome of stars.

Downslope from them, halfway between them and the palisade wall, little Aeia huddled in her blankets, asleep at last. It had been a rocky night for the girl, filled with bad dreams and loud screams.

If there is a hell, Orhmyst, you are surely there.

"Andy," he whispered.

"Yes?"

He quirked a smile. She hadn't been sleeping either.

"I've got to leave, for a while."

She sucked air through her teeth, then rolled over on her side, facing him. She stroked his forehead with gentle fingers. "I know. You're worried about Pandathaway."

"Not worried: terrified. If I stay here too long, I'm not just endangering myself." He patted her barely distended belly. "There's others involved, too."

"Like Karl, Junior?" She grinned at him.

"Even if it is a boy, we're not naming him after me. With a mother as pretty as you, he'll have enough of an

Oedipus problem without saddling him with his father's name. Besides, it's probably a girl."

"It will be a boy, Karl." Her face grew somber. "We women know about these things."

"Bullshit." He snorted. "I think we know each other a bit too well for you to give me that sort of nonsense."

"We *do* know about these things," she said, shrugging, "and we're right about, oh, fifty percent of the time."

"Funny. Very funny. But you're changing the subject. Or trying to."

"I'm starting to get fat, is that it? You're going to run off and find some sixteen-year-old—"

"Shh." He put a finger to her lips. "*Shh.* Not even in jest. Please."

A long pause. "How long will you be gone?"

"Don't know for sure. Six months, at a minimum. Maybe closer to a year."

"When?" she asked, her voice a low whisper.

T'were best done quickly. "In a day or two, I think. It won't take long to pack. I don't know if you've noticed, but Chak's getting itchy."

"And so are you."

There was more truth in that than he cared to admit. "No, it's not that. But this vacation has gone on long enough; it's time to get back to work."

She rolled onto her back and stared up at the sky, her head pillowed on her hands. "Slicing up people. Some work."

"Slicing up *slavers.* Or, if you want to be more accurate, my work is murdering slavers. But it isn't the words that matter, Andrea. You know that." *Please, Andy, don't ever let the blood come between us. Please.*

She sighed deeply, and then closed her eyes. She lay quietly for so long that Karl began to wonder if she had fallen back asleep. "Who are you taking with you?"

"Well, Chak, for one. He's seen more of the Eren regions than any of the rest of us, and he's pretty handy with a sword." *Besides, he rankles at taking orders from anyone except me. I'm not leaving a time bomb behind.* "I'd like to take Ellegon, but he's just too conspicuous." *And he's also the most deadly being I know. He stays here, and keeps an eye on my wife and unborn child.*

I am honored, of course. But I will miss you, Karl. Don't do something stupid and get yourself killed. Please?

Just as a favor to you.

Thanks.

"Who else?" she asked, a decided edge to her voice.

"Well, I can't take Walter, not this time; somebody's got to run the farm." *And if I did take him along, I'd never know whether it was because I wanted him along, or because I didn't trust both of you enough to leave him here.* "I think I'll invite Ahira to come along; he'll want to go. He's just as good in a fight as I am—"

Better.

"—and he's got a fine strategical sense. His darksight might come in handy; it's even better than Ellegon's."

"How's he going to take your being in charge, Karl?"

"Huh? Who said anything about—"

"As Walter would say, think it through. You've always thought he was too conservative, too eager to avoid a fight. So you're going to let him be in charge when you're going out *looking* for trouble?"

He snorted. "We'll work it out. What we're doing is too important to let who's-in-charge games screw it up. And . . ."

"And? I don't recall your mentioning *my* name."

He snorted. "Don't be silly."

"*Silly?*"

"This isn't a time for reflex pseudo-feminism. We're going to be gone for six months, at least. If you think I'm going to let a woman at term bounce along on the back of a horse, try thinking again. Case closed; you stay here, where it's safe."

"Always the diplomat, Karl." She dismissed the issue with a wave of her hand. "But I guess you're right. It's just going to be you, Chak, and Ahira?"

"Can't expect any of the new people to do any good in a fight. The best is Fialt, and he wouldn't last ten seconds against a real swordsman. On the other hand, he's trying hard to learn. If he wants in, he's got it. Chton, Kirah, Ihryk, and he are happy here, or I'd escort them somewhere safe. Tennetty, though . . ."

"Tennetty wouldn't be happy anywhere."

"Exactly. But she's hot to kill some slavers. I can't say as I blame her; she can come along if she wants to. Which she will."

"Is that all?" She frowned. "It sounds like an awfully small group."

"It is. But I think it's the best one, for now." *I may as well get it over with.* "There's one more person we're taking along, Andy."

"Karl, you are *not* taking Aeia."

"We're taking her home." He shrugged. "Might as well swing through Melawei. The hunting should be good; there've been slaving raids all along that coast." Mainly by sea, according to Chak; to the best of his knowledge, Ohrmyst had been the only slaver to try the difficult overland route to Melawei.

Question: How does one take on a slaver's ship?

Answer: very carefully. Do you have any more stupid questions?

No.

"No!" Andy-Andy said, echoing his response to Ellegon. "You can't. She's getting used to being around us; she'll adjust. I'll take care of her."

"We're not her family, Andrea. She's been through hell. You should know that, better than I do; let's let her grow up in her own country, with her own people."

Andy-Andy sat up, angrily pulling the blankets around

her. "What good did *they* do her? Tell me. Her *people* let her get caught by slavers, raped. Karl, you can't take her back to them. I won't let you."

He tried to put his hand on her shoulder, but she shrugged his arm away.

"Shall we leave it up to her?" he asked.

"She's too young to decide. She needs someone to take care of her." She looked away from him, toward where Aeia slept.

"Like you?"

"Yess," she hissed, "like *me*. Don't you think I'm good enough to take care of her? *Don't you?*"

He shook his head. "No, I don't."

Her head spun around. "You bastard." Tears filled her eyes.

"Andy, it's not that there's anything wrong with you. The thing of it is this: She's a little girl. Somewhere, she has family. And they probably miss her as much as she misses them."

She sneered. "Just as our families back home will be missing us? You didn't seem so worried about *that*."

"Different case. For one thing, we're adults; we have to make our own decisions. For another, with the time differential between here and home, the fact that we're gone hasn't even been noticed yet; at home, we've only been gone a few hours.

"But, again, you're dodging the issue. Think about this: If someone stole little whatever-her-name-is from you, you'd want her back." He laid a palm on her belly. "Wouldn't you? Or would you think that some stranger could take better care of her?"

She didn't answer for a long time.

Then: "Leave it alone, Karl. You're right, as usual. Bastard." She daubed at her eyes with a corner of the blanket. "But it's going to be a boy." Gathering her robes about her, she rose and walked down the slope toward where Aeia lay sleeping. She seated herself beside the girl and took one of Aeia's small hands in both of hers.

And sat there, watching her, until the night fled, and the sun sat above the treetops.

PART THREE:
The Middle Lands

CHAPTER EIGHT: *Ahrmin*

Revenge is a dish that tastes best when eaten cold.

—Sicilian proverb

The windowless room was dark and musty, redolent with the smells of aging paper and parchment; the only illumination was a single overhead lamp. In a dark corner, a tall brass censer burned, sending vague fingers of smoke feeling their way into the air. His eyes stung.

Ahrmin repressed a shudder. He never liked being near wizards at all, but it was even worse to confront one on the wizard's own territory. That was one thing his father had always said: "Stay away from the wizards, son, whenever you can." In Ahrmin's nineteen years, he had never seen a reason to doubt that advice.

He stood motionless in the middle of the blood-red carpet, not daring to interrupt Wenthall's unblinking study of the crystal ball.

Though why the thing was called a ball was something Ahrmin couldn't understand. The "ball" was a head-sized crystal model of a human eye, the iris and pupil etched on its front, complete down to a spoke that projected from the back, to symbolize the cords that connected the eye to the brain.

The fat wizard gripped the spoke as he held the crystal before him, staring at the back side of the ball as if he were sitting behind a giant's eye, looking out through it.

Finally, he shook his head, sighed deeply, then carefully set the ball down on a wooden stand before turning to Ahrmin. "Good. I see you received my summons."

"Yes, sir." *Why me? I'm just barely a journeyman. If you have a need for my guild, why not send for a master?*

He didn't say that; Slavers' Guildmaster Yryn had spent most of his tenure trying to improve the often uneasy relations between the Slavers' Guild and the Wizards' Guild, and was known to have little patience with any apprentice of journeyman who did anything to offend wizards.

If the apprentice or journeyman survived. The rapprochement between the slavers and the wizards, while tentative, had paid well; it had opened up both Therranj and Melawei for frequent slaving raids. The Wizards' Guildmaster was thought to be lukewarm about the loose alliance; Yryn tolerated no action that might change that indifference to opposition.

Wenthall walked to a water bowl and splashed water on his face, drying his black beard with his gray robes. "You recall that there is a reward out for the one who stole our sewer dragon," he said, seating himself on a stool, his hands folded over his bulging belly.

"Of course." Despite himself, Ahrmin voiced it almost as a question. After all, the reward had gone unclaimed for more than a year. Undoubtedly, the culprit was dead somewhere, or had fled the Eren regions, past the range of even Wizards' Guildmaster Lucius' location spells. "But hunting dragons isn't something I can do, Master Wenthall; I don't have that kind of experience. Even if there are any small ones left."

The wizard's eyes flashed. "Just listen, fool. I do not want you to hunt a dragon—you and I have further grievances against the one who freed our sewer dragon. The same one believed responsible for the deaths of both Blenryth, of my order, and Ohlmin, of yours."

Ohlmin? That had to mean—no; it was impossible. "But Karl Cullinane has to be dead, or must have fled the region, at least, sir. None of you wizards has been able to locate him."

Wenthall rose to his feet, sighing. He walked over to a scrollrack set into the nearest wall.

"There is one other possibility," the wizard said, rummaging through the scrolls, finally selecting one.

He unrolled it; it was a well-worn map of the entire Eren region. "He could have been in the one place in the region that is protected from both the erratic sight of my crystal ball and my more reliable spells of direction. And a message I've received from Lord Mehlên of Metreyll suggests that that must be the case. He was . . ." The wizard tapped at a spot on the map. "*There.* The home tabernacle of the Healing Hand Society. That is where Cullinane hid. He is not there right now. But he has been. Protected by the Hand."

"You're certain?"

"*Yes,*" Wenthall hissed, "I am certain. I haven't been able to see him with the ball, but there is no doubt that Karl Cullinane is alive, boy. He is *alive.* Look."

Puffing from the exertion, the wizard reached up to a high shelf and brought down a chamois-wrapped parcel, almost a foot high. He unwrapped it carefully before gently setting it down on a table, a baked-clay statue of a bearded man, holding a long sword.

Ahrmin looked closer. The statue was incredibly detailed, down to individual hairs carved into the head. "Karl Cullinane?"

"Karl Cullinane." Wenthall rewrapped the statue and put it away. Then, from the folds of his robe, he produced a strange device: a hollow glass sphere the size of his fist, containing a murky yellow oil. "Look here."

Reluctantly moving closer, Ahrmin peered into it.

A mummified finger floated in the sphere's center. The finger had been messily severed from its owner's hand; a shard of bone projected from its hacked-off end, and shreds of skin and tendon waved slowly as it floated.

"Hmmm." Walking quickly to a compass on its stand in the corner of the room, the wizard took a sighting.

"He's moved again. Not far—but south and west. *Still* south and west. . . ."

"Your pardon, Master Wenthall, but I don't understand."

For a moment, the wizard's nostrils flared. "Stupid little—" he stopped himself. "Never mind. Listen closely.

"This device works like a location spell. After much effort, I have managed to attune it to the body of Karl Cullinane." As the wizard slowly spun the sphere in the palm of his age-withered hand, the dismembered finger maintained its position, pointing unerringly to the southeast. "Too much effort; getting that statue accurate enough for the spell to work was the most precise, most finicky work I've had to do in ten years. But never mind that.

"As long as Cullinane remains within range, this will show you in which direction he is. If, as you turn the ball, the finger fails to point consistently in one direction, there are four possible explanations. First, he has fled the Eren regions. Second, he is inside the Hand sanctuary." Wenthall grimaced. "Third, he is otherwise magically protected. Or, last," the wizard said, smiling thinly, "he is dead."

"Will it tell me where he is? Not just the direction, but how far?"

"Yes." Wenthall nodded. "But only indirectly." The sphere disappeared in the folds of his cloak. Two quick strides brought the wizard across the room. He shuffled through a pile of papers and parchment on his desk and produced a map of the Eren regions, spreading it out on a low table.

"We know," he said, picking up a charstick, "that he is in this direction. But where on this line?" Wenthall shrugged, then drew a solid line that stretched from Pandathaway into the Middle Lands, through Holtun and Bieme into Nyphien and beyond. "We can't be certain. And there is no way of knowing, at any given moment, whether he is moving or stationary; the device is not as precise as we would wish. That could be critical. Were he on his way to Aeryk, your task would be easy; were he traveling to Therranj, it would be more difficult. Your guild is not in the good graces of the western Therranji these days."

"True." Ahrmin smiled; slave-taking raids did have a way of making one's guild unpopular with the locals.

"But I have been tracking his progress for the past tenday. It seems that he is traveling through the Middle Lands, possibly bound for Ehvenor."

"Ehvenor, Master Wenthall? Could he have dealings in Faerie?"

"That seems unlikely," the wizard said, scowling. "It's too risky for humans. Particularly normals. But there are other reasons for going to Ehvenor besides trying to beg passage into Faerie. As you should know, slaver."

"Melawei. He's bound for Melawei."

But why? There were only two reasons for traveling to Melawei: copra and slaves. Neither seemed to apply to Karl Cullinane.

"Quite possibly," Wenthall said. "But possibly not; it's conceivable he has dealings in the Middle Lands. I suggest you begin by taking passage to Lundeyll—here." He tapped the map. "Take another sighting, with both ball and compass. If Cullinane hasn't moved, the two lines will intersect at his location.

"Now"—the wizard raised his finger—"if ever you do lose him, you can use that technique to locate him precisely.

"In any case, from Lundeyll you can take the southern route through the Aershtyls, if he is still in the Middle Lands. There is a land route to Melawei; that could be his intention. If so, you should be able to beat him there by ship, no?"

"Certainly, Master Wenthall. The overland route is said to be very difficult."

"Fine. I will speak to your guildmaster later today. See him before you leave Pandathaway; he will give you a writing that will allow you to commandeer a raiding ship. If, that is, Cullinane is bound for Melawei."

"Perhaps he'll take ship to Melawei." *I could catch him at sea. If the* Flail *or* Scourge *are in Lundeport . . .*

"Perhaps." The wizard extended his hand, the sphere cradled in his palm. "Treat this device carefully; it is the product of far more time and effort than I would like to recall. A finger from a freshly killed maiden elf is difficult to obtain these days."

Accepting the proffered sphere, Ahrmin nodded grimly. "I'll find him, sir, and bring him back to you," he said. He started to turn away, but caught himself.

No. His father wouldn't have wanted him to leave it just at that; by profession, slavers were supposed to be cold and bloodless. "The reward still stands? There will be expenses in this, Master Wenthall. I'll have to hire a team. And if I commandeer a ship in Lundeyll, I'll have to pay the seamen's wages. That is the law, master."

The wizard chuckled thinly. "Quite your father's son, eh? Very well, the reward is doubled. Trebled, if you bring him back alive." The wizard smiled. "I have a use for his skin, but it must be taken while he lives."

Despite himself, Ahrmin shuddered. But he forced a smile and a nod. "You will have it, sir. I swear." With a deep bow, he turned and left the wizard's room.

So Karl Cullinane was alive and well. Probably, Cullinane often snickered over killing Ohlmin. He wouldn't be snickering soon.

You killed Ohlmin, Karl Cullinane. You shouldn't have killed my father.

CHAPTER NINE:
Baron Furnael

When we are planning for posterity, we ought to remember that virtue is not hereditary.

—Thomas Paine

"Relatively speaking, I'm beginning to like the Middle Lands," Ahira said, looking up at Karl from the back of his dappled pony. "Bieme in particular."

"Relatively speaking," Karl answered, tired.

Ahira nodded. "We've seen a few slaves, but neither slavers nor whips. By local standards, this isn't bad."

"By local standards."

Ahira snorted. "What are you today? A Greek chorus? Like you and Slovotsky in Chem?"

Karl laughed. "I didn't know you knew about that."

"Walter told me. Swore me to silence, until the statute of limitations runs out. Not that it matters anymore." His smile faded. "What's bothering you?"

"A touch of homesickness, I think."

"You miss Andrea."

"Yes, but . . . actually, I was thinking about home-home, not the valley-home." Karl loosened his tunic to scratch at his ribs. "I think I'd trade a finger for a bar of Lifebuoy, or a pound of Kenya double-A coffee, or a case of toilet paper . . . hell, even for a pizza."

"You complain too much. Why let it get to you? At least we're not camping out every damn night, for now. The beds may not be Posturepedics, but they are soft."

Karl nodded. The dwarf had a point. In the forty days of traveling since they had left the valley and worked their way into the Middle Lands, they had gone through some hard times.

Not dangerous, particularly; the only slaver caravan they had run across had been easy pickings, so much so that Karl didn't consider the encounter a proper shake-down for Fialt and Tennetty.

The slavers hadn't even bothered to set out a watch-man. The *late* slavers.

Karl had been able to send seventeen former slaves toward the valley, one of them carrying a letter to Andy-Andy. He hadn't worried that the group might not find the valley, as long as they passed nearby. Ellegon would be flying watch at night. Once the dragon spotted them and flew close enough to read their minds, they would be met and guided in.

No danger there, not for anyone.

The closest Karl and the rest had come to real danger was when Fialt accidentally slashed Tennetty across the belly during a fencing lesson. Two quickly administered healing draughts had taken care of that; a switch to wooden swords for training purposes ensured that they wouldn't again have to use up more of their small supply of expensive healing draughts for that sort of accident.

It wasn't the danger that bothered Karl. It was the drudgery.

Moving camp every day had been fun during the summer when Karl's Scout troop had gone up to Mani-toba to canoe down the Assiniboine, but part of the fun of that had been knowing that the primitive life-style was temporary, that hot showers, clean clothes, fast food, and air conditioning awaited them at the end of the trip.

But that wasn't true here. The endless grind of stopping to camp, finding firewood, lighting a fire with flint and steel, cooking, cleaning pots and pans with dirt clods, pitching their tents, watering the horses, breaking camp in the morning—all of it had started to wear on him, bringing him almost to the breaking point.

Perhaps crossing the border from Nyphien into Bieme hadn't saved his sanity, but sometimes it felt like it.

Bieme was possibly the oldest of the Middle Lands; certainly it was the best developed. Tilled by drayhorses and oxen, the farmland produced an abundance of grains and legumes, one-tenth of the fields lying fallow under strict rotation. The productivity of the land and its people had brought both wealth and trade to Bieme; grain sellers and hostlers came from as far away as the Katharhd and Lundeyll to do business there.

Few armsmen were evident, and then only singly, or in small groups. They functioned primarily as a constabulary, rather than a standing army. While there was no love lost between Therranj and any of the Middle Lands, an attack on Bieme would have to go through one of the surrounding principalities first, giving the Biemei ample time to prepare; there was no need to have a large nonproductive soldier class standing by, although all freefarmers were required to produce a well-honed sword for inspection on two different holidays each year.

The best thing, though, was the inns along the main thoroughfare. By law, each community of five hundred or more along the Prince's Road had to sponsor a well-kept inn, the high standards maintained through frequent inspections by the local baron's armsmen—where there was a local baron—and infrequent but potentially more penalty-bearing ones by the Prince's.

Throughout most of the Prince's Road, the village inns were no more than a day's ride apart. In the few places where villages were more widely spaced, there still was an inn, directly supported by the crown. And the Prince's Inns were the most luxurious and least expensive of all.

"There's a trick to all of this," Karl said, as he reined in Carrot, forcing her to keep close to the rest of the group. "Easy, girl." He stroked the rough hair on her neck. She was still dry, even after half a day's ride. His only complaint about her was her tendency to go at her own quick pace, her sneering disdain for the slower pace of the other horses.

"A trick?"

Karl nodded. "Remember Kiar?"

"That inn with the marble floors? Not quite as lush as the Inn of Quiet Repose, but a nice place." The dwarf nodded. "This sour beer isn't all that good, but that cook really knew how to use it as a marinade. Although," he added under his breath, "I guess I do miss some things from home. I'd kill for a Genesee, or a Miller. Or even a Schlitz."

Karl raised an eyebrow. "Kill?"

Ahira shrugged. "Well, maim. I really do love a good beer."

"Don't remember you being much of a beer drinker back home."

Ahira frowned. "I had to be careful about when I drank. It used to really start my kidneys going."

Karl shot a glance over his shoulder. That had become a reflex, and one that he didn't intend to give up, even in the relative safety of the Prince's Road.

But there was no problem. Tennetty, Fialt, and Aeia rode behind, Chak bringing up the rear. The little man favored him with a friendly nod and a slight, open-handed wave.

"So?" Karl asked. "Beer does that to everyone."

Ahira chuckled. "You're forgetting." He raised a thick arm and flexed it, the chainmail tightening around his biceps. "I wasn't just anyone. Muscular dystrophy, remember?"

"I know, but—"

"What does that have to do with it? Karl, I couldn't go to the *john* by myself; couldn't even lift myself out of my wheelchair and onto the toilet. Going out for a drink with the guys wasn't something I could do, unless I had my roommate-slash-attendant with me, to drag me off to

the bathroom. I used to envy the hell out of the way all
the rest of you were so mobile."

"You don't anymore."

"Well, no," the dwarf said, unconvincingly.

Karl nodded to himself. There was something he had
that Ahira didn't, and that was the memory of always
being sound of body, of being able to take for granted
something as trivial as going out for a few beers.

As if he were reading his mind, Ahira cocked an eyebrow. "Let's leave it alone. 'What cannot be cured . . .'
You were talking about the inns?"

"Right," Karl said. "There's a trick there. If you
notice, a lot of the inns were originally built by the
crown. Back in Kiar, they'd taken down the Prince's coat
of arms, but the outline was still on the stone. A prince
built it, and supported it for a while."

"And then?"

"People moved nearby, probably got a good deal from
the Prince on the land, and such; the crown brought in a
cleric, probably sponsored a smith or two."

"Cute. And then, when the population was large
enough, the Prince gave the territory to a baron, and
made the locals support the inn."

"Right." Karl nodded. "At least, that's the way I read
it." And, if it had worked that way, it spoke well for the
local form of government, despite Karl's admitted bias
against feudalism. There was nothing wrong with a bit of
economic encouragement. It was coercion that was the
problem with feudal societies.

"Hmm.' Ahira considered it for a moment. "Possible.
And it's not as oppressive around here as we've seen else-
where. That why you haven't signaled for a fight?"

Karl shook his head. No, that wasn't it at all. The plan
didn't call for them to attack every slaveowner they ran
into; that would quickly result in their being buried
under a flood of bodies: Anyone who either owned a
slave, wanted to own a slave, or had owned a slave would
see them as the enemy.

Attacking slavers was different. Outside of the markets, slavers were unpopular; locals always knew that in a slaver's eye, everyone was potential merchandise.

"No," he said, "we fight slavers, and in self-defense."

"Liberally construed." Ahira threw back his head and laughed. "Like the way you and Walter decided that attacking Orhmyst was self-defense."

"Well, it felt like self-defense." Karl dismissed the subject with an airy wave. He stood in the saddle and turned, raising his head. "Chak?"

"Yes, Kharl?"

"Where are we stopping tonight?"

"Furnael." Chak dropped his reins to rub his hands together. "Best inn in the Middle Lands. We might even meet Baron Furnael himself."

Tennetty snorted. "What a thrill."

"Time for some practice, Fialt, Tennetty," Karl said, gesturing at them to follow him out of the common room and into the courtyard. Chak was ready; he had the bag of practice swords slung over a shoulder.

Ahira yawned and stretched. "I'm going to get some sleep. See you folks in the room."

Aeia put down her rag doll and lifted her head. "Me, too?"

"Well . . ."

"Please, Karl? You didn't let me, last time. Please?"

He smiled down at her as he nodded genially, then gently rubbed his fingers through her hair. "Sure." *Sure, little one, I'll be the gracious father substitute and teach you a bit more about how to disembowel a rapist.*

Goddam world. An eleven-year-old girl should be thinking about dolls and boys and stuff like that. "Let's go."

Wordlessly, Chak followed, carrying the canvas bag of wooden swords.

The courtyard of the Furnael inn was a large open

square, surrounded by the windowed walls of the inn proper. Slate flagstones checkered the ground, well-trimmed clumps of grass separating them.

Heavy with fruit, evenly spaced orange trees dotted the courtyard. Karl unbuckled his sword and hung it on a low branch, then reached up and pulled down a couple of oranges, tossing one to Chak before quartering the other with his beltknife.

Nothing for the other three; they would get theirs later, as a reward for a good session. If at all.

He ate quickly, not minding that some of the juice dripped down his chin. The fruit was cool and sweet. He tossed the peels to Chak, who stashed them under the equipment bag. "Now," he said, wiping the remaining juice and pulp from his chin, "we're going to start with a bit of hand-to-hand today." Karl slipped out of his jerkin and unlaced his sandals, stripping down to breechclout and leggings.

It promised to be a hot session; he slipped out of his leggings, awkwardly balancing on each foot alternately.

Already down to his breechclout, Chak hung up his sword and nodded. "This keeohokoshinkee stuff of yours?"

"Kyokoshinkai. And yes."

"Good." Chak nodded his approval.

Fialt frowned, rubbing a finger through his salt-and-pepper beard. "Rather do swords," he said. Which was, for Fialt, being unusually talkative.

Tennetty recoiled in mock horror—and probably a bit of real disgust. "Not around me. Not even with a wood sword. Liable to put my eye out while you're trying for a thrust to the kneecap."

"Fialt," Chak said, "you'll do swords with me, later. After Kharl's done with you." He shot a grin at Karl. "I'll make him sweat a bit. A bit more."

Karl nodded. When it came to fencing, Chak was the better teacher. There was a good reason. Karl had gained his skills with a sword as part of the transfer to this world.

He'd never had to go through the long hours of learning. There was no deliberate method to his swordplay; his arm and wrist just *did* it, as of their own volition.

A gain? Well, yes; his instantly acquired fencing skills had saved his life on more than one occasion. But it was a loss, too; he'd never had the experience of learning, of knowing how to improve his skills. While he had run into only one swordsman more adept than himself, there were undoubtedly others.

The loss went beyond his inability to teach. Without knowing how to learn swordfighting, his skills were frozen at their present level. He would never get better.

Guess I'll have to live with it.

But with his karate skills, there was the possibility of improvement, enhanced by the innate agility, balance, and reflexes of his body on this side. Here, he could easily have won enough in competition—if they had competitions here—to qualify for a brown belt; back home, the best he had been able to do was green.

"Loosen up, first," Karl said, breaking into a series of bends and stretches. The others followed his example; working out without first warming up was an invitation to wrenched muscles and torn tendons.

After his joints and tendons stopped protesting and settled down to a nice, quiet ache, he straightened. "Enough. Let's start."

Tennetty, Fialt, and Aeia lined up opposite him, bowing Japanese-style, their eyes always on his. Karl returned their bows.

Were the traditional customs irrelevant here? he wondered, not for the first time.

Possibly. Quite possibly the customs of the Japanese dojo were out of place; probably they had been silly back home. Probably it would be easier for him to use simple or compound Erendra names for punches, kicks, blocks, and strikes.

But the traditions seemed to have worked back home;

there was no sense in violating custom without a compelling reason.

"*Sanchin dachi*," he said, swinging his right foot past and slightly in front of his left and planting his feet a shoulder width apart, toes canted slightly in. *Sanchin dachi* was the best practicing stance for strikes and punches, as well as snap-kicks. Not necessarily the best fighting stance—Karl had always favored *zenkutsu-dachi*, a split-legged, forward-leaning stance—but a natural one that could be assumed without triggering a violent response.

"We'll start with a few *seiken*."

"*Chudan-tsuki, sensei?*" Chak asked, as he took his position at the end of the line, next to Tennetty.

"Fine. Start with your right hand." As always, he began by demonstrating. *Seiken chudan-tsuki*, a punch to the midsection, began with the nonpunching hand extended outward as though it had just been used to block, the punching hand pulled back, the fist inverted, resting at his side, just under the pectorals.

He moved slowly, pulling his left hand back as he brought his right hand out, turning his wrist so that the back of his hand faced upward, tensing his entire body just at the moment that the blow would have made contact, had there been a real opponent.

"And now the left." He demonstrated, then dropped his hands. "Now . . . on my count, *seiken chudan-tsuki*; groups of four." He moved closer to them. "*One*—keep it slow, now; follow the pace. *Two*—better, better. *Three. Four*. Speed it up a bit, now. One, two, three, four. Full speed, just as if it were for real. One-two-three-four. Keep going."

Chak was doing it properly, as usual; his stance easy, he punched smoothly, his arms moving like greased pistons.

Karl passed behind the little man and moved to help Tennetty. "No, keep your wrist straight," he said, adjusting her hand. "Mmm . . . better. A bit more tensing of the belly when you strike. *Don't* rise to the balls of your feet. Flat-footed blows have much more power." He moved on to Fialt.

Fialt was still throwing the shoulder of his striking arm forward. Standing in front of him, Karl reached out and grasped his shoulders. "Try it now. Ignore me." With Karl's much longer reach, Fialt's punch wouldn't land.

Fialt punched the air in front of him, pushing his shoulder forward against Karl's hand. "No good," Karl said. "You've got to keep the shoulder steady. Chak?"

"Not the knives, again?" The little man frowned.

"Knives, again. Tennetty, Aeia, keep it up."

Chak walked over to the tree where his clothes and equipment hung and drew his two beltknives, tossing them hilt-first to Karl. Karl caught them, then rested the knifepoints gently against Fialt's shoulders. "Now try it."

Fialt scowled, and punched timidly.

"That was better. At least your shoulders didn't move. But," Karl said, increasing the pressure of the knives against Fialt's shoulders, "you didn't have any force behind the blow. Wouldn't have squashed a bug. Do it right, now."

Still a timid punch.

"*Do it better or I swear I'll stick you*," he said, just as his karate teacher had once said to him. Karl wondered for a moment if Mr. Katsuwahara had been lying, and dismissed the notion as blasphemous.

This time, Fialt struck properly, his shoulders rock-steady, his body tensing at the moment of impact.

"Nice." Karl nodded, handing the knives back to Chak. He turned toward Aeia, and—

Fialt struck, a perfectly executed *seiken chudan-tsuki* that landed just below Karl's solar plexus, knocking him back.

Blindly, Karl brought his right arm around to block Fialt's second blow, then swung his right leg into a fast but gentle roundhouse kick that bowled Fialt over.

"Very pretty," a voice called from the balcony overlooking the courtyard. Karl glanced up. A man stood, looking down at them, his hands spread on the balcony rail.

"Chak. Handle it." Karl jerked his thumb in the direction of the voice as he stooped to help Fialt up. "Nicely done, Fialt."

Fialt's grizzled face broke into a smile. "I did it right?"

"Very. You hit me legally, and hit me hard. If you'd really been aiming here,"—Karl tapped himself on the solar plexus—"you would've had me." He clapped a hand on Fialt's shoulder. "Keep it up and we'll make a warrior of you yet."

"Just a man who can protect himself and his own. That's all I ask." Fialt nodded grimly. "That's all."

"I said, *very pretty, sir.*"

"And who are you?" Karl turned.

"Zherr, Baron Furnael, sir." He bowed. "May I join you?"

At Karl's nod, Furnael walked back into the building, reappearing just a few moments later at the door into the garden, two armsmen and an old man in gray wizard's robes at his side.

Baron Furnael was a tall man in his early fifties, perhaps an inch or so over six feet. Despite his age, he seemed to be in good shape: His thick wrists were heavily muscled, his leggings bulged with well-developed calves and thighs, only a small potbelly puffed out the front of his leather tunic.

Furnael's face was deeply lined, and stubble-free enough to suggest that he shaved himself both carefully and frequently, or else had someone else shave him. On his upper lip, a pencil-thin mustache was heavily streaked with gray, although his short-cropped hair was as black as a raven.

Karl kept his chuckle to himself. That bespoke a bit of vanity. But why hadn't Furnael dyed the mustache, too? A bit of self-honesty? Or was it just that whatever dye they used here would have stained his lip?

"Baron." Karl bowed slightly, Fialt, Tennetty, and Chak following suit.

Aeia glanced up at him, looking ready to break into tears. Strangers often affected her that way. Particularly male strangers. Which was understandable.

"Easy, little one." He smiled. "I think it's time for your nap."

She nodded and ran away, her bare feet slapping the flagstones.

Furnael smiled. "A pleasant child. Yours?"

"No. But in my care. She's a Mel. I'm not."

"So I see." Furnael turned to the armsmen at his right and snapped his fingers. The armsman produced a bottle of wine, and uncorked it with his teeth before handing it to Furnael. "A drink for luck?" Furnael asked, his voice making it clear it was more a command than a question. He tilted back the bottle and drank deeply. "Zherr Furnael wishes you luck, friend." Smiling thinly and wiping his hand on a purple silk handkerchief he produced from a sleeve, Furnael handed the bottle to Karl. "Enjoy."

In the Eren regions, a drink for luck was a custom that was invariably followed by an introduction, whether the drinkers already knew each other or not. Typically, a drink for luck would take place between two strangers meeting on a road, the provider of the wine drinking first to assure the other that it was unpoisoned.

The fact that Furnael had suggested—ordered—a drink for luck in a situation where the custom wasn't really appropriate was suspicious. The fact that his armsman had an opened bottle ready was more so.

Karl drank deeply. The rich, fruity wine was icy cold. "Karl Cullinane thanks you, Baron."

Furnael's smile broadened. "So. I was wondering if it was you, in this company; it's said that you travel with a Hand cleric and another warrior from a land called Seecaucuze. Not a Mel child and a Katharhd."

Secaucus was Walter's hometown. So it was only

known that Karl had been traveling with Doria and Walter. Which suggested that someone had seen the three of them at the cesspit when Karl had freed Ellegon, or that some spell had been able to look back, into that time and place. But how would anyone on this side have known that Walter came from New Jersey? Slovotsky hadn't mentioned it, as far as Karl knew.

Probably Walter *had* mentioned it to some local, at some time, and that local had talked to someone else about the stranger he had met, and someone in Pandathaway had started putting two and two together. That didn't sound good at all. Too damn many unknowns.

"There has been a price on your head for more than a year, friend Karl," Furnael said. "It seems that Pandathaway wants you."

Chak started to edge toward his sword; one of Furnael's armsmen, hand near the hilt of his shortsword, moved between the little man and the tree where Chak's falchion hung.

Even if Furnael meant them harm, this wasn't the right time to do something about it. The odds were poor, with the wizard right there, behind Furnael. "Stand easy, Chak," Karl said. "Stand easy. That goes for you, too," he said, holding up a palm to forestall any move by Tennetty or Fialt. "I don't think the Baron is out to collect the reward."

Furnael spread his hands. "You are wanted in Pandathaway, friend Karl. This is Bieme. And here we have no love for the Guilds Council." He gestured at the wizard who stood behind him. "Sammis, here, once was a guild master, studying daily in the Great Library. Today, he uses his death spells to kill corndiggers; he was thrown out of the Wizards' Guild, forced to flee Pandathaway."

"What'd he do, give out a spell for free?"

Furnael cocked his head to one side, his forehead furrowed. "How did you know?" He shrugged. "In any case, it is fortunate for you that my Prince is neither allied with Pandathaway nor particularly hungry for coin," he said, laying his hand on the hilt of his sword. "Even if you are as good as they say, we do have the advantage."

"That depends on how you look at it, Baron." Ahira's voice came from the balcony above.

About time. Karl glanced up. Beside Ahira, little Aeia stood, the spare crossbow held clumsily in her arms, leveled at one of Furnael's armsmen.

Ahira held his own crossbow easily, the bolt lined up not on Furnael, but on the wizard. "Aeia can't cock the bow, but she can put out a sparrow's eye at sixty paces."

Karl suppressed a smile. Aeia could probably hit a *cow* at *five* paces, if the cow was big enough. The little girl tried hard, but she had no talent for bowmanship at all.

Ahira went on: "And I'm not too bad with a crossbow, myself. We're generally peaceable folk. How about you?"

As usual, Ahira had picked his potential target correctly. If the wizard opened his mouth to use a spell, Ahira could put a bolt through his back before the first words were fairly out.

Karl folded his arms across his chest. "You were saying, Baron?"

Furnael smiled broadly. "Again, very pretty, sir. I was saying that I must have a word with my chief man-at-arms; he didn't tell me about the others, just you. And I was also saying that you simply must be my guests at dinner, at my home. We dine at sundown. And . . ." Furnael let his voice trail off.

"And?"

"And, as long as you break no law, harm no one, do not offend my Prince, you are safe here. Within my barony, at least. You have my word on that, Karl Cullinane."

And even if you're eager to try to collect the reward, you'd rather do it over my dead body than yours. Karl hesitated. If they had to take on Furnael, there probably wouldn't be a better time.

But he couldn't kill everyone who *might* present a threat. "We are honored, Baron. And accept."

The baron's smile made Karl's palm itch for the feel of his saber's sharkskin hilt. Furnael gestured at the nearer of his armsmen. "Hivar will conduct you to the estate." He turned and walked away, the other armsman and the wizard at his side.

"What was that all about?" Chak asked, his swordbelt back around his waist.

Karl shrugged. "I think the Baron wants to know what we're up to. What I'm up to. Seems that freeing Ellegon has gotten me some interesting word-of-mouth. It also seems that word about what we're doing hasn't gotten to Bieme yet.'

"So? How do we handle it?"

"We'll see." Karl turned to the others. "Well, what are you all standing around for? This practice isn't over. You, there. Hivar, is it? These aren't Pandathaway's Games. If you want to stay around, then strip down and join in."

Sitting in the honored-guest position at the foot of the long oaken table, Karl wiped his mouth and hands with a linen napkin. *Just what are you up to, Zherr Furnael?* he thought. Lifting the wedge with both hands, Karl took another nibble of the sweetberry pie. He ate carefully; the dark filling was bubbly hot.

"I must admit to a bit of embarrassment," Furnael said, pushing his high-backed chair away from the table. "I've never had a guest go hungry at my table before. And two?" He daubed at his mustache and the corners of his mouth with a purple silken napkin, then dropped the napkin back to his lap as the white-linened servitor at his side held out a washing bowl for his use.

"I wouldn't have thought it possible," he said, drying his hands on a towel, gesturing at the servant to continue down the table to Fialt, Tennetty, Aeai, and Karl.

Karl considered another helping of pie, but decided against it. Overeating any further wasn't the way to cap the best meal he'd had in months. *Whatever your flaws may be, Zherr Furnael, you do set a fine table.*

"Normally it wouldn't be possible, Baron," Karl said. A fresh washbowl was presented to him; Karl washed the meat juices and berry stains from his fingers. "At least as far as I can imagine."

With a slight nod and a vague frown, Furnael sat back, knitting his fingers over his belly. His face a study in concern, he cocked his head at Chak and Ahira, who sat side by side, across from the others, their silver plates clean and empty in front of them. "Is there anything you would eat? Anything?"

Ahira shook his head. "My apologies, Baron, but it's a religious matter. It's the fast of St. Rita Moreno, you know. My ancestors would never forgive me if I let food or water pass my lips today."

Furnael furrowed his forehead. "I must admit I'm not familiar with your faith, friend Ahira. Which warrens are you from?"

The dwarf frowned at the question, as though surprised at Furnael's prying. "The Lincoln Tunnels. Far away." Ahira sighed, the picture of a dwarf far away from home, missing the comfortable familiarity of his own warrens.

Furnael opened his mouth as though to ask just exactly where, and how far away, then visibly reconsidered. Dismissing the subject with a wave and a shrug, he turned to Chak. "Surely a Katharhd doesn't have religious objections to my food."

Chak glanced at Karl. For once, the little man didn't seem pleased with him. Chak didn't relish having had to pass on the Baron's fare. Platters of juice-dripping roast beef, the slices crisp, brown, and garlicky around the edges, purply rare in the middle; spit-roasted potatoes, so hot that they had to be nibbled carefully from the end of a knife; tiny loaves of warm, pan-baked bread, each with a dollop of sweet, icy butter at its core; bowls of a pungent mixture of chotte and burdock, sauteed together in wine and fresh garlic—it had been a delightful meal, much better than Karl had had since Pandathaway.

But I don't think we're going to trust you any too far, Baron Zherr Furnael. You reek of hidden intent. Never did like people who do that. Furnael had politely sampled all of the food first; eating from the same table as the baron probably wasn't risky.

But only probably.

The cover story, such as it was, had more than a few holes in it. But for all of them to trust Furnael's food was too much of a chance. Best to keep up the pretense.

Karl nodded.

"My apologies," Chak said, glancing with apparently real regret at the silver platters, still well laden with food, that lay invitingly on the table. "But this western food doesn't agree with me. Haven't been able to stomach what you eat here; I've been living on my morning meals of oat stew and greens for more tendays than I like to recall."

"Oat stew?" Furnael shrugged. "Well, if that's what you desire . . ." He gestured to one of his servitors, a short, plump, round-faced woman. "Enna? Would you—"

"No," Chak said. "Please."

The Baron's face clouded over. "And why not?"

Good question. They hadn't worked out what to say if Furnael was able to provide such a bizarre and disgusting dish.

Ahira spoke up. "With all due respect, you're not thinking it through, Baron."

"Well?"

"If all you were able to keep down was oat stew, how eager would you be to eat more than once a day?"

Karl chuckled. "Or even that often." He looked over at the dwarf. *Nice going, Ahira.* "Baron?"

"Yes?"

"It was a wonderful meal and all, but what's this really all about?"

"What do you mean?"

"What I mean is this: I'm wanted in Pandathaway; there's a large reward on my head. You say you're not interested in collecting that reward. Fine; I'll accept that."

The Baron lifted a razor-sharp eating knife and considered its bright edge. "Although you are not convinced of it." Furnael smiled thinly. "Perhaps that's wise under the circumstances; perhaps not." He tested the edge of the knife against his thumbnail, then replaced it on the table, the point, perhaps by chance, aligned with Karl's chest.

"What I'm not convinced of," Karl said, "is that you invite everyone who stops in the Furnael inn into your home. And it'd be impossible to believe that you'd provide this sort of wonderful fare—"

"I thank you, sir." Furnael inclined his head.

"—for all guests of the inn. It seems to me that there has to be something else on your mind."

"Point well taken, Karl Cullinane. I do have a business proposition for you. If you are as good with that sword as your reputation suggests."

"I doubt I'd be interest—"

"Would you at least listen to it, as a courtesy?" Furnael stood, dropping the napkin on his chair. He lifted his swordbelt from the rack next to his chair and buckled it on. "Let's take a short ride together and talk about it privately. These days I get little enough chance to ride just for the pleasure of it. Enna, see to the needs of our other guests, if you please."

Karl stood and buckled on his own sword. "Very well." He walked with Furnael toward the arching doorway.

Ahira cleared his throat. "Baron?"

Furnael turned, clearly irritated. "Yes, friend Ahira?"

The dwarf steepled his hands in front of his chin. "It's

occurred to me that you may have a fallback position in mind, if Karl turns you down. And, since you are a wise man, that fallback position is undoubtedly something terribly wise, such as wishing us well, as we go on our way."

"And if my, as you put it, fallback position isn't so wise?" Furnael gestured vaguely. "As an example only, what if the alternative I present Karl Cullinane with is my taking possession of a young girl who is manifestly an escaped slave, and returning her to her proper owners?"

"Aided by, no doubt, your full complement of twenty or so armsmen, some of whom you have stationed outside, as a precaution."

"No doubt." Furnael smiled.

"Baron, may I tell you a story?"

"This hardly seems the occasion."

"Please?" The dwarf smiled thinly. "At least listen, as a courtesy to a guest? It's a very short story, Baron. And it might amuse you."

Furnael gave in, seating himself on the empty chair next to Ahira. "Since you insist."

"Good. Let me begin it like this. There once was a slaver named Ohlmin. A master of the blade, Ohlmin won the swords competition in Pandathaway's Games every time he entered. With one exception.

"One man defeated him. Karl Cullinane, fighting in his first competition, ever. As you perhaps can understand, Ohlmin resented that."

Karl quelled a smile. That was true, as far as it went, but Ahira's rendition left out a few critical facts. For one thing, Ohlmin had been a better swordsman than Karl; Karl had won only by a judicious application of a hole in the rules of the swords competition.

Ahira went on: "For that reason and others, Ohlmin hunted our party down, and caught us in the Waste of Elrood. Along with a hired wizard, Ohlmin had fifteen slavers with him, all good with their swords.

"Ohlmin put Karl, Walter Slovotsky, and me in

chains. He spent a bit of time working Karl over with his fists, as well. After a number of hours, we managed to break free."

"How?" Furnael raised an eyebrow. "Slavers' chains are too strong to be broken, even by a dwarf."

Ahira smiled. "Trick of the trade. In any case, break free we did. I managed to account for four of the slavers before a crossbow bolt struck me down. The wizard who was with us killed their wizard. For the sake of the injured among us, Karl put us all in a wagon and fled, leaving one of their wagons aflame, and half of the slavers dead."

"Most impressive," Furnael said. "But I already knew that Karl Cullinane is a great swordsman."

"I'm sure you did, Baron." The dwarf inclined his head. "What you didn't know is this: Eight of the slavers were alive when we fled. Ohlmin was among them."

Ahira sighed. "I wanted to leave it at that. We were away, and free, and alive. We all hurt a bit. Karl had used the last of our healing draughts to save me. And Karl wasn't at his best; having your arms chained over your head for hours leaves your shoulders weak and stiff. I wanted to call it a day, leave the slavers behind."

The Baron cocked his head to one side. "But Karl Cullinane didn't." The pallor of his skin belied his calm tone.

"No. With another of our party, Karl went back for Ohlmin and the rest. Two against eight."

"I suppose Karl Cullinane and his companion gave a good account of themselves."

"Karl left seven of them lying dead on the ground. All save Ohlmin."

"But Ohlmin got away." Furnael started to rise. "Nevertheless, a very impressive feat. I thank you for telling me, friend Ahira. Now, Karl Cullinane, if you would walk this way?"

Ahira laid a hand on the Baron's arm. "No, Baron, I said that he left seven of them. He didn't leave Ohlmin;

Karl brought Ohlmin's head back, as a remembrance."
The dwarf removed his hand, and smiled amiably. "Have
a nice talk."

The night was bright, lit by the shimmering of the
million stars flickering overhead and the score of smoking
torches along the ramparts of Furnael's keep.

Sitting comfortably in Carrot's saddle, Karl rode
beside Furnael. The Baron was mounted on a slightly
smaller, snow-white mare whose black marking over her
right eye made her look like an equine pirate.

As they rode slowly along the narrow dirt road outside
the keep, Furnael paused beneath each of the four guard
stations. At each station the noble silently raised a hand
to greet the watchman peering out through an
embrasure, leaning lazily against a jutting stone merlon.
Each guard nodded and waved in response.

By the time they reached the Prince's Road, Karl was
tired of Furnael's silence.

"Baron?"

"Bear with me awhile longer, Karl Cullinane." With a
flick of the reins, he turned his horse east onto the Prince's
Road, Karl following.

Soon, the walls of the keep were far behind; Furnael
picked up the pace as they topped a hill, then started
down toward a cluster of low wooden buildings, half a
mile away, wisps of smoke rising from their chimneys
and twisting into the night. "Those are the slave quarters
of my own farm," Furnael said. On both sides of the
road, fields of chest-high cornstalks waved and
whispered to themselves in the light breeze. "I have been
keeping loose security," he said, with a deep sigh. "No
passwords; I have a few armsmen, and no soldiers at all.
But that's going to have to change. Everything's going to
change."

"Things look peaceful enough, Baron," Karl said. "If
you'll forgive the contradiction."

"If I wouldn't forgive being contradicted, would that

make things look one whit less peaceful?" Furnael
smiled. "Enough of this formality: if I may call you Karl,
I would be honored if you would call me Zherr. When we
are by ourselves, that is." At Karl's nod, Furnael smiled,
then pursed his lips, shaking his head. "And it is truly said
that looks can be deceiving. Do you know the Middle
Lands well?"

"Not at all."

"Except for some problems with the Therranji, it's
been peaceful for most of my life, and unless the
Therranji push much harder than they have been, they're
not going to threaten Nyphien, much less Bieme.

"It's been peaceful for a long time. For all of His Highness' reign, for that matter. His father and mine settled
the boundary disputes with Nyphien to the west; our
grandfathers fought Holtun. Most of His Highness'
soldiers have long settled down to their farms. In all the
country, it'd be hard to find a score of Bieme-born men
who've been blooded in combat. Displaying a shiny,
well-honed sword on Birthday or Midsummer doesn't
make a man a warrior."

Furnael indicated the keep behind them with a wave
of his hand. "I have forty armsmen. Only Hivar is native
to Bieme—his father served mine, as did his grandfather.
The others are slephmelrad, too, but originally outland
mercenaries. I'd thought we could grow fat and happy
through my life, and that of my sons. I'd thought that.
And I still hope so."

"But you don't believe it anymore?" Karl shook his
head. "The reasons don't show, Baron."

"Zherr."

"The reasons don't show, Zherr. I haven't seen any
signs of war or any sort of deprivation in all of Bieme."

"Ahh, you see war and deprivation as linked?"

"Obviously, Zherr. War causes deprivation."

"True. But it can be the other way around, as well."
Furnael pursed his lips. "There is danger in wealth, even
if it's only enough wealth to keep your people well fed,

clothed, with perhaps a bit more to pay the cleric. What if your neighbor isn't wealthy?

"The border wars with Nyphien started because of a two-year case of dustblight that hit western Nyphien and part of Khar. The first year, they paid the Spidersect to abate the blight, but barely recovered half their corn, less of their wheat, and none of their oats or barley; the second year, there was no money left for the Spiders, and the Nyphs tried to push their borders east, into Bieme.

"By the third harvest, the war was fully underway." The Baron shook his head. "I've heard tales of it. Not a pretty war. Not pretty, at all."

"And that's happening again?"

"No, not exactly. Mmm, hold up a moment." Furnael stopped his horse, then bent to pick a fist-sized stone from the road. He threw it onto the road's rough shoulder, then remounted. "A different direction; a different problem. Less than a day's ride to the east, both barony Furnael and the Principality of Bieme end, and Holtun and the barony of my good friend Vertum Adahan begin. And Vertum Adahan *is* a good friend, though I've never crossed his doorstep, or he mine."

"Why?"

The Baron shook his head sadly. "There was a blood feud between our families. Depending on which side you believe, my great-grandmother was either stolen from her husband, Baron Adahan, or left him voluntarily. The Baron took another wife, but Adahan men raided into Furnael throughout the rest of my great-grandfather's rule, and into my grandfather's."

"Which side do you believe?"

Furnael smiled thinly. "Sir, I will have you know that I am a dutiful great-grandson; of *course* great-grandmother left her husband of her own free will to go to my lecherous great-grandfather, and even insisted that he give her a room in the keep that locked only from the outside, in order to reassure him that she didn't want to go back to Adahan." He shook his head. "I'll show you her room, if you'd like. You can decide for yourself.

"But, as I was saying, while the feud died down during my father's time, the old feelings still run deep; there are family graveyards on many of my freefarmers' holdings with tombstones that read 'murdered by the swine Adahan.' I'd hoped that in the next generation . . ." He caught himself. "But I talk too much. I hope you'll forgive me, Karl, but it's so rare that I see anyone who isn't either one of my slephmelrad, or slaves, or a foreigner trying to grub a few extra wagonloads of corn for his coin; it's a pleasure to speak freely."

"I . . . appreciate that, Zherr." Karl didn't believe for a second that Furnael was speaking freely. The Baron was trying to gain his sympathy. Why? Was it just that Furnael didn't think he could intimidate Karl into taking on whatever job Furnael had for him? Or was there something more?

As they neared the cluster of wooden shacks, each about twenty feet square, the door of the nearest swung open and a woman and three children walked out, smiling and calling out greetings.

Though calling them all children might have been an overstatement; the tallest was a black-haired boy of sixteen or so, who looked much like a younger version of Furnael, although he was, like the other two children, dressed in a farmer's cotton tunic and loose drawstring pantaloons, instead of leather and wool. He ran up and took the reins of Furnael's horse in hand, gesturing to another to do the same for Carrot's.

Furnael dismounted, urging Karl to follow him. "Karl Cullinane, it is my honor to present my eldest son: Rahff, the future Baron Furnael. Rahff, this is Karl Cullinane. Yes, son, *the* Karl Cullinane."

What was the son and heir of a baron doing in the slave quarters, dressed like a peasant, his face streaked with dirt and sweat, his hands blistered?

Karl didn't ask; when Furnael was ready, he'd tell Karl whatever he wanted Karl to know.

Rahff bowed stiffly, his eyes wide, his jaw sagging. "The outlaw, sir? Really?" An expression of awe flickered across Rahff's face.

Karl was uncomfortable; he'd never had to deal with a case of hero worship before. "That depends on your definition of outlaw," Karl said. "But I'm probably the one you're thinking of."

"It is a . . . pleasure to meet you, sir," Rahff said, the formality of his manner in comical contrast to his humble dress and grimy face.

The smallest of the children, a boy a year or so shy of Aeia's age and a few inches short of her height, ran up and threw his arms around Furnael, burying his face against the Baron's waist. With a warm smile, Furnael ran his fingers through the boy's hair. "And this is Rahff's brother, my son Thomen. Don't be offended at his silence, Karl; he is always shy around strangers."

"Of course, Baron. I am pleased to meet you, Rahff. And you, Thomen."

"Not 'Baron'—Zherr, please," the baron said, picking Thomen up with a sweep of his arm. "This isn't a formal occasion."

"Zherr."

The woman walked over. She looked something like a slightly younger female version of Furnael, with the same high cheekbones, though she had a more rounded jaw. Her hair was the same raven black.

"Karl Cullinane," Furnael said, "my cousin, wife, and the mother of my sons: Beralyn, Lady Furnael." Furnael's voice was more formal now, carrying in it a hint of distaste. Or anger, perhaps.

"Karl Cullinane," she said, taking his hand in both hers. In the light streaming through the open door, her hands were red and swollen; some of the blisters on her fingers had broken open. "I hope you will forgive me for not greeting you at our home."

"Of course, Lady." He blowed over her hands. "Of course." *What the hell is a baroness doing here?*

"And," Furnael went on, casting a quick frown at Beralyn, "the youngster holding your horse is Bren Adahan, son and heir of Vertum, Baron Adahan, of whom I have spoken." Furnael set Thomen down and walked over, clapping a hand to Bren's shoulder. "Good to see you, Bren. Is your tenday going well?"

"Very well, Baron." Raising an eyebrow to ask for permission, Bren reached up to stroke Carrot's neck the moment Karl nodded. "A fine horse, Karl Cullinane." He ran sure hands over her withers, patted at her belly and flank, then gently felt at her left rear hock.

All the while, Carrot stood proudly, her head held a bit higher than normal, her nostrils flared, as though daring Bren to find any hint or trace of a flaw.

"She's Pandathaway-bred, isn't she? What's her name?"

"That's where I bought her. And her name is Carrot," Karl said. "I take it that you like horses."

"Oh, very much." Bren was a sandy-haired boy of about Rahff's age, with a broad, easy smile. "My father has a stallion I'd love to see cover her. Has she foaled yet?"

"No. She's been a bit too busy to take time out for that." Like an assassin in the night, longing for Andy-Andy stabbed at him. *God, how I miss you.* It was hard to think of her visibly pregnant, her belly swollen, and know that he wouldn't see her, wouldn't touch her for months. At best.

In the back of his mind he could almost see her standing in front of him, hands on hips, her head cocked to one side, a whimsical smile playing over her lips. *So? Who told you this hero business was supposed to be easy?*

Bren went on: "If we have time, later, would you listen to some advice? I think breeding Carrot with a Katharhd pony might produce a—"

"Your manners, Bren," Furnael said, shaking his head, a warm smile making his stern tone a lie. "You're forcing me and my guest to stand outside in the cold wind." He shivered violently, although the breeze from the north was only refreshingly cool. "Would you like to unsaddle and curry the horses, and then join us inside?"

He turned to Karl. "May I? Please?"

"Certainly. No need to tie her; she'll stay around as long as she knows I'm inside."

"Of course," Bren said disapprovingly, miffed at being told something so patently obvious.

Furnael led him into the shack. It was small, but well kept: The stone floor was smooth and clean; the spaces between the wallboards had been filled with fresh clay by a careful hand. No draft disturbed the fire that blazed merrily in the stone hearth, with its cast-iron stewpot bubbling as it dangled over the flames.

Furnael unbuckled his sword and hung it on a peg before pulling a stool to the rough-hewn table that stood in the center of the room, beckoning Karl and the others to join him. There were only three remaining stools; Karl, Rahff, and Thomen sat, while Beralyn stood next to her husband, frowning down at him.

Furnael chuckled. "You must forgive my wife. She doesn't approve of this."

"And why should I?" Beralyn sniffed. "It's nothing but nonsense. My beloved husband," she added, her voice dripping with sarcasm.

The Baron threw his arm around her waist and patted at her hip. "You'll forgive me. As usual."

"Until the next harvest."

Rahff frowned; Furnael caught the expression and turned to the boy. "And none of that, not in front of our guest. You will show proper manners, boy." He gestured an apology to Karl. "This is a family tradition. Before each harvest, the sons of the Baron spend three tendays in slave quarters, working the fields as hard as the slaves—"

"Harder, father," little Thomen piped up. "Rahff says we have to show we're better."

"—eating the same food, wearing the same clothes as do the field slaves. Gives a sense of proportion. Vertum thinks well enough of it that he's sent Bren to join our boys this year. I think Bren is profiting from it."

"Nonsense," Beralyn said. "You should listen to your children. When Rahff is the Baron, he won't put his sons through this."

Furnael snorted. "Which is exactly what I said when I was his age. Karl, feel free to wander around, later; you'll see that this cabin is no better than any of the others. We treat both our fealty-servants and slaves well, here."

"This cabin is worse," Beralyn said. "You sent your men down to chip the clay out of the walls. Again."

"As I *will*, each and every time you clay the walls for the boys. If Rahff or Thomen want to do it for themselves, that's fine. I've tolerated your living with them to cook for them; don't test my patience further."

He shook his head. "Karl, my wife thinks to blackmail me into giving up the tradition, by living down here when our sons do."

"Zherr, you wanted to talk about some problem?" Karl asked, uncomfortable at finding himself brought into a family argument.

"Indeed." Furnael leaned on the table, steepling his fingers in front of his face. "There have been raids into Holtun. A band of outlaws has taken up residence somewhere on the slopes of Aershtym. Perhaps two, three hundred of them. They ride down at night, punching through the idiotic line defense the Holtish—" He cut off as Bren opened the door.

The boy shook his head sadly. "Please don't stop on my account," he said. "I don't have any delusions about Prince Uldren."

Furnael smiled a thank-you at the boy. "They carry off women and food, killing any who raise a hand against them. Behind them, they leave the farms ablaze, cutting the throats of all the cattle and sheep, like a dog covering with vomit that which he can't eat. It seems they've found a large cache of salt, somewhere, and they have lately taken to salting the ground behind them."

He shook his head. "I've talked to Sammis about it, and there is nothing his magic can do. He could kill the weeds, of course, as he does for the farms in my barony. But salted land will grow no grain, whether the weeds are left standing or not.

"If this goes on, Holtun will find itself in the midst of a famine. To the west lies the soda plain; they will have to turn east. They will have to invade Bieme, just as the Nyphs did in my father's time. These two friends"—he gestured at Bren and Rahff—"will find themselves blood enemies. And not just in theory, but in fact."

"And you can't take on the raiders yourself." Karl nodded. "Holtun wouldn't stand for it."

"At the first sign of Biemei soldiers crossing into Holtun, the war would start. Already, there have been a few clashes along the border. I know that this sounds disloyal, but if only the raiders had ventured into Bieme . . . perhaps Prince Uldren would have swallowed his pride and seen the wisdom in some sort of alliance."

"I doubt it, Baron," Bren shook his head. "His Highness is, as my father says, a pompous ass. And one who'd be as likely to grip his sword by the blade as by the hilt. Fancies himself a great general, though."

Furnael nodded. "Karl, I'd like you to stop that. I hope you'll see that we are good people here. And we are people who are willing to pay, and pay well. Perhaps you could pretend to join the raiders, lead them into an ambush? Or track them to their lair, take them on yourselves, chase them into my barony, where we could deal with them? Or something—anything."

Karl closed his eyes. The strategy wasn't a problem. Not Karl's problem, in any case. Ahira could probably work something out.

Still, three hundred against five was not Karl's idea of

good odds. Then again, they wouldn't have to take on all three hundred at once.

But that wasn't the issue. *The question isn't can we, it's should we.*

And that was harder. Granted, Zherr Furnael was—or at least appeared to be—a good man for this world; given, any war between Bieme and Holtun would be bad for everyone concerned, including the slaves of both sides.

But . . . I'm Karl Cullinane, dammit, not Clark Kent. I can't do everything; I've already made a promise I'm not sure I can keep; I can't let other things divert me.

His conscience pricked him. How about Aeia? Taking her home didn't constitute carrying the war to the slavers.

No. Aeia's case was different. Melawei was suffering from slave raids; it was reasonable to take her home, since that path would lead to some good opportunities to strike at the Slavers' Guild.

What would helping Furnael have to do with ending slavery? Anything?

No, there was no connection.

I'll have to turn him down. I—

Wait. "There . . . is a price, Zherr. A large one."

Furnael spread his hands. "We do have money, Karl."

"I don't really need money. But, in return for me and my friends solving your problem, would you be willing to give up all your slaves?"

Furnael smiled. "That's a high price, Karl. It'd cost me much time and coin to replace all the slaves in my barony. Perhaps we could consider—"

"No. Not replace. Your payment would be to give up the owning of slaves throughout your barony. Forever."

For a moment, the Baron's face was a study in puzzlement. Then Furnael sighed. "I . . . I thank you for the politeness of not turning me down directly. But it wasn't necessary; I understand. You don't want to make our battles yours."

"Baron, I'm completely serious."

"Please. *Don't* insult my intelligence." Furnael held up a hand. "Let it be, Karl Cullinane, let it be."

Karl opened his mouth, then closed it. It wouldn't work. To Furnael, the concept of slavery was so normal that he couldn't take at face value any suggestion he give up owning people. It wasn't really offensive to Furnael, just incomprehensible. But trying to explain further could only be an affront.

Furnael's face grew grim. "I'd thought to try to frighten you into serving me, you know. Threatening to hold that little girl—Aeia, is it?—as hostage against your success." He drummed his fingers on the wood. "You do seem to care about her welfare."

"That wouldn't leave me any choice, Baron."

Furnael nodded. "Then—"

"No choice at all. I'd either have to take on three hundred raiders, relying on your word to release Aeia if I did, *or* I'd have to take on you and your forty or fifty armsmen, none of whom seem to have done much recent fighting." Karl left his hand fall to the hilt of his sword. "That would be an easy decision, Baron. Granted, my friends and I would probably all die, but we'd take some of you with us. And how would that leave you in the war that's coming?"

"It was just a thought. But a silly one." He sighed deeply. "The sort of warrior I need wouldn't be frightened into doing something unwillingly." The Baron shook his head as he rose to his feet and walked to the peg where his sword hung. "But, as your friend Ahira put it, I have prepared a fallback position. A ruler, even a lowly baron, should always keep an option ready."

"Baron, you—"

Furnael lifted the scabbard and drew the sword.

Karl leaped away from the table, sending his stool clattering on the floor. Drawing his own sword with one fluid motion, he spun around into a crouch. *Got to be careful. Can't let the woman or the children get behind me; they might grab my swordarm.*

The sword held loosely in his hand, Furnael drew himself up straight. "Karl Cullinane," he said, his voice dripping with scorn, "put up your sword. You are in no danger here, not from me. I swear that on my life, *sir.*"

What the hell was going on? First Furnael had tried to buy his services, then intimidate him, then he had gotten ready to attack Karl. "I . . . don't understand." Karl lowered the point of his sword.

"On my life, sir," the Baron repeated.

To hell with it. I've got to trust somebody, sometime. Karl slipped his sword back into its scabbard.

The Baron turned to Rahff. "Hold out your hands, boy."

Silently, Rahff shook his head.

"*Do it.*" The Baron's shout left Karl's ears ringing.

Slowly, Rahff extended his palms. With exquisite gentleness, Furnael laid the flat of the blade on the boy's palms, then untied his pouch from his own waist. Carefully, Furnael tied the leather strands about the middle of the blade. "There are ten pieces of Pandathaway gold here."

White-faced, Beralyn laid a hand on Furnael's arm. "Don't do this. He's just a boy."

Furnael closed his eyes. "This gives us a chance, just a chance, Bera. If Rahff survives, he may be strong enough to see the barony through the coming years, through the war. I . . . I don't see any other way. Please, please don't make this any harder."

He opened his eyes and turned back to Karl, tears streaming down his cheeks. "Karl Cullinane. I offer my eldest son to you as apprentice, sir, to learn the way of the sword, bow, and fist. I offer as payment my horse, this gold, this sword, and the services of my son, for a period of five years."

Karl looked down at Rahff. The boy's whitened face was unreadable. "Rahff?"

"It's not his choice, Karl. I'm the boy's father."

Karl didn't look at Furnael. "Shh. Rahff? Do you want to be my apprentice?"

Clenching his lower lip between his teeth until the blood flowed, Rahff looked from his mother, to his father, and back to Karl. Slowly, he walked over and extended the sword and pouch, his arms shaking. "It's . . . my father's wish, sir."

"But is it yours?"

Rahff looked from his father, to his brother, to his mother, to Bren. Hero worship was one thing; agreeing to leave his home and family was another.

Bren nodded. "Do it. If you stay, we'll soon be enemies, be after each other's blood."

"And if I go? Will that make any difference?"

"I don't know. But it will give us five years' grace, five years until I have to kill you, or you have to kill me." Bren clapped a hand to Rahff's shoulder, gripping tightly. "Five years, at least."

Rahff swallowed. Then: "Y-yes. Will you accept me as apprentice, Karl Cullinane?"

Karl looked at Baron Zherr Furnael with a new sense of admiration. It took a certain something for a man to see his own limitations, to accept the likelihood of his own destruction, while planning to protect at least a part of his family from the storm of arrows and swords that would certainly leave him dead.

Not necessarily just part of his family; perhaps Furnael had other plans for Thomen and Lady Beralyn.

Apprenticing Rahff to an outlaw was a cold-blooded act, but that didn't make it wrong. If Rahff survived an apprenticeship, he might be strong enough to hold the barony, perhaps even all of Bieme, together through the coming year.

And what if he dies, Zherr Furnael? We're heading into danger; what if he's not quick enough or lucky enough to live through it?

Karl didn't voice the question. The answer was clear:

If Rahff couldn't survive a five-year apprenticeship, then he wasn't the ruler that the barony needed.

Zherr Furnael would either have a worthy successor. or a dead son. Not a pleasant gamble.

But what other choice do they have? Karl accepted the sword and pouch on the palms of his hands. "I accept you, Rahff, as my apprentice. Spend some time saying goodbye to your family and friends; we leave in the morning. Oh, and you can sleep at the inn, if you'd prefer." He untied the pouch from the sword, then accepted the scabbard from the Baron.

"I'd rather stay."

"You're his apprentice, boy." Furnael's low voice was almost an animal's snarl. "You will sleep at the inn."

Karl drew himself up straight. "I'll thank you not to interfere with my apprentice, Baron. I gave *him* the choice, not you." He took two copper coins from his pouch and dropped them on the rough table. "This should cover his lodging; he'll spend the night here, as he chooses."

Slipping the sword into the scabbard, Karl handed it to the boy. "Take good care of this, Rahff. You're going to be spending many hard hours learning to use it."

And may God have mercy on your soul.

The boy nodded somberly.

"But I think you'll do just fine."

A smile peaked through Rahff's tears.

And through Furnael's.

PART FOUR:
Melawei

CHAPTER TEN: *To Ehvenor*

Practice is the best teacher.

—Publilius Syrus

As they rode down the shallow slope toward Ehvenor, the freshwater sea called the Cirric lay below them and ahead of them, rippling off across the horizon. Off in the distance, Karl could see the rainbow sails of a wide-beamed sloop, tacking in toward the harbor.

Ten, perhaps twelve small ships huddled around Ehvenor's docks, as seamen bustled like ants to load and unload their cargo. Just harborside of the breakwater, three large ships lay at anchor, attended by half a dozen small launches that swarmed around them like pilotfish around a shark.

The low stone buildings of Ehvenor cupped the harbor, flat and ugly. The streets were narrow, crooked, and strewn with refuse; the town of Ehvenor looked like one large slum.

There was only one exception: A cylindrical building, seemingly three or four stories high, stood in the center of town like a rose on a pile of dung. It shone whitely.

Karl rubbed his eyes. It was hard to make out the details of that building; the edges and details fuzzed in his eyes, as though he couldn't focus on it.

"Ahira?"

The dwarf shook his head. "It doesn't seem to suit my eyes, either."

"You think that's the Faerie holding, or embassy, or whatever they call it?"

155

The dwarf snorted; the snort was immediately echoed by his pony. "Not likely to be anything else; I doubt the locals build out of mist and light."

Karl nodded. "I'd like to know how they do that."

"Ever hear of magic?" Ahira fell silent.

After a reflexive check to see that the others, riding behind him, were doing fine, Karl patted at Carrot's neck. "I wonder how you're going to take to being on a ship."

Did horses get seasick?

And how about the others? Chak, Tennetty, and Rahff had never been on a boat before. Fialt wouldn't be a problem; he was a Salke, and apparently everyone on Salket spent a good deal of time at sea. Ahira wouldn't be a problem, fortunately. A vomiting dwarf wouldn't be any fun to be around. And Aeia was a Mel; according to Chak, everyone in Melawei was practically conceived at sea.

Well, at worst, we're going to have four upchuckers among us. Probably including me.

Karl rubbed at his belly. *Maybe this time will be different. God, please let this time be different.* His only other time at sea had been on the *Ganness' Pride.* The trip from Lundeyll to Pandathaway on the *Pride* was not one of Karl's fondest memories; he had spent the first few minutes throwing up his breakfast, the next couple of hours vomiting up food he didn't even remember swallowing, and most of the rest of the trip with the dry heaves.

Ahira chuckled.

"What is it?" Karl looked down at the dwarf. "You think seasickness is funny?"

The dwarf shook his head. "No. I wasn't thinking about seasickness at all."

"Oh. So it's my nervousness about going on a boat again that's funny?"

Ahira scowled. "*Your* nervousness? Karl, you don't know what nervousness about being on a boat is."

That was strange. Ahira hadn't shown a trace of nausea while they'd been aboard the *Ganness' Pride*. "Iron-guts Ahira, that's what we'll have to call you. You hid your seasickness well."

"No, I wasn't seasick. There are other problems than seasickness," the dwarf said, scowling. "Think it through, Karl."

"Well?"

"How much do you weigh?"

"Huh?" What did that have to do with anything?

"A simple question, actually. How much do you weigh?"

"Mmm, about two-twenty or so, on This Side. Back home, about—"

"How much do I weigh?"

"About the same, I'd guess." A dwarf was built differently than a human. Ahira's body wasn't just shorter and disproportionately wider than Karl's; his muscles and bones were more dense.

More dense. "Oh. I hadn't thought about that." A human's body was, overall, less dense than water. But the dwarf . . . "If you fell overboard, you'd sink like a stone, chainmail vest or no."

"Exactly. I could easily drown in five, six feet of water. A bit more serious than a spot of projectile vomiting, no?"

"But what was so funny about that?"

Ahira smiled. "You were the one thinking about boats. I was thinking about towns."

"Well?"

"Think about it. What was the first town we ever dealt with on This Side?"

"Lundeyll. We just barely got out of there with our lives." Not all of them had gotten out alive. Jason Parker had died in Lundeyll, spending the last few moments of his life kicking on the end of a spear. *Someday, if I can find the time, I think I'll look up Lordling Lund and feed him his fingers, one joint at a time.*

"Exactly. We left Lundeyll just about ten seconds

ahead of the posse. The next town was Pandathaway. We got out of there a couple days before Ohlmin left, chasing us. We didn't spend any time worth talking about in a town until you and Walter went into Metreyll. And look at the time frame there: From the time you killed Lord Mehlên's armsmen until Metreyll found out must have been . . . at least a week, maybe a tenday." The dwarf held out a stubby finger. "One: ten seconds." Another finger. "Two: three days." A third finger. "Three: a full week." Ahira shot a glance at Karl. "Now, think about Bieme, and Furnael. For once, we left a town without anybody after us, even though the Baron wasn't pleased about your turning down that job. I was a bit nervous about that for a couple of weeks, but now that we're almost in Ehvenor, it's clear that he's not coming after us."

"So?" Karl didn't see the point of it all.

"So, it seems to me it's sort of a progression; looks like we're learning to get along better and better with the locals. If this keeps up, eventually we might even make friends somewhere, be invited to stay. *If* this keeps up . . ."

"Well?"

"Well, yonder—I'm starting to like saying yonder—lies Ehvenor. All we have to do there, all we *want* to do there, is book passage to Melawei."

"Do you always have to belabor the obvious before you ask me a favor?" Karl couldn't help returning Ahira's smile. "Try just asking."

"Fair enough: While we're in Ehvenor, try to avoid sticking any locals through the gizzard."

Karl shuddered. *You're talking as though I like bloodshed.* He opened his mouth to protest, then closed it. *Keep it light, just keep it light.* "That's asking a lot. What'll you do for me?"

Ahira thought about it for a minute. "Ever hear of positive and negative reinforcement?"

"Of course. Use to be a psych major."

"Good. Let's use both. Negative reinforcement: If you get us into trouble here, I'll bash you with my axe."

"And the positive reinforcement?"

"If we do get out of Ehvenor without any bloodshed, I'll give you a lollipop. Fair enough?"

"Fair enough." Karl chuckled a moment, then sobered.

Even though it was hidden by the banter, Ahira was serious.

And he had a point. If they ran into slavers in Ehvenor, the city wasn't the place to take them on. The locals wouldn't like it; Karl had no illusions about his group's ability to take on a slaver team *and* a large detachment of local armsmen.

Though the group was shaping up nicely, come to think of it.

Tennetty was getting better and better with a sword. She didn't have the upper-body strength to parry more than a few solid thrusts without tiring, but she did have an almost instinctive feel for the weak points in an opponent's defenses.

Rahff was coming along well, although he didn't seem to have Tennetty's natural bent for swordplay. The boy had to work at it. But he did work hard. A good kid, although the way Rahff hung on Karl's every word was quickly getting old.

Fialt's swordsmanship was still lousy, but his hand-to-hand skills had come a long way, and he had developed a nice feel for both manriki-gusari and staff.

Chak was a good man. Not a fancy swordsman, but a reliable one. With Chak on watch, Karl could sleep peacefully; with Chak bringing up the rear of the group, Karl could concentrate on what lay ahead, with only an occasioned glance behind. Chak was . . . solid, that was it.

Even little Aeia's bowmanship was coming along. She

wasn't as good as Ahira had told Furnael, of course. But not too bad, either. Aeia and a cocked crossbow could be a nice hole card in a fight.

Wait a minute. "Ahira?"

"Yes?"

"I've got one question, though. If you don't mind."

"Well?"

"Where are you going to get the lollipop?"

CHAPTER ELEVEN: *Ehvenor*

Remember that no man loses other life than that which he lives, or lives any other life than that which he loses.

—Marcus Aurelius

Him? Karl started. The aging, wide-bellied ketch tied at the end of the narrow dock didn't look familiar, but the man in the sailcloth tunic, directing the loading crew, did. *Avair Ganness, what the hell are you doing here? And if you're here, where's the* Pride?

It had to be him. While sweat-stained sailcloth tunics weren't at all rare around the docks, there couldn't be a whole lot of short, dark-skinned sailors with waist-length pigtails and thick, hairy legs who carried themselves with the rolling swagger and easy confidence of a ship's captain.

"Captain Ganness?"

Avair Ganness shouted a quick command at a seaman, then turned.

His swarthy face paled. "You? Not *again.*" He opened his mouth to call to one of the bowmen at the foot of the dock, then pursed his lips and shrugged, beckoning to a crewman. "Quickly," he said, "finish loading and prepare to cast off."

"But we don't sail until—"

"*Smartly*, now. We may not have to, but I want to be able to cast off and up sails in half a score heartbeats. We may need to show Ehvenor a fast set of heels. Understood?"

"Aye, sir." The sailor shrugged and vaulted over the

splintered railing, calling out to crewmen to halt the loading process and prepare for casting off.

Ganness turned back to Karl, a tragic smile spreading over his face. "What is it now, Karl Cullinane?" He spread his hands. "If you've managed to get the Ehven as angry as you did Lord Lund, I'd at least like to know why I'm going to die on this wretched dock."

Karl raised a hand. "I'm not wanted here. Pandathaway, yes. But I understand that Ehvenor isn't interested." As Chak explained it, there was no love lost between Pandathaway, the center of trade, culture, and magic of the Eren regions, and Ehvenor, dominated by the outpost of Faerie.

Ganness nodded, conceding the point. "True enough. As far as official Ehvenor goes. But not all Ehvenor is official Ehvenor."

He pointed a blunt finger shoreward. At his motion, a group of filthy, rag-clad men scurried for the shadow of a warehouse, all the while gibbering at each other in strained, high-pitched voices. "Watch your back, Karl Cullinane. Being around faerie too long does strange things to some humans; drives them crazy. I don't keep bowmen at the foot of the dock for the pleasure of it; in the past, crazies have fired boats—with themselves aboard, more often than not. Some of them would slit you open, throat to crotch, just for the fun of it." Ganness smiled. "Instead of the money."

Karl rested his hand on his swordhilt. "Perhaps you'd like the money?"

Ganness sneered. "Me?" He spat on the dock. "Of course. But while the notion of carrying your head back to Pandathaway thrills me, the idea of becoming a side attraction in the Coliseum doesn't. I don't dare set foot in Pandathaway or Lundeyll, not anymore. Not since I was fool enough to carry you from Lundeyll to Pandathaway. The wizards have long memories. I won't have any further dealings with them, for as long as I live." He laughed ruefully. "And that's a safe claim, come to think of it. Now," he said, drawing himself up straight, "what are you doing here?"

"I'd heard that a ship called the *Warthog* was leaving for Melawei tonight. Is this it?"

"Yes. And she's mine, such as she is."

Karl looked the ketch over, from the gashed bow all the way to the stern, where a pair of seamen worked a bilge pump, sending a constant stream of brown water over the side and into the harbor. "Not quite the *Ganness' Pride*, eh?"

"Not quite."

"What happened?"

"Lund wasn't pleased with my carrying you from Lundeyll; he hired himself a brace of pirate ships to hunt her down. They caught up with me just off Salket. The *Pride* went down; I barely escaped with my life. All thanks to you." Ganness sighed. "But you haven't answered my question."

"I think I have. I need to buy some passages to Melawei: seven people and two horses going, six and two coming back. Are you willing to carry us?"

"The same you were with before?" Ganness brightened. "Including Doria?"

"No, the only one you'd know is Ahira. The dwarf."

"Too bad." Ganness pursed his lips. "I may regret asking this, but are any of the others good with a sword or bow?"

"All of us. You might be able to use an extra sword or two. There's been a bit of trouble on the Cirric, I hear." That was a bald lie. Karl hadn't heard anything of the sort. But, given that slavers were raiding Melawei, it was reasonable to assume that they might pounce on a few merchantment. And if Ganness was even considering carrying them, it was certain that the captain was afraid of just that.

"True enough." Ganness stood silently for a moment. "Are you sure that you're not wanted here? I'm not about to let you close another port to me."

Karl patted the hilt of his saber. "I'm certain. I'll swear it on this, if you'd like."

Ganness nodded. "Fine, then. I can put the horses in the hold, but the only other accommodations I've got are deck passage—unless you'd prefer to sleep with your animals?"

"No thanks."

"Very well, then. It'll be six gold for each human, five for the dwarf, two for each horse. Each passage, each way. Payable now." He held out his hand.

Karl raised an eyebrow. "On this? That's almost ten platinum. I could almost buy this ship for that."

"No, you couldn't. I wouldn't sell." He smiled. "Besides, *Warthog* is faster than she looks. In some ways, she's better than the *Pride* was."

Karl held back a laugh. The *Ganness' Pride* had been a lean, shapely sloop, not a floating leak. The only way this scow was better than Ganness' former ship was that it would hurt Ganness less to lose her. "Well, at least she's here."

One hand on his hip, Ganness held out a palm. "The coin, if you please."

Karl hefted the pouch. "I don't have that much with me." But should they take passage on Ganness' ship? Maybe it would be better to wait for the next one.

No. It could be a long time before another Melawei-bound ship left. And if he turned Ganness down, the captain might be tempted to let it be known there was a wanted man around, for whose head Pandathaway would pay well. The threat was implicit in Ganness' ridiculously high price for passage.

Karl opened the pouch and counted out six gold coins. "You can have this as a deposit; I'll have the rest for you at the time we sail."

"Agreed. And I will see you then."

Karl started to turn away, but Ganness' shout stopped him.

Wait. "Aren't you forgetting something?" Ganness asked.

"What?"

The captain gestured to Karl's sword. "I think there's still a bit of swearing to be done. On your sword, if you please. If, that is, you do want passage."

Karl hesitated.

"Truly," Ganness went on, "she is a good ship. Sea-worthy and fast."

"Of course." Slowly, Karl drew his sword then balanced it on his palms. *I may as well get this over with. Next thing I know, he'll be telling me she made the Kessel run in three parsecs.*

Ahrmin clung to one of ten rope ladders secured to the dock, restraining a shiver.

The Cirric was cold this late at night, but it and the darkness provided good cover for Ahrmin and his ten men. He had spent several hours considering how many of the forty men from the *Scourge* to take with him. Too small a group wouldn't be able to take on Cullinane and his friends; too large a group would be impossible to hide. The element of surprise was always a huge advantage, and Ahrmin believed in having every advantage available.

Ten seemed about right. Enough to overpower Cullinane's group; not too many to hide.

It would take sharp eyes to see their heads and the few inches of rope that had been tacked to the side of the dock. The dock was a thick and sturdy one, rising more than two heads' height above the smooth black water.

Near the ship, sandals slapped against wood and voices called out orders, as the crew made the final preparations for the *Warthog* to sail.

Clinging to the ladder next to Ahrmin's, Jheral nudged him. "Shouldn't you check that ball again?" he whispered. "Or are you afraid of losing it?" Jheral shook his head to clear the water from his eyes and his long, pointed ears.

Ahrmin rewarded him with a scowl. The damned elf was more trouble than he was worth. Jheral had been a journeyman slaver for more than twenty years, and made no secret of his strong distaste for Ahrmin's promotion to master.

Not that Guildmaster Yryn had had any choice; he couldn't place Ahrmin in authority over senior journeymen without promoting him, and this job was clearly too much for Ahrmin and a group of junior journeymen and apprentices.

Probably Jheral and the others could have taken that. But the guildmaster had gone further, taking the unusual step of expressing his confidence in Ahrmin in the Writ of Mastery, by way of trying to avoid any conflicts. Normally that would have settled the matter; Guildmaster Yryn was known for being stinting in his praise.

It hadn't settled it; in fact, Yryn's strategy had backfired, acting as fuel to the journeymen's resentment—Jheral's, in particular.

"We could have just waited for them at sea," Jheral went on, "instead of floating here like a bunch of silkies."

"Be quiet. Do you want them to hear us?" That suggestion was ridiculous; it just couldn't work. In a sea battle, it would be impossible to capture Karl Cullinane alive. Stealth was the only chance.

But Jheral's first idea did make sense. Grudgingly, Ahrmin reached over to the inflated pig bladder that was tied loosely to the ladder and reached underneath, pulling on the slim rope to haul up the fine-mesh net bag containing the device Wenthall had given him.

"Light," he whispered.

Jheral drew his knife, cupping his hands around the blade to prevent the bright glow from shining through the cracks in the dock. Thyren, the *Scourge's* wizard, had refused Ahrmin's request to help them catch Karl

Cullinane, saying that he had signed on only to neutralize the Mel wizards during the slaving raid. But he had agreed to Glow a knife . . . in return for Ahrmin's promise of share of the reward.

The finger floated in the yellow oil, pointing unerringly toward the city, toward Karl Cullinane.

Ahrmin waited, watching the finger.

With agonizing slowness it moved, until it came to rest parallel to the dock.

Silently, Ahrmin pushed himself away from the ladder, pulling the bladder with him, beckoning at Jheral to follow.

Like a compass needle, the finger swung. Karl Cullinane was nearing the dock; he was somewhere in the shadows of Ehvenor. Somewhere near.

"He's almost here." Ahrmin tugged on the netting to make certain that it still secured the ball, then checked the rope fastening the netting to the bladder. The knots were still tight; he let the ball sink below the surface, then beckoned to the others bobbing in the dark water. "On my signal, we move," he whispered. "Remember, we can kill the others, but I want Karl Cullinane alive. And, Jheral—put that knife away."

"For a moment." Jheral smiled. "For a moment."

At the foot of the dock, Karl held up a hand and climbed down from Carrot's saddle. "Rahff, has Pirate ever been on a boat before?"

The boy shook his head. "No." The white horse snorted and stamped her feet, pulling back against the reins as Rahff tried to lead her. He stroked at the horse's neck with his right hand as he held the reins in his left. "And she's getting a bit skittish. I'm sorry, Karl."

"Don't apologize, Rahff. You do just fine with the horses."

Rahff drew himself up straight, standing proudly.

Karl suppressed a pleased chuckle. A few words of

mild commendation did wonders for the boy's posture. Whatever his virtues, Zherr Furnael had clearly never been unstinting in his praise.

Karl tried to calm Pirate down, but the horse snorted and snapped at his fingers.

It was just as well that they had sold the other horses, instead of trying to bring them on board. While Carrot wasn't a problem, Pirate's skittishness could quickly have become contagious.

Chak tapped Karl's shoulder. "Let me try."

"Go ahead."

The little man reached into his sack and produced a strip of cloth. With a quick motion, he whipped it around Pirate's eyes, fastening it in place as a blindfold.

The blindfold worked; Pirate calmed instantly, as though someone had thrown a switch.

Fialt hoisted his bag to his shoulder. "You should keep the horses toward the middle; gives you a bit of room for error if the animal gets twitchy."

Tennetty threw an arm around Fialt's waist. "Hmm." She smiled. "I guess you are good for something, clumsy. Something else, that is."

Ahira raised an eyebrow; Karl shook his head. Something else? Apparently both of them had missed what had been going on between Fialt and Tennetty.

"Can't put the two of them on watch together anymore," Karl whispered. "They'll be paying too much attention to each other to keep a proper lookout. That's probably been going on for a while."

"Happens." Ahira nodded. "But don't be too critical, eh? Let he without sin cast the first stone, and all that."

"Right." Karl raised his head. "Let's go. Slowly, now."

As he led Carrot onto the dock, Aeia skipped ahead, her little feet flying across the wood. She stopped just a few yards from the *Warthog*, nervously eyeing the strangers on board the ship.

Ganness held out a hand. "Welcome aboard." He raised his head and called out, "You have the coin?"

"As agreed," Karl called back. "Go ahead, Aeia. Get on. We'll be there in a moment." After the slightest of pauses, she walked up the ramp and onto the deck.

Karl pulled on Carrot's reins. "Easy, girl. It'll just be another—"

A hand reached out of the water and fastened itself on Karl's ankle. Another hand stabbed a glowing knife into his calf.

Pain cut through him; he fell, landing hard on his side, his left arm caught beneath him. A shrill scream forced its way through his lips.

Swords and knives in their hands, eleven men slipped out of the water, surrounding them all in a circle of steel points and edges.

Karl reached for the hilt of his sword, but the same glowing knife stabbed through his right wrist, pinning his hand to the wood.

His fingers writhed; his nails clawed at the wood.

Another hand grasped his hair. "Don't try to move." An elf's thin face leered inches from his. "That will only make it hurt more."

"We only want Karl Cullinane," a low voice rasped. "The rest of you can go. Or die."

Karl couldn't move his head, and the reflexive twitching of his right hand sent red-hot currents of pain shooting through his arm. He could only see Carrot's rump, Fialt, Tennetty, and two swords, just at the edge of his vision, menacing them.

Fialt raised his hands. "We don't want any trouble—"

He slapped at Carrot's hindquarters, sending the horse galloping down the pier. He snatched the manriki-gusari from his belt, then leaped out of Karl's vision.

Fialt staggered back, blood fountaining from between his hands as he clutched his chest, while Carrot's pounding hooves set the dock shaking.

"Chak," Ahira shouted, *"now."*

Karl struggled to free his left arm as the elf's fist pounded against his face.

Blood filled Karl's eyes. Blindly flailing his arm, he managed to fasten his left hand on the elf's throat.

Karl squeezed, ignoring the pain, ignoring the clatter of steel and the splashes of bodies falling in the water. The ony thing that mattered was his left hand, and his grip on the elf's throat.

Karl squeezed.

The blows grew more frantic.

Karl squeezed. The flesh of the elf's neck parted beneath his fingers, bathing his arm in blood.

The blows eased, then stopped.

"You can let go of him now," Ahira said, bending over him. "He's dead. And the rest are gone." A sudden stab of pain, and the knife was wrenched from Karl's hand. "Rahff, the healing draughts. Quickly, now."

Karl shook his head, clearing some of the blood from his eyes. "No." Pain pounded redly in his hand and calf, making each word a hideous labor. "First. Get on board. All of us. Take off. Then."

The dwarf pulled him up, helping Karl balance on his good leg. The dock was slippery with blood. Three bodies lay face down on the wood.

Tennetty knelt in a pool of Fialt's blood. Her fists drummed a rapid tattoo on his back. "You *idiot*," she trilled. "Never were any good against a sword. Never." She beat against his back as though trying to pound him back to life, tears streaming down her face.

Chak sheathed his sword and grasped her hands in his. "There's nothing more you can do for him," he said gently. "We have to go." He pulled her to her feet, then stopped to pick up Fialt's body and throw it over his shoulder.

Ganness ran over, two bowmen at his side. His face was ashen, his lips white. "I thought you said—"

Rahff reached over and grabbed the front of Ganness' tunic. "You heard Karl. Just shut up. We'd better get out of here; they may come back."

"But—"

Rahff raised his bloody sword. "Shut *up*."

Karl tried to listen, tried to keep his eyes open, but the darkness reached out and claimed him.

It was a long swim back up to the light. The water rocked him, and tried to force itself into his mouth.

He gave up and let himself sink into the darkness, but a hand reached out and grasped his face, pulling him to the light.

"Karl," Ahira said, forcing more of the sickly-sweet liquid between his lips, "we're safe now. For the time being."

Karl opened his eyes. He was lying on a narrow bunk, sunlight streaming through the oversized porthole and splashing onto his chest. The ship was canted, sailing close to the wind.

"Where?" He struggled to get the words out. "Where are we?"

"Ganness' cabin." The dwarf smiled. "Ganness started to object when we brought you down here, but he took one look at Rahff and changed his mind. That's one loyal apprentice, Karl. Good kid."

Karl nodded. He brought his right hand up, in front of his face.

The wound from the knife was just a pinkish scar on the back of his hand, mirrored on his palm. As he stared at the scar, it continued to fade. Soon it would be gone. It would be just as if nothing at all had—

No. "Fialt."

The dwarf shook his head. "Nothing we could do for him. Healing draughts can't help a dead man. But Chak brought the body on board." He bit his lip. "I . . . I thought you'd want to say the words over him, before we bury him in the Cirric. Tennetty says that's the way they do it on Salket."

Karl raised himself on an elbow. "I'd better go see to every—"

The dwarf planted a hand on Karl's chest and pushed

him back. "Everybody else is fine. I've put Rahff and Chak on watch; the horses are safe in the hold." A crooked smile played across Ahira's lips. "Although I'd better bring Aeia in. She's been crying. Thinks you're dead. Rahff and Chak have been telling her you're unkillable, but I don't think she believes them."

"*I* sure as hell don't. How many of the bounty hunters did we kill?"

Ahira shrugged. "Three for certain; another four wounded and pushed into the water. The rest dove and disappeared."

"And Ganness. How is he taking all of this?"

With a weak smile, Ahira picked up his battleaxe from where it lay on the floor. "I talked to him for a while, and he stopped squawking." He lowered the axe and sighed. "But he got away, dammit."

"He? Who?"

"You didn't notice who was leading that group?"

Karl snorted. "I was sort of busy. What's the mystery?"

"The leader looked to be about eighteen. Dark hair, dark eyes, slim nose. Good with a sword; it took him half a second to spear Fialt through the chest and return to the on-guard position. Had one hell of a familiar-looking and very cruel smile. And that voice . . ." The dwarf shuddered. "Didn't he sound like someone we know?"

Karl tried to remember the voice. No, he had been in too much pain to pay attention. But that description—except for the age, that sounded just like—"Ohlmin? But he's dead." *I cut his head off, and held it in my hands*. There were times that violence bothered Karl, but killing that bastard had been a distinct pleasure.

Ahira nodded. "But maybe he has either a son or a younger brother who isn't."

Karl elbowed the dwarf aside as he pushed himself to his feet. His legs were wobbly, but they would support him. "How would you feel about fixing that?"

"At our first opportunity. In the meantime . . ."

"We bury our dead."

Karl stood at the rail, Rahff and Aeia next to him.

In front of him, Fialt's body lay shrouded on a plank; the plank was supported at one end by the starboard rail, supported at the other by Tennetty, Chak, and Ahira.

Karl laid his hand on the rail. "I never knew Fialt as well as I would have liked to," he said. "Guess it's because I never took enough time. But he wasn't an easy man to get to know. Quiet, most of the time. A private person, our Fialt was.

"I never really understood why he came along. He didn't seem to have the . . . fire in him that Ahira, Tennetty, and I do. And it wasn't a matter of practicing his profession, as it is for Chak. Or of learning through doing, as it is for Rahff.

"But that doesn't tell us much about him. What do we really know about this quiet man? We know that he was awkward with a sword, and none too good with his hands. Although he was learning, and no one ever tried harder. We know that he was a Salke, and a sailor, and a farmer, and a slave. And, finally, a free man. But that was about all.

"*About* all . . ." Karl gripped the rail, his knuckles whitening.

"There were only two times that I had even a peek through the wall he put up between himself and the rest of the world. It seems to me that Fialt wouldn't mind my talking about those two times. And I hope he'll forgive me being frank.

"The first was during a lesson. He had done something well, for once—damned if I can remember what, right now—and I'd said something like, 'We'll make a warrior of you, if you keep this up.'

"He turned to me and shook his head. 'Just a man who can protect himself, his friends, and his own. That's all I ask. That's all I ask. . . .'

"The other time was last night. Fialt must have known that he wasn't good enough to take on a swordsman by himself; he should have waited for a signal from Ahira.

"But he didn't wait. It didn't make *sense*, dammit." Karl gripped the body's stiff, cold shoulder. "You should have waited, Fialt, you should have. . . ." Karl's eyes misted over; his voice started to crack. He took a deep breath and forced his body back under control.

"I . . . guess that tells us something important about our friend. Both virtue and flaw. I will miss that virtue, that flaw, and Fialt, whose body we now surrender to the Cirric." He patted the shoulder and stepped back.

Their faces grim, Tennetty, Chak, and Ahira raised their end of the plank. The body slipped from the plank and splashed into the blue water below, falling behind as it sank.

Chak drew his falchion and raised it to his forehead in salute. Ahira unstrapped his battleaxe, mirroring Chak.

Tennetty stared at the ripples, her eyes red, her face blank.

Karl drew his own sword and balanced it on his palms. "I promise you this, Fialt: You will be avenged." He slipped the sword back in its scabbard.

"Maybe I'm wrong, but I like to think you'd want it just that way."

CHAPTER TWELVE: *The Guardians of the Sword*

I have been here before,
But when or how I cannot tell;
I know the grass beyond the door,
The sweet keen smell,
The sighing sound, the lights around the shore

—Dante Gabriel Rossetti

Karl stood at the *Warthog's* bow, holding tight to the railing as the ketch lumbered slowly across the gently rolling sea toward the small inlet and the lagoon beyond. Overhead, the jib luffed merrily in the wind; below, water foamed, splashed, and whispered against the hull.

Gentle waves lapped against the sandy shore. High above, a slim-winged tern circled in the royal blue sky, then stooped to pluck a small fish from the blue water, bearing its wriggling prey away.

Karl rubbed at his belly, once more enjoying the taut feel of a full stomach. It had taken him time to adapt to being at sea, but his body had made the adjustment. And in less time than it had taken before.

Only six days of feeding the fish this time. Hmm. If this goes on, in a few years I'll only be vomiting for the first few seconds I'm at sea.

A vision of himself stepping on board, immediately vomiting, then smiling and feeling fine rose up unbidden. He laughed out loud.

Aeia looked up at him, raising one eyebrow just the way Andy-Andy did.

"It's nothing," he said. He reached into his pouch and drew out a half-dried orange, peeling it with his thumbnail. Popping a section into his mouth, he waved a hand at the shoreline. "Look familiar?"

"Yesss . . ." First she nodded, then she shook her head. "But I don't see my house."

Little one, as I understand it, Melawei stretches out across about two hundred miles of shoreline, with scads of inlets, beaches, islands, and lagoons. We're not going to bump into your hut. "Don't worry. It may take a few days, but we'll find it."

Her forehead creased. "Are you sure?"

Standing next to her, Rahff gently elbowed the girl in the shoulder. "Karl promised, didn't he?" With a derisive snort, Rahff elbowed Aeia again.

That had to be stopped, nipped in the bud. Not that the boy had done anything terrible, but the point had to be made. "Rahff."

"Yes, Karl?"

"We don't hit the people we're supposed to protect."

Aeia looked up at him. "He didn't hurt me, Karl."

"Doesn't matter. A man whose profession is violence must not commit violence on his own family, or on his friends. You and I are supposed to watch out for Aeia, protect her, not hit her, or bully her."

Rahff thought it over for a moment. "How about you and Ahira? You and he threaten to hit each other all the time."

"Think it through, Rahff. We play at threatening each other; we don't actually hit each other. See the difference?"

"Yes." The boy cocked his head. "But how about practice? We've all gotten bruises from you." He rubbed at his side.

"Good point. That's instruction, not violence. Anyone

can back out of practice at any time. That includes you, apprentice. No more training or no more hitting. Understood?"

"Understood. I'll stay with the training." Rahff turned back to the rail.

Karl smiled his approval. A good kid; Rahff took criticism and instruction as a lesson, not as a blow to his ego.

At Ganness' shouted command, the helmsman brought the ship about again, maneuvering it between two outreaching sandspits. The hull rasped against a sandbar; the ship shuddered free, and swung into the placid water of the lagoon.

Karl shook his head. No wonder the hull was as watertight as a sieve, if this was the way Ganness treated it. Even given Ganness' explanation that the Mel would deal with a ship only after it had grounded itself, there had to be a simpler way than bouncing the boat across sandbars until it got stuck at low tide in the lagoon.

Still, Ganness' seamanship and his confidence in it was noteworthy; on This Side, there was no moon, and the weaker solar tides made for only a slight difference between high and low water. It took guts for Ganness to dare a deliberate grounding; breaking free would be tricky.

Karl turned to Ahira, noting that the dwarf's one-handed grip on a cleat on the forward mast wasn't quite as casual as Ahira tried to make it seem. A casual grip didn't leave the knuckles white. "Any problem?"

Ahira didn't turn around. "No."

Karl switched to English. "Hey, it's me, remember? James, are you okay?"

"I'm fine. I just don't like it when the boat jerks around."

Another bump swung Karl around, sent his hands flying back toward the railing as the ship rocked once, then fell still, grounded. Aeia and Rahff exchanged indulgent smiles over Karl's poor sense of balance.

Look, kids, when you've got a couple hundred pounds of mass to carry around, it isn't as easy to keep upright as it is for you.

But never mind. Let them have a few private chuckles. He scanned the shore, trying to see if there was anyone or anything in the dense greenery. Nothing. Ganness had said that the locals would meet them, but—

"Karl?" Ahira's voice held a hint of amusement.

"Yes?"

"Don't turn around for a second. I've got a question for you."

Karl shrugged. "Sure."

"This shoreline looks like Hawaii, no?"

"I was thinking Polynesia."

"Hawaii's part of Polynesia, Karl. And this is the same thing. Not Diamond Head; it looks more like Lahaina. Palm trees, sandy beaches, almost no rocks, warm, blue water, even though it's fresh and not salt."

"Right." Karl started to turn.

"Hold it a moment," the dwarf snapped. He chuckled. "Now, given all that, when the natives show up, you wouldn't be surprised if they were paddling dugout canoes—outrigger types—would you?"

"It wouldn't surprise me at all."

A similar environment would tend to produce similar artifacts. The simplest, most convenient road—and hunting ground, for that matter—would be the sea. If the Mel didn't have the resources to build large sailing ships, they would build canoes. And if they didn't have animal skins or birch bark to build the canoes with, they'd have to make dugouts. Dugout canoes were inherently more unstable than other sorts—therefore, outriggers. All logical.

"Is that what this is? The natives have dugouts?"

"It makes sense to you, right?"

"Right."

"Then turn around and tell me why their canoes look like miniature versions of Viking longboats."

Karl turned.

Three canoes floated in the lagoon's mouth, each five or six yards long, with an outrigger mounted on the port side, each manned with by oarsmen.

And each with a wooden carving of a dragon's head rising from the prow.

After checking on Carrot and Pirate in the hold, Karl climbed back on deck. He gathered Ahira, Aeia, Chak, Rahff and Tennetty around him, keeping the group well away from Ganness and the three sarong-clad Mel, who were busy at the bow, haggling over the price of Melawei copra and Endell steel.

The locals spoke Erendra with a curiously lilting accent, far different from the flat half-drawl of Metreyll or the clipped speech of Pandathaway. A familiar accent. . . .

"Hey, Karl?" Ahira looked up at him.

"You hear it, too?"

"I sure do. You got any explanation of why these folks talk like the Swedish Chef?"

Chak frowned. "It might help," he said, scowling, "if you would either teach me this *English* of yours, or just keep your conversation in Erendra. At least when I'm around."

"Good idea." The dwarf nodded. "I'll give it a try."

Karl gestured an apology. "We were talking about the accent these Mel have. It sounds familiar. Like something from home."

"Home?" Rahff shook his head. "Not my—"

"Our home." Karl waved his hand aimlessly. "The Other Side. A region called Scandinavia." That was very strange. Differences between here and home were to be expected; he had grown used to them. On the other hand . . . coupled with the dragon-headed canoes, the familiarity of the local accent was vaguely frightening. It had to mean something.

But what?

It couldn't be just a transplanting, as had happened

with their group. After all, the Mel didn't look like
Scandinavians, not at all: Their hair was black and
straight, their skin dark; they had slight epicanthic folds
around their eyes.

Chak shook his head. "That doesn't make sense. I
thought you were the only ones to cross over."

"That's what I thought, too."

The largest of the Mel, a deeply tanned, broad-shouldered man in a purple sarong, walked over. His lined
face was grim as he stopped in front of Karl, planting the
butt of his leaf-bladed spear on the deck in front of him.

"Are you from Arta Myrdhyn?" he asked, his accent
still sending chills up and down Karl's spine. "Has he sent
for the sword?"

Karl shook his head. "I'm sorry, but I don't understand."

The Mel gave a slight shrug, as though that was the
answer he had expected, but it had disappointed him
nonetheless. "Avair Ganness," he said, "says that you are
a man from a land strange to him. He says that your
name is Karl Cullinane, and that you are someone for
whom the slavers have offered a large reward. Is this
true?"

*I'm not sure whether it's the slavers or the whole
Guilds Council that's offering it, but you're close enough.*
Karl nodded, gesturing to Chak to take his hand off the
hilt of his sword. This didn't sound like a prelude to an
attack. And even if it was, the Mel still in the boats were
too far away; Karl, Tennetty, Chak, and Ahira could
easily handle the three spearmen on board. "Yes. It's
true."

"And why do they hunt you?" The Mel's face was flat,
unreadable.

"Three reasons. First: I freed a dragon that Pandathaway kept in chains. Second: I killed slavers and
a wizard who hunted me for doing that. Third: It is
my . . . profession to kill slavers and free slaves." *And*

*there's a fourth reason, it seems. One—at least one—
of the slavers has made it a personal matter.*

He laid a hand on Aeia's shoulder. "This is Aeia; one of
your people. We have brought her here. Home."

"I see. And if slavers were to raid Melawei while you
are here?"

Before Karl could answer, Chak snickered, drawing
his thumb across his throat, sucking air wetly through his
teeth.

Karl nodded.

The Mel's face became even grimmer as he slowly
rotated his spear, planting the point deeply in the wood
of the deck until the spear stood by itself. Placing his
calloused hands on Karl's shoulders, he drew himself up
straight. "I am Seigar Wohtansen, wizard and warleader
of Clan Wohtan. Will you and your friends do me the
honor of guesting with Clan Wohtan while you are in
Melawei?"

Karl looked past Seigar Wohtansen's shoulder to
Ganness, who stood openmouthed in amazement. And
down to Aeia, whose eyes grew wide. Clearly, this wasn't
the standard way to greet visitors from other countries.

Back when he was minoring in anthro, Karl had
learned something of the vast range of acceptable
behavior, and the way it varied from society to society.
But the notion of host and guest was close to universal.
Except for the Yanamamo, of course, the only culture
known by the anthropologists who studied them as "those
bastards." The Mel didn't seem like a This Side version of
Yanamamo.

Wohtansen stood silently, waiting for Karl's answer.

"I am honored," Karl said. "And we accept."

Wohtansen dropped his hands and ran to the railing,
calling down to the men in the dugouts. "There are guests
of the clan here, who require help with their animals and
baggage. Why do you just sit there?"

Aeia let out a deep breath.

"What is it?" Karl asked. "Glad to be home?"

She shook her head. "No, it's not that."

"Why? Afraid I'd turn him down and hurt his feelings?"

The girl shook her head. "If you'd turned him down, he would have had to try to kill you."

Ahira cleared his throat. "I think we'd all better be careful with our pleases and thank-yous. No?"

Sitting down his wooden mug on the grass-strewn floor, Seigar Wohtansen sat back on his grass mat, leaned on his elbows, and shook his head. He sighed deeply. "An acceptable meal, guests of my clan?"

"Not acceptable." Karl smiled. "Excellent." The others echoed him as they reclined on their mats.

The guesthouse of Clan Wohtan was the largest of the seventeen huts in the village, and the most luxurious. It was a long, low structure, somewhat like a bamboo version of a quonset hut, the wrist-thick poles that formed the framework bent overhead, rising to about six feet at the center. Long, flat leaves were woven among the closely spaced poles. The light wind dryly whistled through them.

There was no fireplace in the hut; the slightest spark could easily set it aflame. Their dinner of grilled flatfish and deep-fried balls of coconut milk had been cooked over the firepit twenty yards in front of the open end of the guesthouse, the food brought in on plantain leaves.

The cook—and a good one, at that—had been Estalli, the younger of Seigar Wohtansen's wives; she was a slim, attractive girl who looked to be about sixteen. Now, she knelt attentively beside Wohtansen, the hem of her sarong tucked chastely under her knees while her naked breasts bobbled above, refilling his mug from a clay jug of fermented coconut juice while Wohtansen's seven sons and daughters served Karl and the rest.

Wohtansen's other wife, Olyla, a hugely pregnant

woman in her late thirties, presided over the tail end of the meal from the single piece of furniture in the hut, a cane armchair.

Illumination was provided by seven head-size glowing stones, each suspended in an individual net bag hung from the centerpole that ran lengthwise down the roof of the hut. The light from three of the stones had begun to fade; Wohtansen had spent much of the meal reassuring Olyla that his promise to refresh the spell still stood, and that he would do so tomorrow. Her knowing smirk said that this wasn't the first time he had made that promise.

Understandable. Life in Melawei was lazy and easy; it would always be tempting to put work off to tomorrow.

Karl had another swig of the coconut juice. It was dry and crisp, like a light Italian wine. But how did they get it so cold?

He shrugged. Well, if Romans could make ice in the desert, maybe the Mel could chill a bottle of wine.

He looked over at Aeia, who was sprawled out on her grass mat, sated after the heavy meal, half asleep. "Good to be home, little one?"

She frowned. "I'm not home yet."

Wohtansen smiled reassuringly. "We're not too far from Clan Erik, little cousin. No more than two days by sea." He closed his eyes tightly for a full minute. "If your horses can take just a bit of water, you should be able to ride straight there. And in less time. We can start out in the morning." He shrugged. "I've got to go that way myself. I'll need to arrange for Ganness' copra to be picked up, and I'll have to visit the cave."

Estalli reacted to the last two words as though she had been slapped. "Seigar—"

"Shh. Remember Arta Myrdhyn's words. 'He will be a stranger from a far land.' I'll have to take Karl Cullinane there. And if he's not the one, the sword can protect itself. It has before."

That was the second time Wohtansen had brought up

this sword. Karl spent a half-second debating with himself whether asking might offend the Mel. Then: "What sword is this?"

Wohtansen shrugged. "The sword. I wish Svenna—he was the Clan Speaker—hadn't been taken by the slavers; he could tell you the story, word by word." He raised his head. "Though Clan Erik still has its Speaker. Do you want to wait until you can hear it properly?"

"To be honest, I'm itching with curiosity."

Not particularly about this sword, though. What were a group of Mel men doing with Scandinavian names and Scandinavian accents?

And more.

The figureheads on the dugouts looked like the dragons on Viking longboats; they were stylized, almost rectangular, not saurian, like Ellegon.

The huts were bamboo-and-cane versions of Viking lodges.

That didn't make sense. A climate and environment similar to Polynesia could have given rise to a culture similar to the Polynesian culture, complete with loose wraparound clothing, outrigger canoes, and a loose and easy life-style based on the bounty of the sea. But where had the Scandinavian elements come from?

It was possible that the dragon-headed canoes *or* the accent *or* the similarity of some of the names could have been a coincidence, but not all three.

Seigar Wohtansen sat up, then drained his mug, beckoning to Estalli for a refill.

"Very well. My father's father's father's . . ." He knit his brow in concentration as he counted out the generations by tapping his fingers against his leg. " . . father's father's father's *father*, Wohtan Redbeard, was called a pirate, although he truly was a just man. He sailed his boat on a sea of salt, as he raided the villages of the wicked landfolk, taking from them their ill-gotten grain and gold."

As Wohtansen spoke, the children sat down on the

mats, listening intently, as if to a favorite, often-repeated bedtime story.

" . . . he and his men would appear from over the horizon, beach their boat, then . . ."

One of the little boys leaned over toward an older sister. "How could they sail on salt?" he asked, in a quiet whisper.

She sneered down at him, holding herself with the air of superiority possessed by older sisters everywhere. "There was salt in the *water.*"

"That doesn't make sense. Why would they waste salt by putting it in the water?" he pressed. "Father says salt is hard enough to find as it is."

"They didn't. It was already there."

"How?"

"Shh, Father's talking."

" . . . but this night was dark, and a storm raged on the sea, sending his ship leaping into the air, then crashing down into the troughs between the waves. . . ."

"Why didn't they just land?" The boy nudged his sister again.

She sighed. "Because they were too far out at sea."

"Didn't they know that they weren't supposed to go out of sight of land?"

"I guess they forgot."

" . . . and just as he thought that his ship would founder and sink, the sky cracked open around him, and the ship found itself on the quiet waters of the Cirric. . . ."

"But how did it *get* here?"

"Weren't you listening?" She gave him a clout on the head. "The sky cracked open."

He rubbed at the spot where she had struck him. "I've never seen that."

"You will if you don't be quiet."

" . . . standing at the prow was an old man. White-bearded, he was, dressed in gray wizard's robes. Clutched tightly in fingers of light, a sword floated in the air over his head.

" 'I, Arta Myrdhyn, have saved your lives and brought you here,' he said, in a tongue they had never before heard, but somehow understood, 'to take this to a place I will show you.' His voice was the squeak of a boy whose manhood was almost upon him, yet his face was lined with age. 'You and your children will watch over it, and keep it for one whom I will send.'

"A man named Bjørn laughed. 'My thanks for the sword,' he said. 'But I will take it for myself.'

"As he sprang across the deck at the wizard, lightning leaped from the wizard's fingers, slaying Bjørn instantly. . . ."

The boy looked up at his sister. "Bjørn? What kind of name is Bjørn?"

"An unlucky one. And a stupid one. Now, *shh.*"

" . . . brought them to the cave, and left the sword there, amid the writings that only two of them could see, and none of them could read. 'Watch for strangers,' Arta Myrdhyn said. 'One day, a stranger will come for the sword.'

" 'But how will I know him?' my many-times-great-grandfather asked.

"The wizard shook his head. 'You will not, and neither will your children, or their children. It is not yours to know, but to watch, and wait. The sword will know. . . .' "

"How can a sword know anything?"

"It's a magical sword, stupid."

"Hmph."

" . . . accepted them gladly, and offered their daughters as wives." Wohtansen raised his head. "And so, they settled down to an easier life, raised their children, and grandchildren, down the nine generations." He thumped his hand against his mat. "And here we are." He tapped the jug. "More juice?"

Ahira caught Karl's eye. "What we've had has already gotten to my bladder." He elbowed Karl in the side.

"Oof. Me, too. If you'll excuse us for a moment?"

* * *

"Did you catch all that, Karl?" Seating himself on a waist-high rock, the dwarf drummed his heels against the stone.

Karl's head swam. It made sense, but it didn't. All at once. "I don't understand it. Part of it makes sense, but . . ." What Wohtansen had said boiled down to the sort of story a group of conquering Vikings might tell to their children and grandchildren. "But eight, nine generations? When were the Vikings? About eleventh century, no?"

Ahira nodded. "Something like that. And with the faster time rate on This Side, if a bunch of eleventh-century Vikings crossed over, they should have been here for far more than two centuries. Especially since time passes so much more quickly here."

Karl nodded. That was what Deighton had said, and what they had observed. Their trip from Lundeyll to the Gate Between Worlds had taken a couple of months on This Side, but when they had used the Gate to return home, only a few hours had passed. Once, he had sat down with Lou Riccetti to figure it out: For every hour that passed at home, about four or five hundred flew by here.

"It can't be something as simple as Deighton lying," Karl said.

"No." The dwarf scowled. "Deighton has lied to us more than once, but not this time. We know he was telling the truth. This time. The time rate is faster here, relatively."

"Maybe not." Karl shrugged. "Maybe the time differential fluctuates. That'd explain some things."

"Like what?"

"Think it through." Karl stamped his foot. "Wish I'd had the sense to, before." He gestured around them. "If this side really was four hundred times as old as Earth, that'd make it about sixteen hundred billion years old, no? It'd be that much more worn; most of the atmosphere would have escaped, probably; all the mountains would have worn themselves down."

"Huh?" Ahira's forehead furrowed. "You're telling me that mountains wear out? Too much dry-cleaning?"

"Give me a break. Mountains tend to wear down, just like anything else. The Appalachians are older than the Rockies, which is why they don't rise as high, not anymore. In another couple of billion years, they'll be the Appalachian plains, if tectonic forces don't raise a whole new set of mountains. Entropy."

The dwarf pounded his fist against the rock. "Deighton lied again."

"Maybe; maybe not." Karl shook his head. "So, the time differential fluctuates. But maybe Deighton didn't know that. After all, the time rate could have worked just the way he said it did during his whole life. He could have been telling the truth."

"I doubt it." The dwarf shook his head. "I didn't think you caught it. Remember the wizard's name: Arta Myrdhyn. Sound familiar?"

"Myrdhyn. Well, that kind of sounds like Merlin." Karl shrugged. "I guess it's possible that Arta Myrdhyn inspired the legends about Merlin."

That wouldn't be surprising; he had already seen evidence that happenings on this side had leaked over the boundary between worlds: elves, dwarves, wizards throwing bolts of lightning, the silkies of the northern Cirric, the notion of fire-breathing dragons, the cave beneath Bremon that was echoed in the writings of Isaiah—

"No. Or maybe," the dwarf corrected himself. "But that's not the point. Remember how Wohtansen described the wizard? 'White-bearded . . . his voice was the squeak of a boy whose manhood was almost upon him, yet his face was lined with age.' Doesn't that sound like someone we know?"

Ohgod. "And the name: Arta—Arthur. Arthur Simpson Deighton. But he said—"

"That he had only seen this side, but never had been able to bring himself across. That's what he *said*, Karl. Doesn't make it true."

Karl shook his head. "I don't see what this all adds up to."

"Me neither." The dwarf shrugged. "And I've got a hunch we're not going to for quite a while. If ever. Unless you want to try to slip past The Dragon, again, then go quiz Deighton."

"I'll pass, thanks."

"Thought so."

"I don't see you volunteering."

"I'm not." Ahira flexed his arm, his biceps bulging like a huge knot. "I like it here. No, I think we just keep thinking about it. Maybe Walter or Andrea or Lou Riccetti will have some idea; maybe Ellegon knows more than he's telling. We'll just have to wait until we get back to the valley."

"Well, what do we do in the meantime?"

Ahira smiled. "That's easy. We live. Eat. Breathe. Kill slavers. All the usual stuff."

Karl snorted. "Well, let's get back inside, then. Got a lot to think about."

Ahira raised a finger. "There is one more thing we'd better do."

"Yes?"

"I think we'd better have a look at this sword of Wohtansen's."

"Right."

CHAPTER THIRTEEN:
The Scourge

Her beams bemocked the sultry main,
Like April hoarfrost spread;
But where the ship's huge shadow lay,
The charmed water burnt away
A still and awful red.

—Samuel Taylor Coleridge

"I still say we should have taken them while they were at sea," Lensius muttered to Hynryd, his voice pitched so that Ahrmin could hear him, but only barely. Lensius shook his head, his long, greasy ringlets of hair waggling in counterpoint. "And we would have, were I in charge."

Hynryd nodded. "That's what Jheral thought, too."

"I know. He—"

"*Enough.*" Ahrmin's fingers tightened on the hilt of his sword. Lensius and Hynryd fell silent.

Ahrmin sighed. The fiasco at the dock hadn't done anything to improve his standing with his thirty-seven remaining men. What had once been only a silent resentment had become open doubt, sometimes verging on mutiny.

But that didn't matter. Only one thing mattered.

So I failed, Karl Cullinane. This first time. That's not so important; even Father couldn't beat you the first time. But it isn't the first time that counts, Karl Cullinane. It's the last time.

He looked around the *Scourge's* cramped forward hold. Of the thirty-odd faces, the only one that didn't bear a frown was Thyren's; the wizard held himself

190

above both the sailors and slavers. In contrast to the grubbiness of the rest, the wizard's gray robes were clean and unwrinkled, his drawn face freshly shaved, his thin lips holding a disdainful smile.

"Ahrmin?" Raykh scratched at his head. "I think we should consider letting this Karl Cullinane go. There's enough gold to be had picking up a few dozen Mel." He tapped on the bulkhead behind him. "Enough space in the hold for one hundred and fifty, two hundred, if we pack tightly enough."

Ahrmin's irritation rose. He'd had enough of the tight-pack fanatic. Of all tight-pack fanatics.

It had been proved, over and over again, that there was more money to be made by delivering a smaller number of healthy slaves than by tight-packing them, chaining them all closely together in the hold, leaving them to stew in their own wastes during a sea voyage, having to throw away those who didn't survive, then treat the others with expensive healing draughts before a sale.

Tight-packing was a particularly stupid way to handle Mel. Mel didn't take easily to their chains; many would refuse to eat. Tight-packed, they could lose more than half of the slaves. Even loose-packed, the trip from Melawei to Pandathaway would kill ten, maybe twenty percent of the cargo, and leave the rest sick as dogs.

Of course, they could always sell the surviving slaves as-is. But in Pandathaway—or anywhere else along the coast, for that matter—there was little demand for sickly slaves who had to be either healed or nursed back to health before they would be any use to their new owners. Tight-packing would kill much profit.

Besides, tight-packing the women would remove one of the great joys of the profession.

Ahrmin snorted. "And what would you do? It would take several tendays in a good port to refit the *Scourge* for tight-pack."

Raykh shrugged. "It seems a bit late to point that out. We could have—"

Thyren cleared his throat; Raykh fell silent.

"I believe that was Ahrmin's point," the wizard said
"We're not in Pandathaway. Nor are we in Lundeyll, or
Port Salke, or even Ehvenor. To be precise, we're off the
coast of Melawei. Even if you wanted to take the time
and money to refit the slavehold, I doubt that the locals
would be willing to help you."

Fihka spoke up, his low growl barely carrying over the
rush of water. "We could always make them help us."

The wizard eyed him for a moment, then carefully spat
in Fihka's face.

Fihka reddened, but kept his white-knuckled fists at
his sides, not even daring to raise his hands to wipe the
spittle from his cheek. The others near him turned their
faces away, not wanting to be next.

"Fool," Thyren said, smiling gently. "Who do you
think I am? Grandmaster Lucius? Arta Myrdhyn? I can
easily hold off any one of these Mel wizards and his
apprentices. I could probably take on two, perhaps as
many as three. But if I were stupid enough to allow you
to anchor the *Scourge* offshore for—a tenday, did you
say? two?—we would quickly find the ship surrounded
by every Mel wizard and apprentice that could run,
paddle, swim, or crawl. There is a limit to how many
spells I can intercept."

Thyren rose. "But enough of this nonsense; I have
better things to do than listen to more squabbling." He
rose and left, all of the men glaring in unison at the door
as he closed it behind him.

*You would be able to dispel more if you didn't insist on
keeping other spells in your head, wizard. Like your
lightning bolt, or flame spell,* Ahrmin thought. *But then
you wouldn't be able to abuse everyone with impunity,
would you?*

Then it occurred to him that Thyren had, albeit un-
knowingly, done him a favor. By acting as a lightning rod
for the men's discontent, the wizard had given Ahrmin a
chance to ingratiate himself with the others.

But how?

He thought for a moment, and an idea that had been in the back of his mind suddenly jelled.

"Raykh," he said. "You should trust me more."

Raykh's head snapped around. "What?"

"You assumed that I had no reason for not taking the *Warthog* at sea."

The other sneered. "I know your reason. You want to take Cullinane alive."

"And you'd rather take a share of a much smaller reward? Never mind. There is another reason. One that will fatten all of our pouches, as well. As much as a tight-pack would if all the slaves survived. And . . ."

"And?" Raykh leaned forward, interested.

"And my plan will ensure that we can come upon Karl Cullinane unaware. It will be tricky, granted; and we have to assume that Cullinane has business in Melawei that will take him at least a day's ride away from where they've beached the *Warthog*. I'll be happy to share my idea, if you're interested." Ahrmin lay back on his bunk, cradling his head on his arms. "But my major concern is Cullinane. If you don't mind forgoing some extra slaves, some extra coin . . ." He closed his eyes.

"Wait," another voice piped up. "Don't keep it a secret, Master Ahrmin."

He sat up, making sure that his smile didn't reach his face. *"Master Ahrmin,"* eh? *I like the sound of that.*

"Very well." Ahrmin nodded. "The timing will be tricky, but I'm sure we can do it." He pulled the glass ball from his pouch, unwrapped the soft leather sheets that covered it.

Ahrmin cradled the ball in the palm of his hand. "It all depends on this."

The finger floated in the center of the sphere, bobbing slowly in the yellow oil. From the finger's hacked-off stump, threads of tendon and shreds of skin waved gently, while the slim fingernail pointed unerringly toward the north.

"Listen carefully, now. We'll lie offshore, out of sight, until we're sure that Cullinane has gone a fair distance away, then . . ."

CHAPTER FOURTEEN: *The Cave of Writings*

The great brand
Made lightnings in the splendor of the moon,
And flashing round and round, and whirled in an arch,
Shot like a streamer of the northern morn,
Seen where the moving isles of winter shock
By night, with noises of the northern sea . . .

—Alfred, Lord Tennyson

There are times, Karl thought, *when I like this business a whole lot.* He rode Carrot at the edge of the water, sometimes kicking her into a canter, urging her a short way into the surf. Her hooves kicked up spray, bathing both of them in a cool shower.

"Stop that, Karl. Get back on the beach." Aeia laughed, wiping the spray from her eyes. To his left and a few yards behind, she bounced along on Pirate's back, her feet barely reaching the shortened stirrups.

She patted Pirate's white neck. Aeia had grown fond of that horse; it occurred to Karl that she would probably have a harder time saying goodbye to Pirate than to him.

Almost three hundred yards offshore, four dugouts kept pace with them. The first one held Tennetty, Chak, Ahira, Seigar, Wohtansen, and two other Mel paddlers; the other two, each manned by three Mel, were piled high with trade goods from the *Warthog*. In a couple of days, the men of Clan Wohtansen would free the boat from its sandbar, so that Ganness could sail down to collect his copra.

Ahead, a small island grew closer. Perhaps a quarter-mile offshore, it was heavily wooded and roughly conical, rising to a height of almost a hundred feet at its peak.

Aeia's eyes grew wide. "Karl." She pulled Pirate to a stop and stared at the island, her eyes filling with tears.

He guided Carrot over to her side. "What's wrong?"

"I *remember*. My parent's house is . . ." Her pointing forefinger wavered, then straightened. "That way. Along that path." Her arm trembled; she lowered it.

He dismounted from Carrot's saddle and helped Aeia down from Pirate. "Let's walk, shall we?"

Taking Pirate's reins in her left hand, she clasped Karl's right hand as they walked along the sand.

From the top of a slanting palm tree, a rough tattoo of drumbeats issued, then echoed as they were repeated along the path into the forest.

As the three dugouts were beached, Karl smiled down at Aeia. "Let's wait a moment."

"But—" she tugged on his hand.

"But nothing." He smoothed down the sides of his sarong. "I may be dressed in local costume, little one, but I don't think anybody grows quite this tall or hairy around here. I'd rather your clan finds out that I'm friendly *before* we meet them, rather than after I've gotten a spear through my chest."

Seigar Wohtansen spoke a few quiet words to one of his men; the Mel sprinted across the sands and disappeared into the forest, as Wohtansen and the rest walked over to where Karl and Aeia stood.

They were all dressed in local costume. Karl laughed at the way Chak's sunburned potbelly protruded over the waist of his sarong, although Rahff wore his with dignity. On the other hand, Tennetty actually looked kind of nice in a sarong, if you could ignore the scars along her belly and back. And the way that her right hand never strayed far from the hilt of her sword.

I guess I've been away from Andy-Andy far too long, if Tennetty's starting to look good.

Ahira looked ridiculous. The hem of his sarong brushed the sand, and it didn't really go with the chain-mail vest that he wore over a thin under-shirt. Dwarfs weren't built to wear sarongs.

But who except me would tell him that?

As always, the dwarf had his battleaxe with him, strapped across his broad chest. While Ahira really wasn't as touchy as his scowling face suggested, it was unlikely that anyone would risk finding that out.

Wohtansen tapped Karl's shoulder. "The Eriksens will be down to pick up their goods in a short while. And, I suspect, celebrate their surprise." He ran affectionate fingers through Aeia's hair; his face grew somber. "Which means that you and I had best be getting on to the cave. I know Clan Erik; likely you won't be able to leave the celebration for days without offending someone."

Aeia's lower lip trembled; Karl dialed for a reassuring smile, relieved to find that at least some sort of grimace spread across his face.

It would be hard leaving Aeia here. Karl had never had a little sister before.

"I guess we'd better," he said, handing Carrot's reins to Chak. "Keep an eye on everything."

"No sweat, kemo sabe," Chak said in English, his thick accent leaving a lot to be desired.

Karl raised an eyebrow. *"Kemo sabe?"*

Chak nodded, then turned to Ahira. "I said that properly, no?"

"Close." Ahira shrugged an apology to Karl. "Well, he *asked* to be taught some English. And so did Rahff."

"I can see you started them with the important stuff first."

"Of course."

Wohtansen was getting impatient. Karl turned to accompany him.

"Coming, Ahira?" Karl asked.

The dwarf shook his head. "You have to swim to get there. I think you'd better count me out. But I will want to hear about it, later."

"Swim?"

Wohtansen nodded. "You'd better give your sword to one of your friends. You'd have trouble swimming with it."

Karl unbuckled his swordbelt and tossed the scabbarded sword to Rahff. "Don't lose it, now."

"Of course, Karl." His apprentice nodded gravely. "And . . . up your nose with a rubber nose," he added in English, bowing slightly.

Karl laughed. "Ahira, you cut that out." Karl unstrapped his sandals, then kicked them off, absent-mindedly spraying Ahira with sand.

The dwarf chuckled; Karl and Wohtansen dropped their sarongs on the sand and jogged away.

The water was warm and clear; Karl kept to Wohtansen's pace as they swam toward the island.

But it had been a long time since Karl had been swimming, and a quarter of a mile was more distance than he was used to; by the time Wohtansen pulled himself up onto the flat top of a jutting boulder, then offered Karl a hand up, Karl was grateful for the help.

He mimicked Wohtansen, stretching out on a rock, resting while the hot sun dried his skin. His breath came in short gasps; Karl forced his breathing to slow down. "Any reason we couldn't just take a canoe over?"

Wohtansen smiled tolerantly at Karl's panting. "Yes." He thumped a fist on the boulder. "Whole island is rocky, like this. No place to beach it. Besides, it's better not to draw attention to this place. Just in case." Wohtansen rose to his feet. "This way."

The narrow path twisted sharply upward through the bushes, until they arrived at the summit of the island, a rocky outcropping overlooking the seaward side. A single palm grew there, projecting out of a crack in the rock. A sparkling in the leaves caught Karl's eye; he glanced up. A glass ball, only slightly larger than a lightbulb, hung in midair among the palm's fronds, bobbling slightly in the breeze.

Wohtansen smiled. "A gift from Arta Myrdhyn; you can see what it does when we get below."

Below?

The Mel brought him to the ledge and pointed downward. A few yards from where the waves broke against the rocks almost a hundred feet below, the water burbled. "There's a spring that feeds into the Cirric down there. It will help us coming out, but it does make it difficult to go in.

"Listen closely: After I strike the water, count forty breaths, take as large a breath as you can, then follow me. Dive directly for the rough water, then swim down, as far as you can. The tunnel goes deep, very deep. Don't hesitate, just keep swimming down. It will be difficult for you, but it can be done.

"You must keep your eyes open; when you see light, swim toward it. I'll meet you and help you the rest of the way. Do you understand?"

At Karl's nod, Wohtansen walked away from the edge, took a running start, and leaped outward, away from the edge, his body arching into a classic swan dive, then straightening a scant pulsebeat before he hit the surface.

Wohtansen struck the dark water cleanly; he vanished, only a small splash marking his passing.

Karl took a deep breath and began counting.

One breath. *I don't like this, not at all.* But he kept breathing and counting.

Ten. *Well, at least we know why someone as young and vital as Wohtansen is the wizard around here. Not a job for an old man; one misstep and he'd shatter himself on the rocks.*

Twenty. *If I remember right, the cliffdivers in Acapulco dive more than a hundred feet from La Quebrada—if they can do it; why the hell can't I jump a bit less?*

Twenty-five. *Because I'm not trained for it, that's why the hell I can't do it. Or why I shouldn't, if I had a brain in my head.*

Thirty. *But do I have any choice?*

Thirty-five. *Not if I want to see this sword.*

To hell with it. He began hyperventilating, forcing air in and out of his lungs. He counted out five quick breaths, added another fifteen for good measure, eyed the distance from the rocks to the bubbling water, ran, and dove, his hands forming into fists of their own volition.

The air clung to him like a rubber sheet; the scant three seconds that he fell felt like a long hour.

He hit.

The water slammed into him like a brick wall, knocking the air out of his lungs, as he sank into the smooth tunnel, scraping his right shoulder against the stone. For a moment, he considered returning to the surface, giving up for now, trying again later. But he knew that if he backed away now, he would never regain his nerve.

So he swam down, into the black water, kicking his legs as frantically as he worked his arms.

The pressure in his chest grew; his lungs burned with a cruel fire; his diaphragm ached to draw anything, anything into his lungs.

And just when he finally thought his head and chest would split wide open, a horizontal channel appeared beside him, marked by a flickering light. Karl swam toward the light.

A hand grasped his outstretched arm; Karl went limp and let Wohtansen pull him through the horizontal tunnel, then up through another vertical one.

Two yards above him, the surface rippled invitingly. Desperately, he kicked himself from Wohtansen's grasp and stuck his head through to the surface.

His first breath was the sweetest one he had ever taken.

Karl pulled himself out of the water and lay gasping on the rough stone floor.

Seal-like, Wohtansen slipped from the water, then handed Karl a thick, soft blanket. "Here. Take a moment to dry off. It gets cold in here." Following his own advice, the Mel took another blanket from a cane drying rack.

As he dried himself, Karl looked around. They were in a small, almost spherical room, the stone floor concave to accommodate the pool in the center, the walls rising to a height of perhaps five yards. Glowing crystals speckled the walls.

Just like the crystals in the Cave of The Dragon. An icy chill crept along his spine; he rubbed himself harder, but the chill remained.

A long, jagged crack ran along the ceiling on the far side of the room, letting in shreds of noon sunlight through the green foliage that grew over the outside of the wall.

That wall couldn't have been more than a few inches thick; chiseling a doorway wouldn't have been difficult. Still, it was understandable why the Mel hadn't created another, more convenient way into the caverns. If this was the source of their magic, it would be best to keep it hidden.

On the far side of the cavern, a tunnel stood as the only exit other than the pool.

Wohtansen helped Karl to his feet, and they started to walk toward the tunnel. Low enough that Karl had to stoop to walk through it, the tunnel was only ten feet long, opening up on another cavern. "You won't be able to see the magical writing on the far wall, but I think you'll enjoy . . . *this.*"

Karl started. On the wall beside him, a huge picture window looked down on the sea.

Window? How can there be a window? They wer
inside the island; a window on that wall would open o
rock, not look down on the Cirric. And it wasn't a pain
ing; the waves in a painting didn't ripple; the clouds in
painting didn't move.

"That's just not possible. We're at sea level."

Wohtansen smiled. "Remember the Eye you sav
above. Arta Myrdhyn left it there, and this here, so tha
we would never have to leave this place without knowin
what lies outside."

Wohtansen at his side, Karl walked to the window an
ran his fingers over the cool glass.

The view spun.

"Gently, gently," Wohtansen said, pulling Karl's arr
from the glass. He put his own fingers on the left side c
the glass, and pressed gently for a moment.

Like a camera panning to the left, the picture movec
Now the glass revealed a distant view of the beach, wher
perhaps a dozen people stood.

"It seems that some of the Eriksens have arrived on th
beach," Wohtansen said. He pressed his fingers to th
center of the window, holding them firmly against th
glass. The field of vision narrowed, zooming in until
could hold only four figures, all of them with the fla
appearance brought on by a telescope or binoculars.

Ahira stood smiling, while a fiftyish Mel couple, the
faces dripping with tears, hugged little Aeia so hard tha
Karl thought they might squeeze the air out of her.

Wohtansen removed his hand from the glass, the
lightly touched it on the right side, again removing h
hand when the seaside view slid around. "But this is wha
it's for." He jerked his head toward the exit tunne
"Come."

They walked into the tunnel. This one was longer tha
the other, forty yards of twisting turns. As they neare
the tunnel's mouth, the brightness grew. But it was a di
ferent sort, a whiter, purer light.

Karl stepped up his pace. He reached the final bend in the tunnel and stepped out into brightness.

"I don't—" the words caught in his throat; his head spun.

Above a rough stone altar, gripped tightly by ghostly fingers of white light, the sword floated in midair.

CHAPTER FIFTEEN:
The Sword

Once more unto the breach, dear friends, once more,
Or close the wall up with our English dead!
In peace there's nothing so becomes a man
As modest stillness and humility;
But when the blast of war blows in our ears,
Then imitate the action of the tiger;
Stiffen the sinews, summon up the blood,
Disguise fair nature with hard-favored rage;
Then lend the eye a terrible aspect.

—William Shakespeare

Karl's breath caught in his throat. His hands trembled.

But why? In and of itself, the sword didn't look unusual.

It was a fairly ordinary two-handed broadsword, three inches wide at the ricasso, tapering at first gently, then suddenly, to a needle-pointed tip; a cord-wound grip and long, thick brass quillons proclaimed it a sword for use, not for dress.

The blade was free of nicks and rust, granted, but Karl had seen many swords just as good. Perhaps a sword like this was worth sixty, seventy gold. No more.

So why was just looking at it like an electric shock?

"Part of the spell." Wohtansen chuckled thinly. "It affects everyone that way."

Karl tore his eyes away from the sword and the ghostly hand gripping it. He turned to face Wohtansen. "What . . . ?"

The Mel shrugged. "I don't know much more about

than I've told you. There are two charms on it that I can see." He tapped the middle of his forehead. "With the inner sight. One holds it there, waiting." He gestured at the bands of light clutching the sword. "For the one whom Arta Myrdhyn has intended to have it."

"The other?"

"A charm of protection. Not for the sword, for the bearer. It will protect him from magical spells."

Karl couldn't keep his eyes off the sword any longer; he turned back. His palms itching for the cord-wound hilt, he took a step forward.

"Wait." Wohtansen's hand fell on Karl's shoulder. "What do you read on the blade? What does the blade say?"

The blade was shiny steel, lacking any filigreed inscription. "*Say?* Nothing." Karl shrugged the hand away.

"Nothing? Then we may as well go; the sword was not left for you." Wohtansen stared intently into Karl's face. "I'd hoped you were the one," he said sadly, then bit his lip as he shook his head. "But hoping never did make it so."

Karl took another step toward the sword. It vibrated, setting up a low hum that filled the cavern. As Karl leaned toward it, the humming grew louder.

He reached up and fastened both hands on the hilt, while the radiance grew brighter, the humming louder. The fingers of light dazzled his eyes; they gripped the sword more tightly.

His eyes tearing, Karl squinted against the light and pulled. The vibration rattled his teeth, but he gripped the hilt tightly and pulled even harder. The light grew so bright that it made his eyes ache even through closed eyelids, but the sword didn't move at all.

Goddam it, he thought. *Here I am, trying to grab a magical vibrator when I should be home with my wife and child and—*

The sword gave a fraction of an inch, then stopped, frozen in place.

"*Karl.*" Wohtansen's voice was shrill. "It's never moved before. Pull harder, Karl Cullinane. Harder."

He pulled harder. Nothing.

He gripped the hilt even more tightly, then braced his feet against the stone altar, and pulled on the sword until his heart pounded in his chest, and the strain threatened to break his head open.

Move, dammit, move.

Nothing. He set his feet back on the floor and released his grip.

The light faded back to its original dimness; the vibration slowed, then stopped.

"I can't do it." Karl shook his head. Wohtansen tugged at his arm.

"A pity," Wohtansen said. "When it moved, I was certain you were the one."

He pursed his lips, then shrugged, as he led Karl back through the tunnel, the radiance diminishing behind them. "But it's not the first disappointment in my life; it won't be the last."

Wohtansen waved a hand at the window and walked to the far wall. "I do have to reimprint some spells; if you'd like, amuse yourself with the Eye while I study." He seated himself tailor-fashion in front of the wall opposite the glass, folded his hands in his lap, and began reading the invisible letters, moving his lips as he studied it.

Karl stared intently at the wall. No, it was just a blank wall to him; since he didn't have the genes that allowed him to work magic, he couldn't even see the writing.

That hardly seemed fair.

Then again, damn little was fair; damn little even made sense.

Although some things were beginning to. Arta Myrdhyn and the sword, for one.

Things on this side were often reflected as legends on the other side, at home. A great broadsword, somehow involved with the plans of a powerful wizard, held immobile until the right man appeared to claim it . . . that sounded like the story of Excalibur. The legend had been garbled, granted, but that wasn't unexpected.

The Excalibur story had never made sense to Karl; if whoever could remove Excalibur from the stone were automatically to become king of England, England would quickly be ruled by the first stoneworker to happen along and chisel it loose.

No spell could prevent that; magic worked erratically back home, when it worked at all.

But what does all this add up to? Deighton had brought a group of Vikings through to this side, not primarily to guard the sword, but to guide the right one to the sword, a sword that protected its bearer against magic.

And the right one was supposed to take it. To use it. To use it for *what?*

Karl shook his head. He couldn't follow the thread any further.

What are you really up to, Deighton?

He shrugged. Ahira was right. It would be a long time, at best, before they knew.

Karl turned to the window that looked out on the sea. He pressed his fingers against the left side of the glass and spun the view shoreward. A procession of Mel was engaged in bringing canvas sacks down the beach and depositing them on the sand just above the high-water mark. The pile was already well over six feet high.

Karl shrugged. Ganness' copra, no doubt. Too bad for Avair that he couldn't bring it directly to Pandathaway, but would instead have to sell it in Ehvenor to some Pandathaway-bound merchant. The dried, unpressed coconut meat would bring a high price in Pandathaway; after it had been run through presses, what oil the wizards didn't need would find its way into gentle soaps and balms, while the remaining meat would end up in breads and cakes.

But why were they bringing it down to the beach now? Ganness and the *Warthog* weren't due until tomorrow. Right now, the Eriksens should be celebrating Aeia's return.

Karl spun the view seaward. Just over the horizon, a black speck grew. A ship.

That explained it. Ganness was on his way a day early, and the Clan Erik coastwatchers had spotted the *Warthog*. Undoubtedly, the watchers had sounded the alarm, which had then been canceled when Wohtansen's men explained that there was a friendly ship en route.

Karl opened his mouth to tell Wohtansen about it, but changed his mind; the Mel was still studying the wall, his whole body tensed in concentration.

Wish I'd asked how long this was going to take. Idly, he centered the ship on the screen and pressed his fingers to the center of the glass.

The *Warthog* grew in the screen as it seemed to sail directly toward Karl. The ship rode high in the water, since most of its cargo had been unloaded in Clan Wohtan. As it moved closer, Karl could make out Ganness at the prow.

That was unusual; Ganness generally ran the ship from the main deck, where he was midway between the lookout in the forward mast and the steersman at the stern. That way, he could lounge in his chair while still able to hear warnings and give commands easily.

Only when the ship needed careful handling did he act as either lookout or steersman himself. Beaching the ship in the lagoon had needed that careful handling; beaching it here should just be a matter of sailing the *Warthog* slowly toward shore until it wouldn't go any farther.

Ganness' figure grew in the screen. Trembling, he raised a hand to wipe sweat from his brow.

What's Ganness nervous about? I guess there could be underwater boulders near the shore, but that shouldn't scare him like this.

Karl moved his finger to scan the rest of the ship, but

his control wasn't fine enough; the *Warthog* scudded out of the Eye's field of view.

Damn. He removed his finger from the screen, centered the ship as soon as the field widened, and zoomed in carefully, making fingertip corrections to the aim of the Eye.

Standing next to Ganness was a young man. His face was dark and thin, his hair straight. A cruel smile flickered across his lips as he examined a dark glass ball, slipped it into his pouch, then turned to say something to the men behind him.

He looked for all the world like a younger version of Ohlmin.

Karl's heart pounded.

"Wohtansen, look."

The Mel wizard scowled at him. "Not now, please. This is difficult."

"*Shut up.* This is important. That's the slaver who tried to take me on the docks at Ehvenor. He and his men have taken the *Warthog.* They're going to be sailing right up to the damn beach, and the Eriksens won't know—"

"—that they are slavers." Wohtansen whitened. "We've told them to expect friends."

"Right." Karl's right hand ached for his sword. *Got to figure out exactly what they're going to do.* The slavers had the element of surprise. How would they use it?

They would probably drop anchor or beach the ship, and let some Eriksen dugouts come out to meet them, just as if this were a normal trading session. Then the slavers would kill or capture the Mel in the canoes, and use the canoes to go ashore, their wizard protecting them all the while from the Mel wizard's spells.

They would work it something like that. The slavers had clearly gone to some trouble to gain the advantage of surprise, and they would make good use of it.

"Karl," Wohtansen said, his voice shaky, "they must have already raided my clan. Otherwise someone would have chased after us, to warn us."

"Be quiet for a moment." That was true, but there wasn't anything that could be done about it right now. "We've only got one edge. You and I know what's going on, but they don't know that we know."

But how could they use that single advantage? Karl and Wohtansen couldn't take on the slavers all by themselves. "You swim to shore, and quietly warn my people, *only* my people. Tell Ahira to get into the treeline with his crossbow; have Chak take Tennetty and Rahff, and hide themselves along the path to the village."

"But the Eriksens—"

Karl shook his head. "If we let them know, they'll sound the alarm. All that would do is turn this into a standard raid, with Clan Erik taking to the hills, and the slavers scooping up a few dozen stragglers. We've got to stop them; that wouldn't do it."

The Pandathaway wizard, he was the key; Karl would have to take the wizard out. "Just keep quiet until you hear from me. If you raise a fuss, all you'll do is bring their wizard down on your head. Now, *move.*"

"But you can't take on the wizard, not by yourself. You don't have a chance."

"I won't be by myself. Get going."

Wohtansen ran toward the tunnel that led to the entrance pool.

Karl didn't wait for the splash; he turned and sprinted toward the cavern of the sword.

He seated himself tailor-fashion on the cold stone. "Deighton, can you hear me?"

No answer.

"I know you put this sword here for a purpose."

Still no answer. Nothing. Held firmly by the fingers of light, the sword hung silently in the air. "Arta Myrdhyn, talk to me. *Say something.*"

Nothing.

He stood and walked over to the rough stone altar and gently laid his hand on the sword's hilt. As though he were holding a baby's arm, he pulled on the sword, as gently as he could.

It didn't move.

He pulled harder, harder; the light brightened, the sword vibrated.

Karl loosened his grip. Force wasn't the answer. Reason had to be.

Why would Arta Myrdhyn create or procure a sword that rendered its user immune to magical spells? What was such a sword good for? The answer was obvious: It was good for killing wizards. That was Arta Myrdhyn's intention.

Not all wizards, of course. Myrdhyn wouldn't go to all that trouble to wipe out his own kind; he wanted a specific wizard killed.

So. The sword had been left here for a purpose, and that purpose was for the right person to take it, to use to kill an enemy of Deighton's. That made sense.

But why would a wizard as powerful as Arta Myrdhyn need to do this in such a roundabout way? Why not just kill the wizard himself?

There was only one answer: Deighton wasn't sure that he could win, not in a fair fight.

Unsummoned, a vision of the Waste welled up. It had been lush green forest, until a battle between two wizards had scarred the land forever.

And the Shattered Islands lay across the northern part of the Cirric. Legend had it that they once were one island, one kingdom. But the name of that island had been lost.

Lost? That didn't make sense. There were records of *everything* in the Great Library of Pandathaway; knowledge couldn't be lost as long as the library stood. Unless . . .

Unless the name had been excised. Not just from paper, but from minds. And who could do that better than the grandmaster of Wizards' Guild?

Hypothesis: Deighton fought the grandmaster; their

battle created the waste and shattered the island.

And while Deighton wasn't killed, he had lost, and had either created or found the sword, brought some Vikings across to guard it, then fled to the Other Side.

And, eventually, brought us across.

That had to be connected. If this was truly part of his battle with the grandmaster, Karl and the rest being sent across had to be some sort of attack on his enemy.

Then why hadn't Karl been able to take the sword? If all that was true, then the sword should have practically jumped into his hand. All it had done was move a little.

Then I can't take the sword because, for some reason, I'm not the one who is supposed to kill the grandmaster. But I am somehow connected with the right one, or the sword wouldn't have twitched.

No! Deighton hadn't sent them across until the night Andy-Andy joined the group. That was what triggered it. "Connected with? As in 'the father of'?"

He rested his hand on the sword's hilt. "And if I were to agree to take this for the purpose of bringing it back to the valley, giving it to my son when he's ready—"

Black shapes flickered across the silvery blade, forming themselves into thick black letters.

Take Me.

Karl blinked. The letters were gone.

The ghostly fingers faded, then vanished; the sword clanged on the stone.

Quickly, he stopped to pick it up; the steel was blank, unmarred.

"Okay, Deighton, you've got yourself a deal." *There's going to be an accounting between you and me, one of these days.*

But, in the meantime, I'd damn well better work out how I'm going to use this.

CHAPTER SIXTEEN:
Blood Price

*The world breaks everyone and afterward many are
strong at the broken places. But those it cannot break
it kills. It kills the very good and the very gentle and
the very brave impartially. If you are none of these
you can be sure that it will kill you, but there will be
no special hurry.*

—Ernest Hemingway

Keeping all of himself except his eyes and nose below the
waterline, Karl clung with both hands to a half-sub-
merged boulder.

The sword, wrapped tightly in a blanket from the
cavern, was slung across his back with two strips Karl
had torn from another blanket.

Hiding in shadow, he kept motionless as the *Warthog*
passed, no more than two hundred feet away. At the
bow, the boy who looked like Ohlmin stood next to Ganness, one arm around the captain's shoulders in false
comradery, the other resting on a scabbarded dagger.

All over the ship, thirty, possibly forty strangers
worked in sailcloth tunics, never straying far from their
swords and bows.

So, that's the way they're playing it. All of Ganness'
crew had been replaced by slavers. Probably the crew
was chained below. More likely, they were held captive
in the slavers' own ship. Or, conceivably, they were
dead.

With excruciating slowness, the *Warthog* passed the
island. There was no lookout at the stern; Karl pushed off

the boulder and swam after the ship, struggling against the weight of the sword to keep his head above water.

The ship slowed still further; its huge jib luffed, flapping in the wind, while crewmen doused the mainsail. But they didn't bring the ship about or drop the anchor; the *Warthog* drifted in toward the sandy shore.

So that was the plan: The slavers would ground the ship just as though this were a normal trading session. Then wait until enough of the men of Clan Erik came down to the beach to load the cargo, charge shoreward through the shallow water, and attack the unprepared Mel.

Let's see if I can put a few holes in that plan.

It would have been nice to have Walter Slovotsky around; Walter could have figured out some way to get aboard without alerting anyone, then taken out half the slavers before anyone realized there was an intruder among them.

Hell, Walter would probably have been able to steal all their pouches, file their swords down to blunt harmlessness, then tie all the slavers' sandal laces together without being spotted.

Karl would have to confront all of them, take out the wizard quickly, then do his best to hold on until help arrived.

And that just plain sucks. Too much had to go right. It would work just fine, *if* Karl could take out the slavers' wizard quickly, *if* he wasn't too tired to hold off a score of slavers, *if* the Eriksens arrived quickly enough.

Too damn many ifs.

He gave a mental shrug. *I'm no Walter Slovotsky, but let's see if I can do a bit of Walter-style recon.*

He reached the stern of the *Warthog* and clung desperately to the massive rudder, his breath coming in gasps. His back and thighs ached terribly; the tendons in his shoulder felt like hot wires. Swimming with the sword on his back had taken more out of him than he had thought.

The rudder was slippery, overgrown with some sort of slimy green fungus. The ship's railing and deck loomed a full ten feet over his head. It might as well have been a mile. There was nothing to grip; even rested, he wouldn't be able to pull himself up by his fingernails.

But halfway up the blunt stern was Ganness' cabin. In the *Warthog's* long-ago better days, the captain's cabin had been a light, airy place, the light and air provided by a large sliding porthole made up of glass squares. Or was it a window? Didn't something have to be round to be called a porthole?

The glass had long since broken, and the window was covered by boards, but the window sash might still slide, if he could get a grip on it without stabbing himself on the points of the rusted nails that held the boards in place.

Panting from the exertion, Karl pulled himself up onto the rudder and rose shakily to his feet, balancing precariously, his hands resting on the splintered wood of the windowsill.

He tried to slide the boarded-up window to one side.

It didn't move. Years and years of the wood swelling and contracting in the hot sun and cool spray had welded the window in place.

If he pushed harder, he'd likely lose his footing and splash back into the water. Either that, or his hands would slip and open themselves up on the nails.

The nails—of course! His balance growing even more hazardous, he reached over his shoulder and unslung the sword, then unwrapped it, dropping the blanket and strips of cloth into the water. He held the sword hilt-up.

Careful, now. And I'd better pray that there's nobody inside the cabin. Using the pommel like a hammer, he tapped lightly against the point of a nail, flattening it. It didn't make much sound; no one on the *Warthog* would be able to hear it over the whispering of the wind and the quiet murmur of the waves.

His free hand held flat against the wood to dampen the vibration, he hit the flattened nail harder, driving it back through the wood.

The second nail took less time; the third, only a few seconds.

Soon, he pried the board away, dropped it carefully into the cabin, and went to work on the second board. Within a few minutes, he had cleared an opening large enough to accommodate his head and shoulders.

The slavers were using the cabin as a storeroom; it was piled high with muslin sacks, rough wool blankets, cases of winebottles, and chains.

Karl slid the sword into the cabin and followed it in.

For a moment, he lay gasping on the floor. *No time. Can't afford this.* He rose to his hands and knees, then crawled to the cabin's door, putting his ear to the rough wood. No sound. Good; that meant that the slavers were all on deck.

Using a rough blanket to towel himself off, he took a quick look around the room. Over in a corner was his own rucksack. He opened it and drew out his spare sandals and breechclout, quickly donning them before picking up the sword. *I always feel better when I'm dressed, and a fight is no time to worry about splinters.*

But there was no armor in the room. That was bad; tired as he was, he could easily miss a parry. This was one time that he would have liked to have his boiled-leather armor, no matter how uncomfortable it was over bare skin.

As he moved again toward the door, a familiar-looking brass bottle under a bunk caught his eye. Propping the sword against the bunk, he stooped to examine the bottle, and found that there were eight other, similar ones, all marked with the sign of the Healing Hand.

Healing draughts. Thank God. He uncorked a bottle and drank deeply, then splashed the rest of the bottle on his face and shoulders. The sweet, cool liquid washed away his muscle aches and exhaustion as though they never had been.

Reclaiming the sword, he straightened. *Good. My chances of getting out of this alive have just gone way up.* He tucked another bottle of healing draughts under his arm. It might come in handy.

Next to the stacked bottles of healing draughts were five other brass bottles. These were plain, unengraved.

He unstoppered one and sniffed. Lamp oil. Not necessarily any use, but—

I'm still stalling, he thought, suddenly aware that the dampness on his palms hadn't been caused by either the splashed healing draughts or the water of the Cirric. *I'd better get to it.*

Both of them standing aft of the forward mast, Ahrmin smiled genially at Thyren. The wizard looked silly in a sailcloth tunic, but Ahrmin wasn't about to tell him that.

"Have you spotted their wizard yet?" Ahrmin asked, as he stooped to check Ganness' bonds and gag, then rolled the captain through the open hatch, enjoying the thump and muffled groan as Ganness landed in the hold.

Thyren smirked. "Wizards."

"Wizards?"

Thyren closed his eyes. His forehead furrowed. "There's one on the beach." He opened his eyes. "And another, some distance away, beyond the treeline."

"Are you sure?"

"Yes. My inner sight sees their glow." He raised a palm. "But they can't see me; my own glow is damped. They won't be able to see it until it's too late. I *have* done this before, you know."

"Good." Ahrmin turned to glare at Lensius and Fihka. Lensius was fondling a hooknet, while Fihka had taken his bolas from the rack beneath the mainmast. "Put those *down*," he hissed. "We don't show any weapons until we're ready."

"And when will that be?" Lensius muttered.

"When enough of them gather on the beach." A simple plan, but a good one: The crossbows would kill twenty or thirty of the Mel men, cutting the locals' ability to defend themselves down to almost nothing. That, and the element of surprise, would make it easy to gather up scores of women and children.

The nice part of it was that once Thyren had killed the Mel wizards and Ahrmin's men had gotten down to work, Ahrmin would be able to take Thyren and a few others out in search of Karl Cullinane, leaving the rest of his men to the boring task of chasing down the Mel.

Thyren waved a hand at Ahrmin's pouch. "Best to see where Cullinane is."

Ahrmin shrugged. The last sighting he had taken before they had steered around the tiny island, had shown that Cullinane was in the direction of the Mel village. Since he wasn't on the beach, he was probably up at the village.

Resting comfortably, I hope. It will be the last time you will ever be comfortable, Karl Cullinane. I've put away four bottles of healing draughts, so that I can keep you alive on our trip back to Pandathaway, while I amuse myself with you. I have to deliver you unmarked to Wenthall, but that doesn't mean I can't spend hours cutting you open, then healing you up.

"Take a sighting," Thyren repeated. "If he's within range, I'll put him to sleep before I deal with the Mel wizards. That way, he won't have the chance to run."

Ahrmin sneered. "Run? And abandon his friends? Leave slavers alive behind him?" He turned to Lensius. "Now, if you please."

Lensius smiled, and beckoned to the milling throng on deck. With merry whoops, all except five of the slavers vaulted over the side and charged toward the beach.

Thyren caught Ahrmin's arm. *"Take a sighting."*

Ahrmin shrugged and reached for his pouch. "Since

you insist . . ." He pulled the glass sphere from his pouch and unwrapped the soft leathers that covered it. "Although we don't have to—"

His breath caught in his throat. Bobbing in the yellow oil, the dismembered finger pointed straight down.

"Ganness!" Karl hissed, pulling the other away from the light streaming down through the hatch. When both of them were safely in shadow, Karl shook the captain's shoulder with one hand while he wielded the sword with the other, slicing through the ropes that tied Ganness' hands behind his back.

His face ashen, Ganness shook his head. His eyes cleared. "Cullinane, they want you."

"Shh. Drink this." Karl unstoppered the bottle of healing draughts, then forced the mouth of the bottle between Ganness' lips. Immediately, color started to return to Ganness' face. "You'd better get out of here. Things are going to get very nasty in just—"

"Greetings, Karl Cullinane." A familiar face leaned out over the edge of the hatch. "Please don't move a muscle." Four crossbowmen looked down at him, their bows cocked, the bolts pointing directly toward his heart. "I've been waiting to meet you. If you'll be kind enough to stay where you are, I'll be down in a moment."

There was no doubt in Karl's mind that Ahira was right: The face was Ohlmin's, only younger, smoother. Perhaps the eyes were a bit sharper, maybe the smile was a trifle more cruel, but that was all.

Another man joined the five above. "Don't be foolish. Let me put him to sleep. Then you can chain him at your leisure."

The boy shrugged. "Very well."

The other raised his hands and began to mutter harsh words that were forgotten as soon as they were heard.

Ganness' eyes sagged shut, but Karl only felt a momentary faintness.

He held the sword tighter, while the wizard paled.

"*It's not working,*" the wizard shrilled. "Something's interfering with—"

Karl didn't wait for the wizard to finish; he dove for the companionway, bolts thudding into the deck behind him. He ducked through a door, and looked around while feet pounded on the deck above him.

There was no way out. They would have the aft hatch covered before he could get to it.

The captain's cabin, the way I came in. He ran to the cabin, slammed the door behind him, and threw the bolt.

On the other side of the door, voices shouted, feet thudded. *I can dive out through there, and—*no. If the slavers' wizard hadn't already taken out Wohtansen, he would be doing that at any moment. There just wasn't time to get off the ship and then warn Wohtansen to get away.

I'll have to take them out quickly, then get to the wizard. It's either that or make them come to me. His eye fell on the bottles of lamp oil next to the healing draughts.

I've got to try it. As hard blows shook the door, he uncorked all except one of the bottles of oil, then slathered their contents around the room, soaking himself with the lamp oil in the process. He lunged for his knapsack, jerked it open, then extracted a piece of flint before dropping the knapsack and opening a bottle of healing draughts.

The pounding grew louder.

Another few seconds and they'll be inside. A quick hefty swig of the sweet liquid for luck, then he poured the rest of the bottle over his head, careful to keep both sword and flint dry. He made sure that the healing draughts covered him from head to toe, then tossed the empty bottle aside before opening another, putting it to his lips, and draining it.

He uncorked the last bottle of lamp oil and held it in his left hand. A quick thrust to the oil-wetted wood stuck the sword into the wall beside the door. He coated most of the sword with the oil, then dropped the empty bottle to the floor.

He retrieved another bottle of healing draughts, and waited, while the slavers pounded against the door.

The wood held solid, but the bolt began to give, protesting the punishment with the squeal of metal strained beyond its limits.

As the door crashed inward, Karl took a deep breath and stroked the flint along the sword's length.

One spark caught the oil.

The cabin burst into flame.

Fire seared him; his skin crackled in the flames, the pain taking his breath away. But he healed instantly, only to be burned again.

The fire burned brighter, hotter. As the flames seared his eyeballs, Karl screamed, jamming his eyelids shut.

He smashed a bearded face with the bottle of healing draughts, then jerked the sword from the wall and swung one-handed, slicing through a slaver's neck.

A lancing pain shot through his belly accompanied by the cool slickness of a steel blade; Karl fell back, batting the blade away. He switched grips and threw the sword like a javelin, driving it into a slaver's chest to its brass quillons.

Another hand fastened on his bottle of healing draughts.

No. The bottle was Karl's only chance to come out of this alive. He bit the other's hand, his teeth rending muscle and tendons, a rush of salty blood filling his mouth.

The pain stopped as his wound healed, but the fire still roared, still burned him. Karl reached out with his free hand and caught hold of a slaver's ear. While the slaver screamed, Karl brought his hand down and his knee up, the man's face shattering against his knee like a bagful of eggs.

Screams still filled his ears, but now they were only his

screams. Karl staggered through the shattered door and into the companionway beyond, his whole body on fire.

His right hand fumbled at the bottle's cork, but he couldn't control his fingers. He brought the cork to his mouth, clamped his teeth on it, and jerked it loose.

As he drank the sweet healing draughts, he inhaled some of the fluid. Doubled over in a coughing spasm, he splashed the healing draughts over his body, making sure to get some into his eyes.

The pain receded. He opened his eyes. At first, his vision was cloudy; it was as if he had opened his eyes underwater.

Then his vision cleared. He poured some of the healing draughts onto the smoldering spots of his breechclout, feeling the burns on his thighs and buttocks subside.

The pain was gone. Tossing the empty bottle aside, he let out his breath, then sucked in sweet, fresh air. Behind him, the fire was spreading beyond the cabin. Through the wall of flame he could see unmoving bodies, scattered across the room, crackling in the flame.

Beside him in the companionway, a dead slaver sat against a bulkhead, propped up by the sword stuck through his chest, unseeing eyes staring up as Karl jerked the sword from the body.

The stench of burning flesh filled his nostrils. He gagged, stumbling back through the companionway.

Ganness lay unmoving on the deck.

"Ganness." Karl slapped Ganness' face lightly, then harder. *"Wake up."*

Ganness' eyelids fluttered, then snapped open. He grabbed at Karl's arm.

"Ganness, the ship's burning. Get over the side. Quickly, now."

"My ship—"

"Your life—move." Karl jerked Ganness to his feet, then pushed him toward the companionway. "Get out through the rear hatch; I've got to get to the wizard."

Karl ran to the forward ladder, then climbed it, his

feet touching every other rung. He broke through into daylight.

On the beach, a battle raged.

No time for this. Where's—

At the bow of the *Warthog*, the wizard stood, wind whipping through his hair, rippling his tunic, as he raised his hands over his head, murmuring words that Karl couldn't make out.

Lightning crackled from the wizard's fingers, the sun-bright bolts shooting shoreward.

"*Wizard!* Try me!"

The wizard turned, his sweaty face going ashen as his eyes widened. "Karl Cullinane. *Wait.*" He raised his hands. "Please don't. We can talk—"

Karl took a step forward.

The wizard murmured another spell. Again, lightning crackled from his fingertips, streaking across the few feet that separated Karl and the wizard.

Inches from Karl's chest, the lightning shattered into a stream of sparks that flowed around him, never touching him.

Karl took another step.

"The *sword*—it's the sword of Arta Myrdhyn."

"A sword made to kill wizards."

And another step.

Again, the wizard threw up his hands. "*Wait.* I surrender to you. There's much I can do for you, Karl Cullinane, much I can tell you. Wait, please."

Karl stopped three feet away and lowered the point of the sword.

The wizard relaxed momentarily, a relieved smile spreading across his face.

Karl returned the smile, then slashed. Once.

The smile was still on both of their faces as the wizard's head rolled across the deck and splashed overboard, leaving his body behind to twitch in a pool of blood for a moment, and then lie still.

On the beach, the battle stopped. Slavers and Mel alike

staggered, then dropped to their knees, and to their bellies, unconscious.

Except for one man. Seigar Wohtansen stood at the waterline and lowered his arms. The sand around him was dotted with smoldering black patches.

He sprinted across the sand to the nearest Mel man and kicked him awake, holding a hand across the man's mouth to prevent him from crying out. "Quickly, before they wake." Roughly, the Mel woke another of his fellows, and then another, until all the Mel men stood among the sleeping bodies of the slavers.

And slowly, cold-bloodedly, they picked up swords and knives, cutting the slavers' throats as they slept.

Karl shuddered, but the roar of the fire behind him suggested that the *Warthog* wasn't the place to be right now; he levered himself over the side and dropped into the water, wading toward shore.

As he reached the beach, Wohtansen ran up. "This way—some got by us. Going up toward the village."

They ran up the path, under the overhanging branches. "Just put them all to sleep," Karl said, panting as he ran.

Wohtansen shook his head. "Can't. All out of . . . spells."

Scattered across the trail ahead, the pieces of several dead slavers lay, already covered with a blanket of flies. Karl nodded to himself as he leaped over a part of a leg. Looked like Ahira's handiwork; nothing but a battleaxe could dismember someone so thoroughly.

That boded well.

A break in the trees loomed ahead. Through it, Karl could see the tops of Mel lodges.

Karl picked up the pace, leaving Wohtansen behind.

The lodges of the village were set in a wide circle, surrounding a grassy common area, cleared patches with grids and stones for cooking fires on the near side, water vats on the far side.

Thirty or forty bodies littered the green. Slavers and Mel men, women, and children lay across the grass, some dead, some moaning from their wounds.

But the battle wasn't over. Tennetty parried a slaver's thrust, then lunged in perfect extension, spitting him on her sword. She jerked the sword out and turned to help Chak with his opponent.

A few yards away from Tennetty and Chak, Ahira ducked under his enemy's swing, then swung his battle-axe. The axe didn't slow as it cut through the slaver's torso.

But Rahff was in trouble. Karl ran toward the boy, hoping he'd make it in time, knowing that he wouldn't.

Rahff stood between Aeia and a tall, long-haired swordsman. The boy's bloody left arm hung uselessly; a long, bloody gash ran from elbow to shoulder.

The swordsman beat Rahff's blade aside and slashed.

Rahff screamed. His belly opened like an overripe fruit.

Karl was only a few yards away; he dropped the sword and leaped, his arms outstretched.

As the slaver pulled back his sword for a final thrust, Karl landed on him, bowling him over. Before the slaver could bring his sword into play, Karl grabbed the man's head and twisted, neckbones snapping like pencils.

He pounded the slaver's face with his fists, not knowing if the man was already dead, not caring.

"Karl." The dwarf's face was inches away from his. Ahira gripped Karl's hands. "Rahff's *alive*. He needs help."

Karl turned. The boy lay sprawled on the grass, his head cradled on Aeia's lap, his hands clawing at his wounds, trying to hold his belly closed.

"*Tennetty*," Karl snapped. "Find my horse—healing draughts in the saddlebags."

"On my way," she called back, her voice already fading in the distance.

Rahff's arm was badly gashed; a long, deep cut ran

from the elbow almost to the shoulder. His whole left side and much of the ground underneath it was soaked with dark blood.

Rahff smiled weakly, trying to raise his head. "Karl, you're alive," he said, his voice weak. "I told them you would be."

"Shh. Just lie there." Karl ripped a strip of cloth from his breechclout and slipped it around the upper part of Rahff's left arm. He tied a quick slipknot, then pulled it as tight as he could. That would keep him from bleeding to death from that wound. But what about the belly?

There was nothing he could do. Direct pressure would just spread the boy's intestines all over the meadow; there was no way to clamp all the bleeding veins and arteries shut.

Just a few minutes. That's all he needs. Just a few minutes. Tennetty would be back with the healing draughts and then—

"Chak, Wohtansen's somewhere around. He should know where the Eriksens keep their healing draughts."

Without a word, Chak ran off.

Rahff coughed; a blood-flecked foam spewed from his lips. "Aeia's fine, Karl. I took care of her. Just as you said we were supposed to."

"Shut up, apprentice." Karl forced a smile to his face. "If you'll just keep still for a moment, Tennetty or Chak will be back with a bottle, and we'll fix you right up."

"I did right, didn't I? She's fine, isn't she?" He looked up at Karl as though Aeia weren't there.

"She's just fine, Rahff. Shh."

Ahira laid a hand on Karl's shoulder. "The boy was overmatched. That slaver went for Aeia, and Rahff couldn't wait for me to finish off mine."

"How the *hell* did they get by you?" Karl snarled. "I told Wohtansen to tell you to hide on the path."

Ahira shrugged. "Just too many of them. Six of them engaged Chak, Tennetty, and me, while the others ran past. By the time we killed ours off and got up to the village . . ." He shook his head. "They went crazy, Karl. Most of them didn't bother trying to capture anyone, they just started hacking. Mainly trying to wound the Mel, it seemed. I guess they figured we'd be so busy treating the injured that we wouldn't have time to chase after them. A lot of them got away, Karl. After they had their fill of killing."

Their fill of killing. They're going to learn what a fill of killing is. "Just take it easy, Rahff. Just another moment or two."

Rahff's hand gripped Karl's. "I'm not going to die, am I?"

" 'Course not." *Hurry up, Tennetty, Chak. Hurry. He doesn't have much time.* "Ahira, find the Eriksen wizard. Maybe he knows—"

The dwarf shook his head. "Pile of cinders; the slavers' wizard got a flame spell through to him."

Rahff's breathing was becoming more shallow. Karl laid a finger on the boy's good wrist. His pulse was rapid, thready.

Come on, *Tennetty.*

At a cry of pain, Karl looked up. Coming around from behind a hut, Chak ran toward him, an uncorked brass bottle cradled in his arms.

White-lipped, he knelt beside Karl, pouring the liquid into the boy's open belly.

The healing draughts pooled amid the blood and the gore.

It's not working. Karl slipped a hand behind Rahff's head, prying the jaw open with his other hand so Chak could pour healing draughts into the boy's mouth.

It puddled in Rahff's mouth. The overflow ran down the boy's cheek and onto Aeia's lap.

Chak lowered the bottle. "He's dead, Karl. It won't do him any good."

"Keep pouring." Gripping Rahff's arm tightly, Karl couldn't feel a pulse. He slipped a finger to the boy's throat.

Nothing.

Karl spread the fingers of his left hand across Rahff's chest, and pounded the back of that hand with his fist, all the while cursing himself for never having taken a CPR course.

Live, damn you, live. "I said to keep pouring. Drip some on his arm." He put his mouth over the boy's, pinched Rahff's nostrils with his left hand, and breathed in. And again, and again, and again . . .

He became aware that Ahira was shaking him. "Let him go, Karl. Let him go. He's dead." The dwarf gathered Karl's hands in his and pulled him away.

The boy's head fell back, limp. Glazed, vacant eyes stared blankly up at Karl. Slowly, Chak knelt down and closed Rahff's eyes.

A drop fell on Rahff's face, then another. Aeia wept soundlessly, her tears running down her cheeks and falling onto Rahff.

Karl rose and led Aeia away from the body. At Chak's low moan, he noticed for the first time that the little man was clutching the side of his waist. A bloodstain the size of a dinner plate spread out across Chak's sarong.

"Drink some," Karl said quietly, motioning toward the bottle. "Then give the rest to the wounded. And give them whatever Tennetty comes back with, if it's needed."

"Fine." Chak raised the bottle to his lips, then poured some of the healing draughts into his own wound.

The wound closed immediately. Visibly getting stronger, Chak gripped his falchion. "Can I kill Wohtansen, or do you want to?"

Karl jerked around. *"What?"*

"I'd better show you. Take that sword. You'll be wanting it."

Karl walked over to where the sword lay and stooped to pick it up. "Aeia, go find Tennetty."

"No. I want to stay with you." She clung to him, her

tears wet against his side. "But what about Rahff?"

Ahira sighed. "I'll take care of him."

"There's . . . no rush, Aeia." He blinked back the tears. "It doesn't hurt him anymore." He turned to Chak. "Take me to Wohtansen."

Behind a hut, Wohtansen was ministering to a wounded woman, pouring healing draughts down her throat and into a deep gash in her belly.

"Tell me," Karl said.

Chak spat. "He found *two* bottles of the stuff, but he couldn't be bothered to bring one for Rahff. I had to pry it from his fingers."

Karl stood over Wohtansen and spoke quietly. "Stand up, you bastard."

Wohtansen didn't glance up. "I'll speak to you in a moment."

Karl reached out a hand and lifted Wohtansen by the hair, dropping the sword so that he could slap the Mel's face with his free hand.

In the back of his mind he realized that hitting a clan wizard and war leader might possibly trigger an attack by the remaining Mel; certainly it would make Karl *persona non grata* throughout Melawei.

But he didn't care.

"Why didn't you bring it over there? We could have saved him," he shouted, punctuating every word with a slap. "Why didn't you—" He caught himself, letting Wohtansen's limp form drop to the ground.

Chak felt at Wohtansen's neck. "He's still alive." Laying the edge of his blade against the Mel's neck, he looked up at Karl. "Should I fix that?"

"You leave him alone!" The Mel woman shrilled up at Karl. "That boy was a stranger. Not one of ours."

Aeia launched herself at the woman, pounding her little fists into the woman's face until Karl pulled her off. "Come on, Aeia, let's go."

They gathered on the beach, half a mile away from the

sands where the bodies lay. Off in the distance, the *Warthog* still burned, sending sparks and cinders shooting hundreds of feet into the night sky.

A few yards from where they sat, Rahff's body lay, wrapped in a blanket.

I won't have him buried in Melawei soil. I won't have his body polluted that way. Rahff would be buried in the Cirric. Not here.

Karl looked from face to face. All were grim, although Tennetty's expression was a mix of satisfaction and frustration. Karl could understand the first; after all, she'd gotten her quota of slavers. But the frustration?

"Tennetty? What is it?"

She shook her head, her straight hair whipping around her face. "I can't find him. The one that killed Fialt. I've looked at all the bodies, but . . ." She pounded her fist on the sand. "He got *away*."

"No, he didn't." Karl waved a hand at the burning wreck. "The one who killed Fialt was the leader, right? Black hair, thin smile—"

In light from the burning ship, a smile flickered across her sweat-shiny face. "You killed him?"

"Yes. He and some of his friends trapped me in Ganness' cabin. So they thought."

She looked at him for a long moment, her face blank, unreadable. Then: "Thank you, Karl." She gripped his hand in both of hers for just a moment, then dropped his hand and turned away. She walked a few yards, then stopped, watching the burning wreck.

Aeia stared down at a spot in front of her, picking up sand and letting it dribble through her fingers. Soundlessly, she rose, walked over to the pile of driftwood where Carrot and Pirate stood hitched, and stroked Carrot's face. The horse snorted, then nuzzled her.

Karl walked over and stood beside her. "You're going to miss Carrot, eh?"

"No." Carrot lowered her head. Aeia put her cheek against the horse's neck. "I can't. I can't stay here."

He stroked her shoulder. "They didn't understand about Rahff. They didn't know he was your friend." His words sounded false, even in his own ears. But he couldn't try to push her into leaving home.

"No. They just didn't *care*. I . . ." her voice trailed off into sobs. Aeia turned and threw her arms around Karl, burying her face against him. Tears wet his side.

"Go talk it over with your parents, with your people. If you want to come with us, you can." He ran his fingers through her hair. "You know that."

"No. I won't talk with them. They let Rahff die. I want to go with you."

"Think it over."

"But—"

He pried her arms away. "Just think it over." He turned and walked back to the others.

Ganness sprawled on the sand, visibly relieved to be alive. In a while, he'd once again start regretting the loss of his ship. But it wouldn't hurt him as much as losing the *Ganness' Pride* had.

Chak had been through all this before. Just another day in the life of a soldier of fortune.

Sure.

"Ahira?"

The dwarf looked up at him, not saying a word.

"What the hell do we do?"

Ahira shrugged. "I think it's time we go home. At least for now."

"I know. It's just that I wish . . ."

"But you wish this victory had been bloodless, at least for our side. And you wish that Wohtansen had had as much concern for one of us as for one of his own. And you wish that the world were a fine and simple place, where every problem you can't solve with your head you can solve with one simple blow from your sword. Right?"

Ahira shook his head. "Doesn't work that way, Karl." Ahira pushed the hilt of his battleaxe into the sand and scooped up handfuls to scour the congealed blood from its head. "Just doesn't work that way. You're trying to start a revolution; one that will shake this whole damn world, turn it upside down. Didn't Thoreau say something about revolutions not being hatched in a soft-boiled egg?

"Before we're done, rivers of blood will flow. And not just the blood of slavers, either. A lot of good people are going to die, and die horribly. That's a fact, Karl. Yes?"

Karl nodded. "Yes."

Ahira sat silently for so long that Karl thought the dwarf was finished.

Just as Karl was about to speak, Ahira shook his head. "Karl, what it really comes down to is whether you think the end justifies the means." Ahira chuckled. "Sounds hideous, doesn't it?"

"It does, at that." Still, Ahira was right. The world was not full of nice, clean, easy choices. And wishing that it was would never make it so.

The battleaxe now clean, the dwarf rose to his feet and strapped the axe to his chest.

He flexed his hands, then finger-combed his hair. "You asked where we go from here. I think we take off and walk back toward Clan Wohtan. Ganness says the slavers' ship is there, with only a skeleton guard. We'll take the ship, kill the slavers, and free the Mel and Ganness' crew. Then we can give Ganness the ship—"

"We do owe him a ship."

"Two, actually. We'll have him drop us off as close to the Pandathaway-Metreyll road as he can. We buy a few more horses, and ride back to the valley."

Chak joined them. "Except for losing Rahff, we haven't done too badly here. The wizards lost one of their own; maybe they won't be so eager to send guild members along on slaving raids into Melawei."

To hell with that. Who cares if—He caught himself. So the Mel weren't all nice people. Did that make it okay to clap collars around their necks?

Aeia clutched at his hand. "I'm coming with you. I won't stay here."

Tennetty pulled her away. "Nobody will make you stay here." She patted the hilt of her sword. "I swear it."

"But what do we do about Rahff?" Aeia shrilled.

There wasn't any answer to that. Killing Wohtansen wouldn't change it. Rahff was dead, and he'd stay dead. Like Jason Parker, like Fialt.

And probably like me, before this is all over. He stopped and picked up his own sword, belting it around his waist. He gripped the sharkskin hilt for a moment. It felt good, comfortable, familiar in his hand. "Ganness, you sure that the slavers don't have another wizard with them?"

"Yes." Ganness nodded. "But why do you care? You have the sword."

Karl didn't answer. He lifted the sword of Arta Myrdhyn, holding it with both hands. The bright steel caught the flicker of the *Warthog*'s flames.

Once more, dark shapes moved across the blade, forming sharp letters. Keep me, they said.

No.

Karl walked to the edge of the beach, then into the Cirric until the water rose to his knees.

He held the sword over his head, the hilt clenched in both hands. *Okay, Deighton, you've got me to do your dirty work for you. I'll probably die with my blood pouring out of me, as Rahff did.*

"But not my son, Arta Myrdhyn. *Not my son.*"

He swung the sword over his head three times, then threw it with every ounce of strength he had left.

It tumbled end over end through the air; Karl turned back toward the beach, not caring where the sword fell.

Ahira's eyes were wide. "Look at that."

Karl turned back. Ghostly fingers of light reached out of the water and caught the sword, then pulled it underwater. A quick glimmering, and the sword was gone.

For now.

It doesn't matter if you keep the sword here for him. Karl shook his head. *Not my son.* "Okay, people, let's get going. We've got some traveling to do before we reach Clan Wohtan."

Chak nodded. "A couple days' travel, a quick fight, a day or so getting the pirate ship ready for sea, a tenday at sea, and quite a few more tenday's ride, and then we're home."

Tennetty shrugged. "Sounds easy to me."

PART FIVE:
Home

CHAPTER SEVENTEEN:
Jason

Home is where one starts from. As we grow older
The world becomes stranger, the pattern more
    complicated
Of dead and living. Not the intense moment
Isolated, with no before and after,
But a lifetime burning in every moment . . .

—T. S. Eliot

Tennetty kicked Pirate into a canter, coming even with Karl, then slowing her horse down to a walk.

Carrot whinnied, lifting her feet a bit higher as Karl rode her through the tall grasses.

"Easy, Carrot." He patted her neck, then glared at Tennetty. "Don't do that—she likes to be out in front."

She shrugged. It was possible that Tennetty could have cared less about something than she did about what Carrot wanted or didn't want, but only barely. "How long?"

Fine. On this trip, I didn't have Slovotsky asking "Are we there yet?" all the damn time. Instead, I've got Tennetty asking "How long is it going to be?" Three times in the morning, four in the afternoon, twice when we're sitting around the campfire in the evening. I could set my watch by her. If I had a watch.

It had taken a couple of weeks on the newly named *Ganness' Revenge* to arrive at the little fishing village of Hindeyll, then weeks of travel on the Pandathaway-

Metreyll road to get to the Waste, another month to skirt the Waste and cross into the outskirts of Therranj.

Of course, we could have cut out some time if we hadn't jumped those slavers near Wehnest. Backtracking to chase them down must have cost us a week. At least. Not a bad raid, though; it had added a sackful of coin, three horses, and another member to their party.

Peill was a nice addition to the group; Karl had never met anyone with such a talent for tracking as the elf.

He turned to see the tall elf riding next to Ahira's pony, Chak and Aeia on the dwarf's other side, while Ahira continued the English lesson.

Guess this stuff about elves and dwarves not getting along doesn't apply when the dwarf is the one who shatters the elf's chains.

Peill's skills with a longbow could come in handy, particularly if he could teach others to use it. The trouble with the crossbows was that their rate of fire was just too damn low, although they did have the advantage of greater accuracy.

But from ambush, a few good longbowmen might be able to finish off a group of slavers before they even knew that they were under attack.

Then again, it would be hard for a longbowman to conceal himself; a crossbowman could shoot while prone, or from a perch in a tree. . . .

Well, it was something to think about, anyway. Maybe talk over with Chak.

But I can do that later. We're almost home, and we all deserve a vacation.

"I asked you, 'How long?'" Tennetty glared at him. "If you're going deaf, you can damn well count me out of the next trip."

Perhaps twenty miles across the plain, the ground sloped upward into an area of blackened, burned ground. Beyond that, the valley lay.

"I figure we'll get there sometime tomorrow."

It was almost over. For now. But only for now.

Karl sighed. *I'm never going to be done with blood. Not until the day I die.*

Then again, if you don't learn to keep your eyes open while you're feeling sorry for yourself, that could be anytime now.

"Ellegon!" He scanned the sky. Nothing but clouds, and a few birds to the east. *Where are you?*

Try behind you.

Karl turned in the saddle; above and behind him, a familiar shape dropped out of the blue sky.

I usually come this way on the returning leg of my patrol, the dragon said.

Both Carrot and Pirate snorted and held their ground as the dragon landed; the other horses galloped away in different directions, their riders vainly trying to control the animals' panic.

Tennetty swore as she struggled with Pirate's reins. "Easy, now. Easy, damn you. The idiot dragon's just trying to scare you, not eat you."

Good to see you too, Tennetty.

"Try giving a little warning next time."

"*Cut the crap, both of you,*" Karl snapped. "Ellegon, how is Andy-Andy? And the baby?"

A gout of fire roared into the sky. *Took you long enough to ask.*

Don't play games with me, Ellegon.

Both your wife and son are fine.

My son. Karl shook his head. *If ever anyone wished for a daughter . . .* "You stay away from my son, Deighton," he whispered. "Just leave him alone."

Across the plain, Aeia and Chak had reined their horses down to a canter, while Ahira's and Peill's mounts still galloped away.

"Just as well," Tennetty said. "Might teach them all something about keeping their animals under control." She patted at Pirate's neck, then held out a hand to Karl. "Give me your reins."

"Huh?"

She jerked a thumb at the dragon. "I think you might be able to persuade Ellegon to give you a ride the rest of the way home. I'll gather the others together and bring them all in sometime tomorrow."

It was tempting, but . . . "I'd better stay." The group was Karl's responsibility, until they got home. He could relax then.

Idiot.

"Idiot," Tennetty echoed. She rolled her eyes, looking toward heaven for reassurance. "Ellegon, explain to Karl how his wife would feel about his being gone a day longer than necessary."

Well . . . I don't think Andrea would exactly appreciate it. She's been a bit worried; she was hoping you'd be back by now.

"You sure things are safe around here?"

I was just finishing my patrol, Karl. The dragon pawed at the grass. *Though you could be right, come to think of it. I smell a nest of rabbits somewhere around here; maybe your whole party will get eaten if you're not here to protect them. If it will make you happy, I'll be willing to fly back and baby-sit Ahira and the rest after I drop you off at home.*

"The reins, please." Tennetty snapped her fingers. "Get moving."

He laughed. "You win." He jumped from Carrot's saddle, tossing the reins to Tennetty. "See you tomorrow," he said, climbing up to Ellegon's back.

The dragon's wings began to beat, moving faster and faster until they were only a blur, whipping so much grass and dust into the air that Karl had to close his eyes.

Ellegon leaped skyward. *I've got strict instructions about where to set you down,* he said, as the ground dropped away beneath them.

As they passed over Chak and Aeia, Karl returned their waves. *Ellegon?*

Be quiet for a while; I'm going to put on some speed.

His wings began to work even faster, the wind drawing tears out of Karl's eyes.

Karl put his head to the dragon's rough hide and held on.

Almost home. The rush of wind slowed.

Karl raised his head. They were flying over what had been a burned rise leading to the valley. It had become even more green; soon, the evidence that a fire had once burned would be gone.

The valley spread out below. When Karl had left, the encampment had been one wooden wall, a stone fireplace, and two wagons.

There had been some changes. More than thirty log cabins spread out along the shore of the lake, several of them with split-rail corrals for horses and cattle.

Children scampered around a wooden dock that jutted out from the shore, pausing momentarily in their play to wave to Ellegon as the dragon passed overhead.

Where there had been only forest, there now were fields, stalks of corn, and seas of wheat waving in the breeze.

The fortifications had been completed; they now enclosed a group of five houses, one with a slow-turning waterwheel. Ellegon dove toward the bare-dirt courtyard, braking with his wings.

Mill?

Yes. Riccetti has done well, no?

No. You've all done well.

Deftly avoiding the network of hollowed half-logs that piped water to the five houses, the dragon landed inside the walls. Karl dismounted.

Welcome home.

To his right, a familiar face peeked out of an open-sided cabin whose chimney puffed smoke into the air. Walter Slovotsky, wearing a leather apron and carrying a smith's hammer, ran into the courtyard, dropping the hammer as he ran.

"Karl." Slovotsky stuck out a hand, drew it back, shaking his head. "To hell with it." He threw his arms around Karl.

"Dammit, you're breaking my back," Karl said, untangling himself.

Slovotsky chuckled. "Fat chance." He turned. *"Kirah!* They're—" He caught himself. "Is everyone—?"

"We lost Fialt, but the rest of us are fine." *Except for Rahff. I wish he'd gotten the chance to—*

Later, Karl, later. Homecoming is supposed to be a happiness.

You know a lot about happiness?

I'm learning, Karl. Walter, take him to her.

Slovotsky led Karl toward a cabin on the far side of the courtyard, talking nonstop as they walked. "I wish we'd known you were getting back today. Lou's taken a party to the far side of the valley. He found a cave full of bats a couple of months ago, and we're finally getting them all cleared out."

"Bats?" Karl removed his hand from the hilt of his sword. "Some sort of trouble?"

"No." Slovotsky laughed. "Just garden-variety fruit bats. They can give you a nasty bite, but Thellaren— he's our cleric—can fix you right up."

"Cleric?"

"Spidersect. Showed up one day, half starved; seems he had some trouble with the Therranji. Does one hell of a business, although Andy and I had to reason with him about rates. The bastard was charging—"

"Then why clear out the bats?"

Slovotsky smiled knowingly. "Think about it. What are bats good at making?"

"Baby bats, and bat sh—" *Of course.* Karl raised a hand. "Never mind. I take it you've found some sulfur, too."

"You got it. No willows around here. But oak seems to work okay."

Take the crystals of saltpeter from underneath any

well-aged pile of excrement, add sulfur and powdered charcoal in the right proportions, and *voila!*—gunpowder. Well, it was probably a bit trickier than that, but not much.

Maybe I'm not going to be needing longbows, after all.

"It was Riccetti's idea. He remembered reading that Cortez used bat guano to make gunpowder."

"I didn't know Lou was a historian."

"Only when it comes to making things." Slovotsky nodded. "He's already made some gunpowder—stinks to high heaven when it burns—and I'm working on a flintlock right now."

Slovotsky caught himself as they stopped in front of the cabin's door. "Later; we'll have plenty of time. She's in there, Karl." Slovotsky waved as he jogged off. "I'd better go see Kirah. We've been fattening a calf."

Karl opened the door and walked in.

The cabin was well kept, from the burnished wood of the floor to the ceiling timbers, hung with unlit oil lamps. A beaded curtain covered a doorway on the opposite wall.

On the right-hand wall, a rough table stood beneath a mottled glass window. On the left-hand wall, a pot of stew burbled merrily in the stone fireplace.

Two huge wooden chairs stood side by side in front of the fireplace, both with blankets padding their seats. The arms of one chair was stained with nicks and sweat marks; the other looked new, unused.

He unbuckled his sword and hung it over the back of the newer chair.

"Who is it?" She pushed through the curtain, a wicker basket filled with clothes in her arms. Her eyes grew wide. "Hi."

"Hello."

He wanted to reach out, to run to her, but he couldn't. There was an almost palpable distance between them. The months of separation had changed her, changed both of them.

Worry lines had begun to form around her eyes. Her hair was tangled, matted down. It wasn't just that she looked more than a few months older. Her smile was strained.

He could see her looking at the changes in his face, not sure that she liked what she saw.

There had been a time when Karl took the world lightly, even while he took it seriously. A time when he could push the darkness away, when he could dismiss it, if only for a while, not merely pretend that it didn't exist. There had been a time when Karl had been basically a gentle man, sometimes forced into doing violent things, but always, deep inside, untouched by the violence.

That time was gone. Forever. It could never be the same between them.

The thought cut at him like a knife.

"Andy, I—" He fumbled blindly for the words. For the right words, the ones that would make everything right between them.

He couldn't find them. Maybe they didn't even exist.

"*No*," she shrilled. She threw the basket aside and ran to him.

As he gathered her into his arms and buried his face in her hair, he knew that he was both right and wrong. Yes, there had been changes. No, things could never be the same.

But they could be better.

After a while, he took a loose sleeve of her robe, wiped first at his own eyes, and then at hers.

She looked up at him, her eyes still tearing, still red. "Karl?"

"Yes?" He ran his fingers through her hair.

"If," she said as she rested her face against his chest, "if you *ever* give me another look like that, I swear I'll hit you. Don't you—"

"Shh."

Stupid humans. Ellegon's massive head peeked

hrough the open door. He snorted, sending ashes from he fireplace swirling around the room.

Karl raised his head. *What is it now?*

"You always have to make things more complicated han necessary, don't you?"

"What are you getting at?"

"Tell her you love her, idiot."

She pushed away from him and smiled 'Yeah. Tell me ou love me, idiot." She grabbed his hand. "But later. 've got someone for you to meet."

She pulled him through the beaded curtain and into he bedroom.

Under the murky window, a cradle lay. It was a plain vood box, mounted on two wooden rockers.

He peered inside.

"Don't wake him," she whispered. "It's a pain to get im back to sleep."

The baby, wrapped in a gray cotton diaper, slept eacefully on the soft blankets. Karl reached out a hand nd gently touched the child's soft cheek. Still asleep, the aby turned his head to nuzzle Karl's fingers.

Karl pulled his hand back. "He's so . . . small."

"That's *your* opinion." She snorted. "He sure as hell idn't feel that way when I was flat on my back in labor. ut he'll grow."

"How old is he?"

"Just under two months." Andy-Andy slipped an arm round Karl's waist. "I named him Jason, after Jason 'arker. I hope that's okay; we didn't decide on a name efore you left, so . . ."

"The name's fine."

"I did good?"

"Andy, he's beautiful."

"He takes after his mother. Fortunately."

CHAPTER EIGHTEEN:
The Flickering Candle

*. . . the bravest are surely those who have the cleares[
vision of what is before them, glory and danger alike
and yet notwithstanding go out to meet it.*

—Thucydide[

Walter Slovotsky walked quietly around the bonfire an[
tapped him on the shoulder. "Karl, take a walk wit[
me," he said, his voice slurred. He snagged a bottle fror[
one of the merrymakers, bowing an exaggerated apology[

Andy-Andy leaned over and whispered in Karl's ea[
"He's drunk again."

"I noticed. Has this been happening a lot?"

"Yes." She nodded. "Ever since Kirah started to show[
But I don't think it's just the expectant father jitters[
Maybe you should go see what's wrong. I haven't bee[
able to get him to talk about it. Neither has Kirah." Sh[
cast a glance across the clearing. "And I'd better go chec[
on the baby."

He chuckled. "Between Ellegon and Aeia, I'm sure he[
okay." Ellegon had told him that there were bears an[
pumas up in the mountains. Probably the animals woul[
continue to avoid the village.

But if they didn't, Ellegon could always fit an odd bea[
or puma into his diet.

"Still . . ."

"Okay. See you later."

"Not too much later, I hope. Kirah's going to keep Aei[

and Jason tonight. No interruptions." Her eyes smiled a promise at him.

Karl rose and followed Walter off into the dark, leaving the bonfire behind them. The welcome-home party was in its twelfth or thirteenth hour, but it hadn't let up. Some of the revelers kept the music going with their flutes and drums; others loitered around the cooking fire, slicing off sizzling pieces of roast calf from the slowly turning spit.

Tennetty, Chak, Peill, and Ahira looked road-weary, having arrived only that morning. Still, the four of them held court, a few dozen meters from the fire, standing in a circle of fifty listeners, taking turns relating the story of Karl Cullinane on the *Warthog*.

Six of the listeners drew Karl's attention. A group of battle-scarred men, they listened raptly, occasionally interrupting Tennetty or Chak to press for more details. Karl had been introduced to them, but had forgotten their names. But he hadn't forgotten the fact that they were former mercenaries, now engaged in the profession of taking on slavers.

Which means, he thought, *that the whole world doesn't rest on my shoulders anymore.*

And it also means I'm becoming a legend, he thought, and smiled. *Probably have more volunteers than I can use, next time.* He sobered. That possibility might have its pluses, but it sure as hell had its minuses.

As they walked, Slovotsky passed him the clay bottle; Karl took another swig of the tannic wine that already had his head spinning.

The fire and sound far enough behind them, Karl seated himself on a projecting root of an old oak, gesturing at Slovotsky to join him. "What's bothering you?"

"Me?" Slovotsky snorted. He tilted back the bottle and drank deeply. "Nothing's bothering me, Karl. Not a damn thing." Slovotsky was silent for a while. Then: "How soon are you planning on going out again?"

"Eager to get rid of me?"

"How about an answer?"

"Mmm, I don't want to leave too soon. Maybe si
months or so. I suspect it'll take Pandathaway a while t
put another team together. If they don't just write of
killing me as a lost cause."

Karl folded his hands behind his head and leaned bac
against the bulk of the trees. "Besides, I think that th
Slavers' Guild is going to be a bit too busy to go lookin
for me." He closed his eyes. "How many people have w
got here?"

"Just over two hundred, as of the last census. Seems t
grow every day, practically. But it's not going to get an
easier: The size of the slavers' caravans keeps growing
They're running scared, Karl. Which isn't good; I'
rather have them fat and self-satisfied."

Karl shrugged. "So we'll take bigger raiding parties.

If this scheme of Riccetti's to make some rifles panne
out, he might not need a much larger team. Granted, th
manufacture of cartridges was probably decades away
but even a few flintlocks and blunderbusses would giv
them a huge edge.

"Think it through, Karl. Think it through."

He opened his eyes to see Slovotsky shaking his heac
Karl grabbed his arm. "What the hell is bothering you?

"Take a look at the silo?"

"No, but what does that have to do with anything?"

"It has to do with *everything*. We're getting a dam
fine yield for the acreage. Better than any of the loca
have ever seen. And this is just the first real harvest. Wa
until next year."

"This is doom?"

"Yup. Free societies . . ." Walter interrupted himself
down the last of the wine. He flipped the bottle end ov
end, then caught it by the neck, setting it carefully on tl
ground. "Free societies *produce*. You should see ho
hard these poor bastards work, once they understand th
what they grow or make is theirs."

"Didn't Riccetti say something about taxes?"

"Sure." Slovotsky shrugged. "Two percent of production or income, payable to the town treasurer—that's me, for now. We've been using it to sponsor public works like the mill, pay Riccetti and your wife for running the school, grubstake new arrivals. Matter of fact, I'm going to have to assess what you've brought back. Quite a bit of gold and platinum, no?"

"A bit. Just net, right?" Idly, he wondered what the tax on the sword of Arta Myrdhyn would have been.

"Net. No tax on what you make and spend outside. Only what you bring back, or make here. Keeps things simpler. But can we leave all that for tomorrow?"

"Sure. But would you just come out and tell me what the hell has got you running scared?"

"Running scared is right." Slovotsky snorted. "You still don't see it, do you? Free societies produce more than slave societies. Always have, always will. Right?"

"Right. So?"

"*So*, that means we're going to continue to flourish and grow. *So*, eventually we're going to attract some notice. *So*, when we do, some bright baron or prince or lord is going to work out that we just might overflow this valley and spread out, and eventually, challenge his power." He shook his head. "*So* . . . how long do you think that the slave societies are going to let us get away with it? A year, almost certainly. Five, probably; ten, possibly; twenty, maybe. But not forever, Karl. Not forever."

Dammit, but that made sense. The only reason they had gone unmolested so far was the small size and remote location of their colony.

"*So*," Walter went on, "we're in a race. We have to grow large enough, strong enough, quick enough, so that we can take on all comers. Or . . ."

"Or? You've got an alternative?"

"Or your kid and mine grow up as orphans. If they're lucky. We're going to have to keep our wives pregnant all the time, rescue and arm as many slaves as we can, and work our butts off to have a chance at winning the race.

Any chance at all." Slovotsky smiled in the dark. "Let me ask you again: How soon are you planning on going out again?"

Karl sighed. "Give me ten days." *Dammit.* "I need to spend some time with Andy."

Slovotsky echoed his sigh. "Take twenty. I'd better break in a new treasurer, and I've got some smithing to finish before we go."

"We?"

"We. Slovotsky's Law Number Forty-three: 'Thou shalt put thy money where is thy mouth.' " He rose and held out a hand. "Count me in."

Karl accepted the hand and let Walter pull him to his feet.

"So what do we do now, Karl?"

"We?" Karl shrugged. "*We* don't do anything now. I'm going to let my wife drag me off to our bedroom. You're going to finish getting drunk tonight, because you're going back into training tomorrow." He threw an arm around Slovotsky's shoulder. "And after that . . ." he let his voice trail off. The words escaped him. *Ellegon? Can you hear me?*

No, not at all. Not one—

Please. Give me the words.

No, Karl. You don't need me for that. You already know the words.

But I don't.

Try.

"We . . . survive, Walter. We . . ."

Gentle fingers stroked Karl's mind.

" . . . we protect ourselves, our families, our friends and our own." Fialt had said that, and Fialt was right. But there was something more. "We keep the flame of freedom burning, because that is why we all are here."

"Fair enough."

I told you that you knew the words.

And you're always right, eh?

Of course.

CHAPTER NINETEEN:
The Hunter

I am in blood,
Stepped in so far, that, should I wade no more,
Returning were as tedious as go o'er.

—William Shakespeare

He lived like a jackal, sleeping during the day in a hollow under a palm tree, feeding at night at the garbage pits behind the village, always running for cover at the slightest sound.

He never tried for his own kills; anything that could betray his presence had to be avoided. There were just too many of them.

All of his burns and cuts had long since healed, but the scars remained. The bottle of healing draughts he had managed to drink while the fire burned around his bleeding body had kept him alive, although only barely; it had not brought him back to unmarked health.

He waited, feeding and gathering his strength for the hard trip over the mountains. That was the route he would have to take. The sea was closed to him; even were another raiding ship to come this way, they would hardly recognize him as one of their own.

But he always kept his pouch with him.

And every once in a while, Ahrmin would unwrap the glass sphere and watch the dismembered finger floating in the yellowish oil, pointing unerringly to the north and east.

And smile.

ABOUT THE AUTHOR

Joel Rosenberg was born in Winnipeg, Manitoba
Canada, in 1954, and raised in eastern North Dakota and
northern Connecticut. He attended the University o
Connecticut, where he met and married Felicia Herman

Joel's occupations, before settling down to writing full
time, have run the usual gamut, including driving a
truck, caring for the institutionalized retarded, book
keeping, gambling, motel desk-clerking, and a two-week
stint of passing himself off as a head chef. His majors
while at UConn, surpassed Karl Cullinane's in numbe
and scope.

Joel's first sale, an op-ed piece favoring nuclear power
was published in *The New York Times*. His stories have
appeared in *Issac Asimov's Science Fiction Magazine*
Perpetual Light, *Amazing Science Fiction Stories*, and
TSR's *The Dragon*. He is now a Contributing Editor a
Gameplay magazine, writing a monthly backgammon
column.

Joel's hobbies include backgammon, poker, bridge
and several other sorts of gaming, as well as cooking; hi
broiled butterfly leg of lamb has to be tasted to be be
lieved.

He now lives in New Haven, Connecticut, with hi
wife and the traditional two cats.

The Sleeping Dragon, Joel's first novel in th
Guardians of the Flame series, is also available in a Signe
edition.